Praise for

A DEADLY ROW

"Do the math—this book's a winner! Make this number one on your must-read list."

—Laura Childs, *New York Times* bestselling author

"A dazzling debut indeed. Combining the police procedural knowledge of Zach Stone with the [deductive] reasoning of his wife, Savannah, the equation adds up to a delightfully intelligent couple who are a pleasure to get to know. Fans of mysteries that make you stop and think will find *A Deadly Row* the start of a brilliant series." —*Fresh Fiction*

"Fascinating . . . Character driven with several terrific twists . . . Readers who enjoy mysteries like those of Parnell Hall's Puzzle Lady will enjoy observing the two Stones methodically work separately and together on their first joint case." —*Futures Mystery Anthology Magazine*

"Mayes is quite good at planting clues and red herrings. There are many possibilities for the reader to consider . . . *A Deadly Row* is quite a pleasant traditional mystery, with just enough police procedural thrown in to keep it interesting." —ReviewingTheEvidence.com

"The mystery is engaging and well constructed . . . *A Deadly Row* reads a bit like a younger, hipper Carolyn Hart or Nancy Fairbanks novel. It makes a welcome addition to the cozy scene, and I'll definitely be keeping an eye out for the sequel." —*The Season*

Berkley Prime Crime titles by Casey Mayes

A DEADLY ROW
A KILLER COLUMN

A KILLER COLUMN

Casey Mayes

BERKLEY PRIME CRIME, NEW YORK

THE BERKLEY PUBLISHING GROUP
Published by the Penguin Group
Penguin Group (USA) Inc.
375 Hudson Street, New York, New York 10014, USA

Penguin Group (Canada), 90 Eglinton Avenue East, Suite 700, Toronto, Ontario M4P 2Y3, Canada
(a division of Pearson Penguin Canada Inc.)
Penguin Books Ltd., 80 Strand, London WC2R 0RL, England
Penguin Group Ireland, 25 St. Stephen's Green, Dublin 2, Ireland (a division of Penguin Books Ltd.)
Penguin Group (Australia), 250 Camberwell Road, Camberwell, Victoria 3124, Australia
(a division of Pearson Australia Group Pty. Ltd.)
Penguin Books India Pvt. Ltd., 11 Community Centre, Panchsheel Park, New Delhi—110 017, India
Penguin Group (NZ), 67 Apollo Drive, Rosedale, Auckland 0632, New Zealand
(a division of Pearson New Zealand Ltd.)
Penguin Books (South Africa) (Pty.) Ltd., 24 Sturdee Avenue, Rosebank, Johannesburg 2196,
South Africa

Penguin Books Ltd., Registered Offices: 80 Strand, London WC2R 0RL, England

This is a work of fiction. Names, characters, places, and incidents either are the product of the author's imagination or are used fictitiously, and any resemblance to actual persons, living or dead, business establishments, events, or locales is entirely coincidental. The publisher does not have any control over and does not assume any responsibility for author or third-party websites or their content.

A KILLER COLUMN

A Berkley Prime Crime Book / published by arrangement with the author

PRINTING HISTORY
Berkley Prime Crime mass-market edition / August 2011

Copyright © 2011 by Tim Myers.
Puzzles by the author.
Cover illustration by Bas Waijers.
Cover design by Rita Frangie.
Interior text design by Kristin del Rosario.

ISBN: 978-0-425-24223-0

BERKLEY® PRIME CRIME
Berkley Prime Crime Books are published by The Berkley Publishing Group,
a division of Penguin Group (USA) Inc.,
375 Hudson Street, New York, New York 10014.
BERKLEY® PRIME CRIME and the PRIME CRIME logo are trademarks of Penguin Group (USA) Inc.

PRINTED IN THE UNITED STATES OF AMERICA

10 9 8 7 6 5 4 3 2 1

For Puzzling Looks, Puzzling Glances,
and Puzzling Dedications Everywhere!

AUTHOR'S NOTE

The cities—in particular, Raleigh, North Carolina—featured in this novel are real enough. However, each place has been modified for the sake of the narrative in many subtle ways, and the author hopes that the residents of each locale can forgive him, since they are indeed filled with many gracious people and spectacular sights.

The art of simplicity is a puzzle of complexity.

—DOUGLAS HORTON

Chapter 1

...

NO ONE IS GOING TO GET AWAY WITH TREATING ME LIKE that.

I won't stand for it.

Derrick thinks that he can replace me, that he's so much better than I am, but he's wrong.

Dead wrong.

But I'm not going to be stupid about it. Just because I want him to die doesn't mean I'm willing to trade the rest of my life in prison to see it happen.

Someone else is going to have to take the blame for his murder, or get all of the credit, depending ultimately on how they feel about Derrick.

It's too bad an innocent person is going to have to take my punishment, but the military have a term for it, "collateral damage," and if it's good enough for them, it's going to have to work for me.

As long as Derrick dies and I get away with his murder, I can live with anything else that happens.

I won't be cast off, and it's going to be a lesson he learns, the hard way.

Chapter 2

...

"**A**RE YOU SURE YOU CAN'T COME TO RALEIGH WITH ME?" I asked my husband, Zach, as I packed my things into an overnight bag at our cottage in Parsons Valley, North Carolina.

"I wish I could, but I've got to go back to Knoxville today to testify. Why can't Derrick meet you here in Asheville instead of making you drive halfway across the state?"

"My syndicator claims he's meeting me in the middle between here and Richmond," I said as I added a few more tops to the growing pile. I had a tendency to over-pack wherever I went, and even though I was just going to be gone three days, it felt as though I was taking enough clothes for a week.

"Don't forget your pads and pencils," he said as he added a handful of each to the heap.

I picked them up and moved them to another stack.

"These go in my briefcase. I really wish you were going with me, and not just for selfish reasons. If you drove the four and a half hours to Raleigh, I could come up with two of my puzzles for next week." That was my job, creating logic and number puzzles found in some of the best secondary market newspapers in the country. The puzzles varied from week to week, and sometimes it was a real challenge making everything come out in the end.

"Sorry, Savannah. If I don't testify, the Slasher might not get convicted, and we don't want to live with that on our consciences, do we?" My husband, the former chief of police for Charlotte, North Carolina, had been shot in the chest while off duty, and the bullet had left a scar too close to his heart. He'd been forced to retire, and we'd moved to the Blue Ridge Mountains. His departure from law enforcement hadn't lasted long though, and he was currently working as a consultant to any police department that had a tough case and the budget to hire him.

I shivered at the mention of the case he would be testifying at soon. The Slasher had been a bad one, preying exclusively on single mothers alone in the world. I was sure there was some psychological reason for his obsession, but as far as I was concerned, once he was in prison, he could have all the therapy he wanted until they marched him down the hall to the electric chair.

"I know you have to go. I'll be fine," I said as I finally finished packing. "If I'm going to make it in time for our meeting, I'd better hit the road."

My husband wrapped me up in his arms, and I felt my heart skip a little, despite all of our years together. I couldn't help myself. Whenever he held me, I felt safe, and not just because he was over six feet tall and built like a bear. It was more because he was mine and I was his, and neither one of us would have had it any other way.

After a lingering kiss, he said, "Don't forget to call me when you get to Winston-Salem."

"That's just halfway to Raleigh from here. Should I call you from Hickory, too?"

"That depends," he said as he picked up my overnight bag. "Are you going to go see Tom?"

My Uncle Thomas lived in Hickory, and though I didn't visit him very often, I tried to pop in whenever I could manage it. He was all that was left of my mother's generation, or at least he had been until my Uncle Barton had come back into our lives.

As we walked to my car, Zach had my bag and I had my briefcase. I said, "No, he and Uncle Barton are still in Alaska."

He looked surprised by the news. "I thought they were supposed to be home last week."

"I guess when you have the kind of money Barton has, you can pretty much play things by ear." My prodigal uncle had made a fortune after leaving home with my grandparents' money, and ever since he'd come back into our lives, he'd been trying to make up for his past sins.

"I suppose that's true, though I doubt we'll ever know what it's like," Zach said.

After I unlocked my car door, I slid my briefcase onto the seat beside me.

As I buckled my seat belt, my husband added sternly, "Savannah, I don't want you working on any puzzles while you're driving, do you hear me?"

I laughed. "I'm not crazy. It takes too much concentration to do that. I'm not about to take any stupid chances."

"Good," he said as he slid my bag onto the backseat. "I still think you should have let Barton buy you a new car when he offered to."

"You know me better than that."

"I do," he said with a grin as he leaned in and kissed me again. "Be careful, sweetheart."

"You're testifying in open court against a serial killer, and you're telling me to be careful?"

"Are you kidding? I'd love it if he took a swing at me."

"I know you would," I said. There was a side to my husband that he kept hidden away most of the time, but I knew he could be swift, cruel, and even deadly, if the circumstances called for it. It was as though there was a beast inside him, one he kept carefully chained away unless he needed it.

"Talk to you soon," I said as I drove away.

From Parson's Valley, it was a short drive to Asheville, where I picked up I-40, the road I'd be taking all the way to Raleigh. Interstates were great for getting from one place to another, but they weren't much for scenery. The miles seemed to melt into each other as I drove almost due east. I made a quick stop in Statesville for gas and a bathroom break, and then, against my better judgment, I picked up a Snickers and an icy cold Coke for the road. My husband always protested that he loved me no matter what size I was, but as a rule I didn't want to put that belief to the test.

I was lost in my own thoughts when my cell phone rang on the seat beside me. How sweet. It appeared that my dear husband couldn't wait until Winston-Salem to talk to me.

Unfortunately, he wasn't the one who was calling.

"**W**HY AREN'T YOU HERE YET?"

"Our meeting isn't for another two hours, Derrick," I said as I glanced at my watch. I'd left myself plenty of time to get from Parson's Valley to Raleigh, and if I was being honest about it, I was in no hurry to get there early.

My puzzle editor and syndicator, Derrick Duncan, wasn't a pleasant man on his best days, which were too few as a rule in the minds of anyone who had ever had to deal with him. I'd signed a contract with him to distribute my puzzles, and each of us had grown to regret it many times since. I wasn't that thrilled dealing with his abrasive personality, and he felt that his commission was less than it should be.

"You should have planned better, Savannah."

"I planned it perfectly," I said. The less time I spent with him, the better. Since Zach had to stay at the Slasher trial at least two days, I'd budgeted some fun time for myself once I was finished with Derrick. I planned to go to the North Carolina Museum of Art, have a hot dog at the Grill, and generally just act like a tourist. I had a friend in town I'd be staying with, Jenny Blake. We'd been roommates in college, and we tried to do something together every year, though she was still trying to make partner in her law firm and worked some horrendous hours. She'd been thrilled when I'd told her about my meeting with Derrick in Raleigh.

"I need you here now," Derrick said abruptly.

"I can't drive any faster than I already am," I said. "I'll get there as soon as I can."

"You'd better," he said, and before I could say another word, he hung up on me. I slammed the phone down onto the passenger seat, determined not to let him ruin my trip. We'd have his precious meeting, and then Jenny and I would have fun, and I'd do my best to forget that the man ever existed.

The phone rang again not three minutes later. I was still fuming when I answered. "What do you want?"

"This isn't a good time, is it? You're not in bad weather or heavy traffic are you, Savannah?"

It was my husband, and I'd just bitten his head off for

no reason whatsoever. "I'm sorry. I thought you were Derrick."

"Wow, that's just about the most insulting thing you could have said to me."

"I know. I'm really terrible. Forgive me?"

"Sure, why not? What did your fearless leader want?"

"He expected me to move up our meeting," I said as I clinched the steering wheel with my free hand. "When I told him I wasn't going to be able to do that, he had a fit."

"You should find a new syndicator," Zach said.

"Our contract's pretty airtight, and you know it. We're stuck with each other until Derrick exercises his escape clause, and you know he's not going to do that, at least not as long as I'm making money for him. Don't worry, I can handle him."

"But can you do it without giving him a taste of that famous temper of yours?"

I laughed. "I'm not going to make any promises. Sometimes I think that the only time he really hears what I'm saying is when I raise my voice."

"Fine, yell at him all you want then."

We'd wasted enough time discussing my editor. "Let's change the subject. I thought you were going to let me call you. You're not checking up on me, are you?"

"No, ma'am. To be honest with you, I'm a little lonely here. I decided to go ahead and leave myself, so I'm on the road to Knoxville."

I glanced at my dashboard clock. "You weren't supposed to head out for an hour."

He paused, and then admitted, "What can I say? This cottage feels kind of empty without you in it."

"I'm sorry. I don't like being apart either. We'll see each other soon."

"Sure we will. Listen, I'd better hang up now; traffic's

starting to get a little busy. Don't let Derrick get you too riled up, and give Jenny a hug for me."

"I can promise the latter, but the former's a wasted wish, and we both know it. I love you."

"Love you, too," he said.

BY THE TIME I GOT TO RALEIGH, I'D MANAGED TO GET MYself in a state of mind that would allow me to deal with Derrick without losing my cool.

At least that's what I hoped I'd be able to do.

But as I parked in the guest lot of the Crest Hotel where we were having our meeting, all my good intentions vanished. I didn't like being summoned now any more than I had when he'd ordered me to appear three days earlier, and I was going to make certain that he knew it. I started building up a good head of steam as I walked swiftly toward Conference Room C.

At least that was the plan. However, when I got to the meeting room, someone else was already waiting to see him.

It appeared that my little diatribe was going to have to wait.

"ARE YOU HERE TO SEE DERRICK, TOO?" THE MAN SITTING by the door asked me as I joined him at the empty row of seats. He was a nondescript little fellow, with thinning gray hair and a sallow complexion.

I glanced at my watch. "Apparently not for another twenty minutes." I offered my hand. "I'm Savannah Stone."

His face suddenly lit up. "I love your puzzles," he said. "They're part of my daily routine."

"Why thank you," I said. I wasn't a celebrity in any

sense of the word, but it always pleased me when someone let me know they enjoyed my puzzles. "They're great
fun to create."

"Are they? Honestly?"

"Of course they are," I said, startled by his reaction.
"Why do you ask?"

He shrugged. "I'm Brady Sims. I do the Wuzzle World
puzzles for Derrick," he said. "I struggle with them every
day. To make matters worse, I don't earn much making
them, but they're all I've got." He grew even more somber
as he added, "Even worse, I think Derrick's about to fire me."

"What makes you say that?"

"Come on, think about it. We're all away from our home
bases, and Derrick is lining his clients up like dominoes
ready to push over. This can't be good news any way you
look at it, can it?"

The thought that my syndicator was about to drop me
had never entered my mind. "I'm sure you're wrong."

"Don't kid yourself, Savannah. There are computer
programs to make word jumbles all over the Internet now,"
he said. "The only really creative thing I do is the draw-
ings that go with them, and frankly, they're the weakest
part of my puzzles."

"I don't know; I find them charming." In truth I did, but
much like a mother might enjoy the masterpieces of her
kindergarten children. "Much the same thing can be said
about my puzzles as well."

"Oh, I love your snippets," he said as he smiled for a
moment, referring to my little musings that accompanied
each published puzzle.

"So, there you go. No computer can replace your draw-
ings, or my writing. I'm sure it's nothing."

At that moment, the conference room door slammed
open, rattling it in its tracks. A large woman stormed out
with a red face and unnaturally platinum hair, shouting,

"If you think you can just write me off, you're mistaken. My Bridge column is too popular with the readers; you'll see that when you crawl on your knees begging me to come back, but Sylvia Peters will not budge."

As she stormed off, Brady turned to me and asked, "Do you still think it's just my imagination?"

Before I could reply, a mousy-looking woman with brown hair pulled back into a ponytail and thick glasses perched on her nose came out of the conference room. "Brady, Derrick will see you now." Was that an expression of pity on her face? She said his name so softly it was almost too low to hear.

Brady looked at me for a moment with real sadness in his eyes, and then he got up and started walking toward the door as though he were making his way to the gallows.

Instead of following him inside, the woman approached me and said, "Miss Stone, Mr. Duncan will be with you shortly."

"Actually, it's Mrs.," I said as I stood and held out my hand. "We haven't been introduced."

"Sorry about that. I'm Kelsey Hatcher. I'm Mr. Duncan's new executive assistant." Her hand was cold and a little clammy, and I wondered if the slight tremor in it was from nerves.

"It's nice to meet you, Kelsey. You can call me Savannah."

She looked taken aback by the suggestion. "Oh no, I couldn't do that."

"Of course you can. It's pronounced just like the city in Georgia."

She smiled briefly at me, and then disappeared back into the conference room. It appeared that whatever was going on today would be happening to me next.

* * *

IT DIDN'T TAKE LONG FOR ME TO FIND OUT. SEVEN MINUTES after Brady Sims went into the conference room, the door opened again, and he stumbled back out. He looked as though he'd just been shot, though there was no sign of blood anywhere on him.

I hurried toward him. "Brady? Are you all right?"

He didn't even look at me as he brushed past. What had Derrick said to him?

Kelsey came to the door again, and beckoned me inside. As I looked at her, I could feel a wave of queasiness creep over me, but I fought it back. Now was the time to be strong.

I was two steps from the door when my cell phone rang, filling the small space with the cacophony of ducks squawking. It had been a joke assigning that particular ringtone to my husband, but I wasn't in the mood to laugh at the moment.

I flipped it open quickly, said, "This is not a good time," and then slid it back into my pocket.

"What was that noise?" Derrick demanded as I walked into the conference room. He was a slight man, barely a hundred and fifty pounds, and if I wore heels, I could look down on him, not that I ever wore heels when we met. I refused to dress up for the man. He was a thorn in my side, and I didn't care who knew it, including him.

"That was my cell phone," I explained as I looked around. The room was bare and simple, a plain chocolate brown table with a cushioned chair on each side of it. I looked around and spotted a third seat by the door, no doubt Kelsey's sentry position, Cerberus guarding the gates of Hades.

"Turn it off," he snapped.

"I already did," I said, steeling myself for the coming assault.

"Then sit down, Savannah. I don't have all day."

I hadn't even realized that I'd been doing it, but I'd been looming over him, emphasizing his lack of stature compared to mine. I personally didn't equate height or size with expertise and ability, even though my husband was a big, strapping man who also happened to be intelligent, caring, and a fine human being.

And suddenly the sound of ducks filled the room again. What was he, daft?

I pulled the phone out, flipped it open, closed it without answering it, and then turned the ringer to vibrate.

"I thought you said it was off."

"My finger must have slipped," I lied. "What is this about?"

"It's the day of reckoning," he said with the wisp of a smile dancing on his thin and cracked lips.

"I have no idea what you're talking about. Why the melodrama? If you've got something to say, just say it."

He tapped a stack of papers on the desk in front of him. "Fine, have it your way. Consider this the official notice required in the contract we signed. You've been sold, as of noon tomorrow."

"What are you talking about?"

"The second I sign these deal sheets, your column becomes the property of Harrison Enterprises. I have a feeling you won't like it one bit. They won't put up with the garbage I've had to take from you over the years."

"You can't do that," I said. "I have a say in who I work for."

"That's where you're wrong," he said, his smile becoming broader by the minute. "I can buy and sell you as though you were nothing more than a box of laundry detergent."

"Is that what you told the others, too?"

He frowned. "No, I had different news for each of them. They're being dropped altogether, and with the noncompete agreements I put in their contracts, they can't work for anyone else for five years."

"Derrick, sometimes you can be a real jerk," I said.

"Keep talking and I'll show just what a jerk I can be. Your husband's not around to protect you now, Savannah. This is the real world."

I stood. "You're not going to get away with this."

"I already have, and if you had any sense at all, you'd shut that trap of yours and be a good little girl before I have to spank you and put you in your place. You think you're something special, but in truth, you're just a plain, ordinary hack with no real talent at all."

Normally I'm not a woman of violence. I'm not foolish enough to think that it resolves much of anything, but there are times when the only way to deal with a bully is to stand up to him. I wish my motives were that pure as I struck out and slapped Derrick's face, but honestly, I did it because of the way he'd been goading me since I'd signed that syndication contract with him years ago.

I didn't even regret it as my hand started stinging from the impact of the blow. I looked at Derrick's face and saw the crisp white outline of my hand on his cheek, and tried to keep the blossoming smile from my lips.

"That's it. You're fired," he said with a hard edge in his voice that I didn't recognize.

"You can't fire me," I said. "We have a contract, at least until tomorrow. Remember?"

"I can do whatever I want, Savannah. Now get out."

I walked out of the room, not even glancing at Kelsey as I did. In all honesty, I'd forgotten she was there, watching us the entire time.

What had I done?

And more important, what was I going to do now?

Chapter 3

...

I HAD TO CALL ZACH AND TELL HIM WHAT HAD JUST HAP-
pened. When I flipped open my phone, I saw that he'd
left a message when I'd hung up on him so abruptly before.
I nearly cried as I heard him say, "Sorry about that. I've got
a meeting with the prosecutor, so I can't talk. Hope everything goes well with you. Call me tonight. Bye." Almost as
an afterthought, he added, "Love you."

I wanted to talk to him—I needed to—but I knew that
wasn't going to happen. He was smart enough to turn his
own phone off when he was in a meeting.

I had to think. If either one of my uncles were around,
I would call them, but they were currently near the Arctic Circle, and I'd been warned that they'd be out of cell
phone reach until further notice. It had surprised me when
their voices had sounded so close when they'd last called
from Anchorage, but Chena Hot Springs was a lot farther

north than that. They were taking in the natural springs, the ice sculpture museum, and a plane ride to the Arctic Circle itself, using the trip as an excuse to get reacquainted.

At least for the moment, I was on my own. I thought briefly about going straight to Jenny's place, but I didn't want to burden her with my troubles. Besides, I needed some time alone to think.

I got into my car and started driving around Raleigh, no destination in mind, just a chance to clear my head. I found myself near the capitol building, and by some miracle I found a parking space in front of the promenade across the street. The grounds around the capitol were lovely, carefully manicured and dotted with statues, tributes, and cannons, but I needed a place to sit and think. On my side of the street, there was a tree-lined expanse of geometrically laid gray square pavers, with buildings on both sides, a museum in one direction, and an office building in the other. I walked over to a stone planter and sat down facing three bronze statues perched on the steps to the museum. One of them, a Native American woman, had her hands held up to the sky, as though she were pleading for help from above.

I knew the feeling.

I was in serious trouble, and I fully realized it. Could I fix this? Surely if Derrick had originally intended to transfer my contract to the other group he wouldn't be able to fire me out of hand, not if my columns were part of the deal. Didn't that give me some kind of leverage? I realized that maybe this change would be a blessing in disguise. I didn't mind the idea of not working for Derrick a minute longer than I had to. I certainly wouldn't miss his threats and complaints about my work. Would working for someone else really be that bad? Now that I had some time to think about it, I realized that the jerk might have actually done me a favor by selling my contract to some-one else.

But I'd taken care of that with one swift slap.

I wouldn't deny that it had felt good, but I wasn't about to pay for my rash behavior for the next five years if I could help it.

There was only one thing I could do, no matter how distasteful it was going to be. I had to get down on my knees and grovel until Derrick forgave me and included me in the sale.

It wasn't going to be pleasant, but I didn't see that I had any real choice.

I walked back to my car, glanced at my dashboard clock, and saw that I'd been sitting there for nearly an hour and a half. Was he even still at the hotel? I drove there as fast as I could, pulled into the parking lot, and then slipped inside.

The door to the conference room was closed, but that didn't mean anything. He could be in there firing some-one else, for all I knew. I waited five minutes, and then I knew I couldn't just stand around hoping that he would come out.

I opened the door and instantly saw that something was very wrong.

It looked like I was too late for my apology to matter anymore.

Derrick was slumped over the table, his face buried in prime rib, and even from the doorway, I could see that someone had stuck a steak knife into his back.

I RAN TOWARD HIM. MAYBE THERE WAS STILL A CHANCE TO save him.

"Derrick? Can you hear me?" I tried to find a pulse as I

leaned over him, but there wasn't any that I could find. That didn't mean it wasn't there, though. I flipped open my phone and dialed the first two digits of 911 when his assistant, Kelsey, walked into the room. As I pressed the last 1 she dropped the tray in her hands and started screaming.

I doubted the operator could hear me over her shrieks, but Hotel Security was right behind her, and it was only after they charged in that I realized how this must have looked to them all.

I had just elevated myself to a whole new level of trouble.

I DIDN'T DO IT," I SAID AS I FACED THEM. "WHEN I WALKED IN, I found him like this."

Kelsey was still screaming, and I wasn't sure they even heard me over the noise. I'd expected a pair of weapons to be aimed at me, but all they had were cell phones. Unless one of them had a stun gun in his pocket, I should be all right.

"Would you stop that?" I snapped at Kelsey. She wasn't making the situation any easier.

"You stabbed him," she said, now whimpering.

"I did no such thing. I just got here."

Kelsey wasn't buying it. "Don't lie. You hit him before. I saw it."

That got the security team's interest, and I really couldn't blame them. "It's all very simple to explain," I said.

"Save it for the police," one of the guards said. "Now step away from the body."

I knew better than to try to argue with them. I did as I was told, and a minute later, paramedics arrived, along with a police escort. Before I could say a word, one of the security men pointed to me, and a man in a nice suit walked over to where I was standing.

"What happened here?" he asked me as the paramedics began searching for a pulse.

"We had a disagreement, I left, regretted it, then came back to apologize. When I did, I found him like that."

"You seem pretty calm after just discovering a body."

I nodded toward Kelsey, who was now collapsed in the arms of one of the security men. "I'm not like her. I've been a cop's wife a long time."

That got his attention. "Someone on our force?"

I shook my head. "No, he used to be the head of the Charlotte police department."

"But not anymore."

"He was shot in the line of duty, so he had to retire."

"You're Zach Stone's wife?" he asked.

Maybe things weren't going to be so bad after all. "I am. My name's Savannah," I added as I extended a hand to him.

He ignored it, and I put it back by my side. If he was impressed with the new information, he didn't show it. "My name's Shawn Murphy. Let's go to the station."

"You're arresting me? Based on what?"

"I'm questioning you," he said patiently, as if I were too simple to understand words any bigger. "You're an ex-cop's wife. You should know the difference."

"Fine, I've got nothing to hide. Let's go."

As we started for the door, Kelsey suddenly came alive. "You didn't have to kill him!" she screamed at me.

"I didn't," I said, "and I wish you'd quit saying that I did."

As we walked out to the officer's unmarked car, he asked, "Is she a friend of yours?"

"Did she sound like she was?" I snapped.

"Hey, no reason to take it out on me. I'm just trying to find out what happened."

"I wouldn't mind knowing that myself."

We drove a few blocks, and he pulled into a parking lot

clustered with blue and white police cruisers. An imposing building with rows of glass and red brick faced us, and I was quickly led inside.

"Now, let's start from the beginning," he said as he settled in behind his desk.

"I want to talk to my husband first," I said.

"He's not a lawyer," Detective Murphy said.

"No, but he's the only one I trust. I'm not about to answer a single question until I talk to him."

The detective studied me a few moments, and then said, "Then I guess we've got a problem. I'm trying to investigate a murder, and so far, you're my only witness."

"But I told you, I didn't see anything," I said loudly. "Derrick was already dead when I got there."

"So you say," Murphy said, jotting something down in his notebook. "You two had a fight, didn't you? Or are you denying that now, too?"

I suddenly realized that though I'd claimed I was going to be quiet, I was being anything but. "I'm calling my husband, unless you want to stop me."

"Go ahead," he said.

I grabbed my phone, and then realized that his would still be off.

"Did you change your mind?" the detective asked.

"Just about who I'm going to call." I dialed an entirely different number, and Jenny answered on the third ring.

"You're early," she said the second she heard my voice. "I'm just getting out of court."

"That's handy, because I'm at the police station," I said.

"Where are you parked? I'll swing by and pick you up."

"No, you don't understand. I'm inside. They think I killed Derrick, my syndicator."

"That's not funny, Savannah."

"It's not meant to be. I need you."

There was a brief pause, and then Jenny said, "Don't say another word. I'll be right there."

FIVE MINUTES LATER, JENNY BLAKE CAME INTO THE STATION wearing a suit that must have cost a fortune. She looked good, but there were more frown lines on her face than I'd ever seen before. Jenny was still trim, something I'd always envied, and her long red hair was pulled back in a conservative style.

"Hello, Detective," she said as she walked to us, ignoring me for the moment. "I'd like to speak with my client in private, please."

"Since when has she been your client?"

"Since she called me," Jenny said. With a lighter air, she added, "She's my roommate from college, Murphy."

"And an ex-cop's wife, I know all that," the detective said. "But she's deep into this."

"Let us have the room," Jenny said.

Murphy seemed to think about it, and then he pushed himself away from his desk. "Fine. I'll be just outside waiting."

After we were alone, Jenny hugged me, and then got a legal pad out of her briefcase and sat across the table from me. "What have you gotten yourself into this time, Savannah?"

"I don't even know where to begin," I said.

"Let's start with what happened at your meeting with Derrick," she suggested.

"I didn't kill him. You know that, don't you?"

She looked exasperated. "Of course I do. But I need to know everything that's been happening."

"As my lawyer or my friend?"

"Right now I'm not your old college roommate; I'm trying to keep you out of jail. Have you called Zach yet?"

"He's testifying in court in Knoxville, and I don't want him to know what's going on here, at least not yet."

She looked startled by the admission. "You two aren't having problems, are you?"

"Of course not," I said. "I'm afraid he'll fly here and not testify in court, and trust me, he needs to testify."

"Fine, we'll call him later. For now, it's just you and me."

"The two musketeers, together again."

"Let's get started."

AFTER I BROUGHT HER UP TO SPEED, SHE SAID, "OKAY, WE can deal with this. I'm going to get Murphy in here, and then we'll have a conversation. If he asks you anything, you look at me before you answer. I don't want you admitting that my hair is red without my permission. If you can answer with one word, do it. I know you, Savannah; you have a tendency to overexplain. Fight that impulse. Do you understand?"

I hadn't heard that tone of voice from her often, but I knew enough to abide by whatever she said. "I understand."

"Good, but just a yes would have been better."

She stepped outside for a moment, and I suddenly realized how lucky I was to have her represent me. Jenny was exactly who I needed by my side, not my dear sweet husband. Zach would come in like a bulldozer, knocking down everything in his path until he was sure I was okay. Jenny, on the other hand, would get things resolved without compromising my position. I'd tell Zach what was going on, but not until I was sure he'd finished testifying against the Slasher. What he was doing was too important.

Jenny and Detective Murphy came back into the room, and we started. I was a good girl, not admitting to anything or overexplaining, and there were more questions

Jenny wouldn't allow me to answer than I ever could have imagined.

"Are we finished here, Detective?" she asked.

He glanced at his notes. "I guess we are for now, for all the good this interview did."

She smiled at him. "I'm sure once you begin your investigation, you'll see that my client is innocent."

He just chuckled at that, and Jenny took my elbow, leading me out of the police station.

"Wow, those years in law school really paid off," I said.

"Don't kid yourself; you're not in the clear yet by any means. This is just getting started."

That sobered me instantly. "Then I'm glad you're on my side. Are the partners going to mind you taking my case?" I knew the people she worked for were bottom-line folks, intent on squeezing every cent they could from their clients.

"They really can't say much about it, since I'm one of them now." She smiled at me as I wrapped her up in a bear hug.

"When did that happen?"

"Last week."

"And you didn't tell me the instant you made partner?"

She shrugged. "I knew you were coming, so I wanted to surprise you and tell you in person."

"Congratulations, Jenny. You earned it."

"You bet I did. I was going to take some time off to celebrate, but this is more important."

"I'm ruining your vacation?" I asked. I knew she hadn't had a real one since law school.

"Don't worry, I'll just postpone it. There's no way I'd be able to live with myself if I left town when you needed me."

"Thanks," I said. "I owe you."

"In more ways than you can imagine," she said with a smile that reminded me of our college days together.

"What happens next?" I asked.

She glanced at her watch. "I've got to wrap up a few things back at my desk. Do you need a ride to your car, or do you want to come in with me?"

"No offense, but hanging around in a law office all afternoon isn't my idea of a good time." I looked around and took in the beautiful day. "Why don't you take me back to the Crest Hotel so I can get my car?"

"What are you going to do in the meantime?"

"I'm not leaving town, if that's what you're worried about," I said with a laugh.

"Good. It wouldn't be a smart thing to do right now." She was deadly serious.

"Jenny, am I really a suspect?"

"Until the police get a better one, you're the only one on their radar."

"I can give them more names, if that's what they're looking for," I said.

That certainly got Jenny's attention. "Who did you have in mind?"

"There's at least two other columnists he fired today. Either one of them could have done it. I don't know what Derrick's personal life was like, but I can't imagine he left anyone behind that he didn't infuriate at some point."

"Enough to murder him?" Jenny asked.

"I don't like speaking ill of the dead, but yes, he was just that kind of guy."

"Then I have to make a phone call when I get back to the office. Shawn's not a bad guy, but once he gets his teeth into an idea, he hates to let it go. The faster I can send him looking in another direction, the better off you'll be."

She drove me to the hotel, and as I got out at my car, I

said, "I'll see you at your place in a few hours, if you still want me."

"Of course I do."

"You're going to hide your steak knives though, aren't you?"

She shrugged. "Oh, yes. A girl can't be too careful these days. See you soon."

"Thanks, Jenny. For everything."

"What are friends for?"

"If not this, I can't imagine what," I said as she drove away.

I had a couple of hours to kill in Raleigh, so I headed for the art museum. There might not be anything in the world that could perk me up at the moment, but the collection's pieces would do it if anything could.

I was wrong.

As I tried to take in the artwork, my thoughts kept going back to Derrick's body slumped over the table.

It was not an image I relished, and yet I couldn't drive it from my thoughts, not even staring at my favorite Georgia O'Keeffe, or the Monet that always touched me.

I was still trying to appreciate the artwork in front of me when my cell phone went off, earning me an angry glance from an elderly gentleman standing nearby.

I didn't even need to glance at the screen to see who was calling as the quacking of a hundred ducks suddenly filled the air.

Chapter 4

...

"**Y**OU'RE OUT EARLY," I SAID AS I HURRIED TOWARD A PUB-lic space in the museum where we could talk.

"It's all over," he said, the sound of pure defeat filling his voice.

"He's free?" I asked, not believing what I was hearing.

"I guess you could say that. They found him hanging in his cell this morning. He was too big a coward when it came down to facing the world with what he'd done, I guess."

"I'm so sorry," I said. My husband believed in justice, and I knew that this wasn't any approximation of it in his eyes.

"It happens. At least he's finished terrorizing this part of the world. How did your meeting with Derrick go?"

"Not well," I admitted. I hated to add to his misery, but there was no way I could keep what had happened to myself any longer. As I brought him up-to-date, he interrupted more and more until I finally said, "Just let me talk, Zach. I'll answer your questions when I'm through."

"I can do better than that," he said. "I'm catching the next flight to Raleigh. I'll leave my car in Knoxville at the airport and we can pick it up later."

"Jenny's handling things. There's no need to rush here," I said, though I was heartened by my husband's reaction.

"That's where you're wrong. I'll call you back as soon as I get a flight time," he said.

"Thanks."

"Just hang in there, kiddo," he said.

And that's when I felt myself breaking down. "I will," I managed to get out before I hung up. I'd been bottling everything up inside, but hadn't realized it. Hearing my husband's voice had triggered something in me, and it all came rushing out in a sudden avalanche of tears.

I was standing in front of a modern piece, a collection of paper butterflies and flowers hovering overhead. An older woman walked up to me and handed me a tissue. "It affects me the same way, dear. You have the soul of a poet seeing its beauty as strongly as you do."

I didn't have the heart to tell her why I was really crying. "Doesn't everyone?"

"You'd be surprised."

I walked back out to my car and sat there until I got myself composed again. I wasn't sure how long I'd been there when my phone rang.

"Where are you?" It was Jenny.

"I'm at the art museum. Why?"

"Well, get over to my place. I've got a pitcher of sangria waiting with your name on it."

"You know I'm not much of a drinker," I said.

"Trust me, now is as good a time to start as any."

"I thought you had work to do."

She laughed. "I put most of it off on some of the associates at the firm. Rank does have its privileges. Now, are you coming, or do I have to drink this all by myself?"

"I'm on my way," I said.

AS I WAS DRIVING TO JENNY'S PLACE, MY PHONE STARTED quacking, and I've never been so happy to hear that sound in my life.

"Hey, sweetheart."

"Don't worry about a thing," he said. "I'll be in Raleigh by seven."

"Tonight?"

He laughed. "Yes, tonight. I got lucky. I found a flight and weaseled my way onto standby. They just told me I got a seat, so I'll be there in a few hours."

"I'm so glad," I said, letting the remaining tension flow out of me. I was a brave, independent woman who wasn't afraid to fight her own battles, but that didn't mean that I didn't love having my husband by my side, especially when things got dicey. I knew he felt the same way about me. It wasn't weakness on either of our parts, but we both knew that we were stronger together than we were apart. Our marriage was a partnership, and that was the way we both liked it.

"You can't be any happier than I am about it," he said.

"What time should we pick you up at the airport?"

"Don't bother," he said. "I'm going to rent a car and drive to Jenny's."

"Nonsense. We'll be happy to come get you."

He said solemnly, "Savannah, there are some things I need to do on my own. I can't drag you back to the police station while I'm there asking questions, now can I?"

"Do you know anybody on the force here?"

"I've got a few connections," he admitted. "In fact,

there's one—hang on, they just called my flight. I'll call you when I land. Love you."

"Safe flight," I said, but he was already gone. Suddenly I felt a world better knowing that Zach was going to be on the case. If anyone could get me out of this jam, it was my husband.

By the time I got to Jenny's, I was actually beginning to feel a little better. I started to knock on her door when I saw an odd little man staring at me from the porch next door.

"Hello," he said with a wave.

"Hi," I replied.

I knocked, and Jenny answered, dressed in slacks and a casual blouse. "Who's your friend?" I asked as I gestured toward him.

"That's Charlie. He's harmless. He likes to keep an eye out on my place since he works from home."

"He's a little odd, isn't he," I said, but Jenny just laughed.

"He's fine." To show she meant it, she waved next door and called out, "Hey, Charlie."

"Hi, Jenn . . . y."

"Very good," she answered with a smile. "You're getting better. You caught yourself from using my whole name just in time."

"I'm trying, but it's tough."

"Don't worry, you'll get there."

He nodded. "It's a beautiful day, isn't it?"

"The best," she said.

When Jenny led me inside, I saw that she already had a glass of sangria waiting for me.

"Have a drink," she said before I could take off my coat.

"I'd better not," I said. "Do you have any orange juice?"

"You're not serious, are you? Come on, you need a stress reliever."

"You're right, I do, and I just talked to him. He's on his way."

Jenny pushed the glass aside. "Maybe you're right. We don't need any alcohol in our systems if we're going to drive to the airport to pick him up. How would that look if we got stopped?"

"Not good," I admitted. "But he's renting a car, so that's not really a factor. I just think I need to keep my wits about me right now, do you know what I mean?"

"Sure I do, but I insist you take one sip. I've been dying to toast my partnership with you. We can do it with these, or we can crack open a bottle of champagne. It's your choice."

"Let's save that for when I'm out from under this mess," I said.

"Then in the meantime, this will do nicely," Jenny said as she raised her own glass.

"To you," I said, picking up the fruity but potent concoction and raising it toward her. "Congratulations."

We clinked glasses, and then I took a sip. It was a sweet and icy drink, and the first time I'd had one in college no one had told me that it packed an alcoholic punch. After three drinks, I had slept for twelve straight hours and woke up with the worst headache of my life.

I finished my sip, and then put the glass back down. "I know you were just expecting to house one Stone, so we'll find a hotel in Raleigh." I knew that my Uncle Barton owned the Royal Hostelry in Raleigh, and I had a standing reservation there, along with all of the other hotels he owned, whenever I wanted it. I'd told Jenny a little about my long lost uncle, but I'd purposefully left out the fact that he was rich beyond my ability to describe it.

"Nonsense. I've got plenty of room. Besides, it will be good to see that big bear of a husband of yours again, even if it is under such rotten circumstances."

"I know he'll be happy to see you, too," I said. I looked around her place, a beautiful home in one of the nicer sections of Raleigh. "You've really done well for yourself, haven't you?"

"It beats the place we had on High Street, doesn't it?"

"Your kitchen alone is bigger than our entire apartment," I said. "But we still managed to have fun, didn't we?"

"We did at that. I love my life now, except for the present cloud hanging over it, but we had some good times back then, didn't we?"

"The best."

As we moved into the living room, I admired the elegant Queen Anne style of her furniture. "My, my, my. Your style has certainly improved over time."

"Don't kid yourself. I've always had elegant taste. It's just that I've only recently begun to be able to afford it. I'm not sure how long I'm staying in this house, though."

"What's the matter? Do you need something bigger to impress your partners?"

"Just the opposite. I don't have to care nearly as much now. I'm thinking about getting a condo downtown. Think how nice it would be to walk to the office and the courthouse. My idea of heaven is not having to drive to work every day and fight traffic."

There was a lull in our conversation, and not the comfortable one we usually shared. I knew we were both thinking about Derrick's murder, and the fact that I was involved in it, but neither one of us would say anything about it.

Finally, I couldn't take it anymore. "It's bad, isn't it?"

The great thing about our friendship was that I didn't have to explain any more than that for her to understand.

"I won't lie to you. It's not good."

"Zach seems to think he can help," I offered.

She paused for a moment, and then said, "Maybe he can. To be honest with you, I'm glad he's coming. I'm sure he'll have more luck getting something out of Murphy than I would."

"Did you two ever go out?" I asked, noticing the hint of something in her eyes when she spoke his name.

"Savannah Stone, have you been spying on me?"

"You mean I'm right? It was just a stab in the dark."

"Well, you hit what you were aiming at," she said as she stood. Jenny walked around the room, her fingers lightly trailing over furniture as she moved. It was clear that she'd be more comfortable without direct eye contact, and that was fine with me. After a few moments, she said, "Two years ago, he asked me out. I figured, what could it hurt? He's a nice-looking man, and he's very good at what he does. We went out for a while, but there just wasn't any spark there for me, you know? I finally turned him down when he asked me out, but he kept asking, all the while I kept saying no. Persistence is an excellent trait in police detectives, but in unwanted suitors, it's not so wonderful. I finally had to tell him bluntly that I would never go out with him again under any circumstances, and what should have faded away into oblivion suddenly became a barrier to my work. I made it a point never to date another cop or lawyer since, and I haven't regretted the decision."

"I'm so sorry," I said.

"I'm the one who should be apologizing. It's going to make things a little tougher on you."

I smiled at her. "I'm a big girl. I can take it. Besides, I shouldn't be the only suspect on his list. There were other folks there today who had just as much motive as I did to want Derrick dead."

"So you said. Hang on a second, I want to start digging into that. Let me get a legal pad so I can take some notes."

"Are you billing me for this?" I asked.

She grinned. "I'm officially on vacation, so this isn't

any of the firm's business. Besides, I've got some pro bono work figured into my workload."

"Seriously, I can afford to pay you."

She mentioned her current hourly billing, and I whistled under my breath. "Okay, I might have to do it in installments, but I can still handle it."

Jenny frowned, and then suddenly brightened. "Do you remember back in school that you loaned me money whenever I needed it without a word about me ever paying it back?"

"You were on scholarships and student loans. Anything I had was yours, and I was glad to do it."

"Well, consider this return payment in full."

I stood and approached her. "Jenny, we both know it couldn't have been more than five hundred dollars altogether."

"So, think of it as compound interest. It might not sound like much now, but it saved me back then. Let me do this, Savannah."

I grinned at her. "Well, if you insist."

She hugged me, and then said, "I've really missed you."

"I've missed you, too."

"Before we get started, I've got something you're going to want to see," she said as she reached into one of the drawers of an end table.

"What is it?"

She produced a photo album, and the second I saw the cover, I knew what it held. "You still have that?"

"Are you kidding? The photographic chronicles of the two musketeers is never far from my side."

We moved to the couch and started leafing through the past, amazed that the two silly girls in the pictures were now the women sitting side by side reliving cherished segments of their lives.

* * *

THE DOORBELL RANG, AND JENNY LEFT ME TO GET IT. A troubled look crossed her face for just an instant, and it was gone so quickly I wasn't even sure I'd really seen it. "I hope that's our pizza."

"I can't wait. I'm starving," I said.

She came back a minute later, but there was no box in her hands.

"Where's the food?"

"I've got something better," she said with a smile, and Zach suddenly appeared. Without a word between us, we rushed together, and he wrapped me up in his arms. I held onto him a great deal longer than I usually did. It was as if I were pulling strength from him for my soul. I couldn't explain it if I had to, but I could swear his energy transferred to me, and I felt myself growing stronger, calmer, and more able to deal with what I was going to have to face.

"I'm so glad you're here," I said softly.

"There's no other place I'd want to be," he answered.

The doorbell rang again, but I barely noticed as Jenny left the room.

"I'm sorry I've gotten myself into this jam," I said.

"Don't worry," Zach replied as he brushed a little lock of hair from my face. "We'll fix it."

"How can you be so sure?"

"You've got me on your side, and having Jenny in your corner will help, too. It's going to be all right."

"I hope that's true, but forgive me if I don't fully believe it just quite yet."

He laughed. "Don't worry about it. Leave the faith part up to me."

Jenny came back into the room and said, "I hate to interrupt, but the pizza's here."

"Never apologize for feeding me," Zach said. He spied

the large size of the box, and then asked, "There is enough to share, isn't there?"

"We were hoping you'd make it in time to eat," I said.

"Excellent. I'm so hungry I could eat the box."

"Then if you're good, we'll let you," Jenny said.

As we sat down at the table and got started, Zach asked Jenny, "Do you mind a little shoptalk while we eat?"

"I don't, if Savannah doesn't," she said.

"I can hardly complain since you two are trying to keep me out of jail, now can I?"

Zach nodded. "Tell me everything then, and try not to leave anything out, no matter how mundane it might seem."

I took a bite of pizza, added a sip of Coke, and then began to relay everything that had happened that day. The pizza was soon forgotten as my husband and my old college roommate started listening, and soon began taking notes. Neither asked me any questions as I went, allowing me to focus on the narrative, though I knew I'd be peppered with queries as soon as I finished. I recounted my conversation with word scramble creator Brady Sims, the reaction that bridge columnist Sylvia Peters had when she'd stormed out of her meeting, and the way Kelsey Hatcher had discovered me leaning over Derrick's body. Once I was through, Zach looked through his notes and began asking questions. I did my best to answer, but mostly I didn't know.

"Who else haven't we discussed yet would want to see him dead?" he asked at one point.

"I have no idea," I replied.

"Savannah, I've heard you complain about the man enough in the past to know that's not true. There was a business partner of his at one time, wasn't there?"

I nodded. "Yes. It was Frank Lassiter. Evidently Derrick drove him out of their land development partnership just before the company struck it big. The only way I knew about it was Derrick's bragging. Could he have had something to do with it? He lives in Richmond, as far as I know."

"Richmond is just a few hours away," Jenny said. "It would be easy enough for him to drive here, murder Derrick, and then get back across state lines before anyone even realized that he was gone."

"How about the women in his life?" Zach asked.

"Derrick has a wife, but that's about all I know about her. I think her name is Terry, or Cary, or something like that."

"Do you think he fooled around on her?" Jenny asked.

I looked at her and shook my head. "What makes you ask that?"

"Hey, I've been an attorney long enough to realize that most men are dogs at one time or another in their lives."

"Not Zach," I said.

When he didn't answer, I looked at him and asked, "Right?"

"What? Oh, right. No, I'm not a dog. But that doesn't mean Derrick wasn't. It's an angle worth pursuing."

"When did you get so cynical?" I asked Jenny.

"I'm not sure if it's that, or if I'm just being realistic. I've seen some pretty dark things over the years, especially lately."

"I hope it's not spoiling you for a chance at finding love."

"Don't worry, I'm not there yet." She looked over at Zach, and then added, "I've got to say, you're not bad at interviewing people."

He smiled at her. "Thanks. It's not my first time."

"I know it's not, but that still doesn't mean it's not impressive. I picked up a few things myself."

"Glad I could help. I don't envy the detective working this case. There appears to be a lot of angles to follow up on."

"Are you going to offer the police here your help?" I asked.

"Not directly, not with my ties to the case. But I am going to ask some questions, and maybe see if I can point them in some other directions. I called the station on the way over here, but the lead detective was out, and they aren't expecting him back until morning." Zach looked at Jenny. "Do you know anything about this Murphy fellow?"

Jenny and I exchanged glances and then she recounted much the same story about the detective to Zach that she had told me.

He shook his head. "That might make things a little stickier, but we'll work something out."

My husband stifled a yawn, and then said to me, "We'd better find a hotel room before I fall asleep at the table."

"We're staying here," I told him.

"We don't want to put you out," Zach told Jenny.

"Nonsense. I've already settled this with Savannah. Don't make me start with you."

He held up his hands. "Then I give in. Just point me in the right direction." Zach turned to me. "Are you coming, Savannah?"

"No, if you don't mind, I think I'll stay up a little while longer and catch up with Jenny."

"Suits me just fine," he said as he gave me a quick kiss and then disappeared into the guest room.

After he was gone, Jenny said, "Maybe you're right after all."

"Of course I am," I answered. "About what?"

She laughed. "Perhaps I'm letting the people I deal with on a daily basis cloud my perception about the world around me."

"I said that?"

She nodded. "You did."

"Wow, I sound really smart when you say it."

Jenny grinned. "Come on. We both know you have to be sharp to create those puzzles of yours. I have a tough time finishing them most days."

"You do my puzzles?"

"Absolutely," she answered. "They're a nice way to unwind at the end of the day."

"I'm honored," I said, "But don't give me too much credit. Sometimes I think they're easier to make than they are to solve."

"I suppose that makes sense. After all, you've got all of the answers, don't you?"

"If only life were like that."

She patted my arm. "Don't worry. We'll figure this out."

"I hope so." I stifled a yawn. "In the meantime, I think I'd better join my husband."

"That's not a bad idea. We have a big day tomorrow."

"What do you have planned?"

"Well, seeing some of the local sights is out. I thought we might do a little digging into Derrick Duncan's life and see what we turn up. What do you say to that?"

"I'm all for it."

Chapter 5

• • •

THE NEXT MORNING, I FOUND JENNY AT THE KITCHEN table drinking a cup of coffee and looking through the newspaper.

"You're a star," she said as she handed me the front page.

I took it and scanned the headline. SYNDICATOR SLAYING A REAL PUZZLE, it said on the front page of the Local section. There was a blown-up photo of Derrick, and below the fold, I was appalled to find headshots of Brady Sims, Sylvia Peters, and me.

"Don't you love how clever they can be with their headlines," I said as I handed the paper back to her.

"Wake that husband of yours up and I'll make us all some breakfast."

"I'd love to, but he was already gone when I got up," I said.

"Is he always such an early bird?"

"When he's working on a case, he barely sleeps at all. Since I'm involved in this, I was surprised he even closed his eyes."

"It must be nice having him on your side."

"It is, but it's great having you there, too. Tell you what. Why don't I cook for us this morning? It's the least I can do."

"Are you saying you don't like my cooking?" she asked.

"That depends. Have you had any more chance to practice since the last time I stayed with you?"

"Hey, I've been trying to make partner. There wasn't exactly a lot of time to take any cooking classes."

"I'm not complaining, I'm just offering my services."

"Then I'll gladly accept. How about some blueberry pancakes?"

"Do you have the ingredients?" I asked as I headed for the refrigerator.

"I just happened to lay in some supplies yesterday," she said with a smile.

I laughed as I started measuring the flour and other ingredients and mixing the batter. As I worked, we talked about our plans for the day.

"I don't see any way around it," Jenny said as the first pancake hit the griddle. "We have to go to Richmond to Derrick's home base if we're going to learn anything about him."

"I'm guessing Detective Murphy isn't going to be too thrilled about me leaving town, let alone the state."

"I could go on my own," Jenny offered.

"I don't think so. There's no way I'm going to put you in jeopardy for my sake."

"You'd do it for me, wouldn't you?"

I flipped the pancake when tiny bubbles started to form in the batter. "Of course I would."

"Then it's not fair to try to keep me from doing the same." She leaned over and looked at the single pancake browning on the griddle. "Why just one?"

"I always do a test pancake first," I said.

"Does that mean I can't have it?"

"It might not be very good," I admitted. "Sometimes the first ones are real duds."

She held out her plate. "I'll take my chances."

I grabbed a few small pancakes myself as I cooked the rest of the batter, and we were still chatting about our investigation when there was a knock at the front door.

Zach came in, smiling as he smelled the pancakes. "Any chance there are some left for me?"

"I might be able to scrape up enough batter," I admitted. "You didn't even leave me a note this morning."

"Sorry, I wasn't sure where I'd be. I found out something interesting, though."

"What's that?"

"Feed me first, and then I'll talk."

I did as he asked, and after he finished three large pancakes—and the last of the batter—he said, "First off, Murphy's not a bad cop."

"I never said that he was," Jenny answered. "Just a bad boyfriend."

"Be that as it may, he was willing to open up a little with me." Zach pointed to me as he added, "You're no longer their only suspect, if that means anything to you."

"But I'm still on the list," I said.

"Hey, I'm good, but nobody's that good. At least he's looking beyond the obvious now. I went over our list with him, and he seemed open to it. As a matter of fact, I found out someone else we should be looking at."

Jenny appeared to have a hard time believing that. "Shawn actually gave you a lead?"

"Not exactly, but I spotted a name on his bulletin board, and there was a line tying it directly to Derrick. Savannah, does the name Mindi Mills mean anything to you?"

"No, why? Should it?"

"That's what we're going to find out." He glanced over at the bowl that had once held blueberry pancake batter and saw that it was empty. "No more?"

"No more," I agreed. "Sorry."

"I've probably had enough, anyway," he said as he kept staring at the bowl.

Jenny asked, "What now? Savannah and I have been thinking about going to Richmond to see what we can dig up on Derrick."

"That's the right idea, but the wrong execution."

"What do you mean?"

Zach said, "I'm going myself as soon as I grab a few things, but you two have to stay in town."

"Why do you get to go?" I asked. "You shouldn't do it alone."

"Think about it. There's a good chance Murphy's going to have an eye on you, but I'm not a suspect in anything. It's just a few hours' drive from here. I'll be back tonight, and then we can compare notes."

"If you go to Richmond, what are we supposed to do?"

"From what I understand, your fellow columnists are still in town. I suggest you talk to Brady Sims and Sylvia Peters and see just how much they hated Derrick Duncan. Can you do that?"

"Yes, but I still don't like the idea of you going off on your own."

My dear husband frowned at me. "Savannah, believe it or not, I'm perfectly capable of watching out for myself."

I patted his chest where the scar from a bullet remained, but I didn't say a word.

"That was a fluke, and we both know it," he said.

"Flukes happen though, don't they?"

He kissed me quickly, and then said, "You worry too much. I'll see you tonight."

"Call me when you get there," I said.

"Yes, ma'am. I promise."

After he was gone, I looked at the dirty dishes. "We should do these before we go out."

"Don't you just love dishwashers," Jenny said as she loaded hers up. "The griddle can wait. Why don't you get dressed, and then we'll go do a little snooping."

W HEN WE WALKED OUT OF JENNY'S HOUSE, SOMETHING fell through the door onto her welcome mat. It was a half dozen roses, bloodred and in full bloom.

"It looks like you've got a secret admirer," I said, and then I saw Jenny's frightened face. "Hey, I was just kidding. Are you all right?"

She stared at the flowers, and then at me, before she burst into tears.

"What is it?" I asked her as I led her back inside.

"He's back," she said through her tears. "I thought this nightmare was over, but it was too good to be true."

"Tell me what's been happening," I asked as I handed her a nearby box of tissues.

"It started a month ago," she said once she calmed down enough to speak again. "The first thing I got was a note."

"What did it say?"

"Hang on, I've got it in the other room." A few seconds later she came back with an orange folder. As she took a note wrapped in cellophane from it, she said, "Read it yourself."

I picked it up and read.

Why don't you wear your red blouse anymore?
Red's my favorite color.
Do yourself a favor and wear the blouse, Jennifer.

"That's creepy," I said.

"Wait. There's more. I didn't wear the blouse, I couldn't, since I'd given it away. The next note was even stranger.

Wear the blouse.
You don't want to make me mad.

"Did you call the police?"

"I phoned Shawn Murphy, as a matter of fact. He said it was probably just some random kook, but the guy knew my name, what I drove, and even where I lived. Shawn said he'd keep an eye out on my place, and he had a few cruisers come by to check on me, but they never saw anything."

"What did you do? You must have been scared to death."

"I'm ashamed to admit it, but I went out and bought another red blouse. I thought that might be enough to get him to leave me alone."

"Did it work?"

"Judge for yourself. Here's the last note I got from him."

Close, but not quite.
It's just not the same, is it?
I'm through warning you, Jennifer.

"Needless to say, the police stepped up their patrols, and Shawn suggested I trade my car and move, but I wasn't about to let this creep win. I tried my best to forget what had happened and I threw the blouse away."

"You must have been petrified."

"Savannah, at that point, I was angry more than anything else. I hung a sign on my car door that said, 'I'm done with you,' and I went about my business. When I didn't hear from him again, I figured it was over. And then I saw those roses, and my name on the card."

"What does it say?" I asked as I reached for it.

She pulled it away from me. "There might be fingerprints, though he's been careful so far. Let me."

She pulled out a pair of latex gloves, slipped them on, and then opened the card. Inside, something fluttered to the ground, and Jenny's face went pale as she said, "It's part of my blouse. The one I threw away. How did he get it?"

"What's on the card?" It was killing me not knowing. I looked over her shoulder as she opened it.

Roses the color of blood.
They match your blouse nicely.
Remember, this was your choice, Jennifer.

"Call Murphy," I said as I handed her the telephone.

"He's just going to say the same thing," Jenny protested.

"I'd say the threat level just elevated, wouldn't you?"

She took the phone from me and dialed the number she obviously knew by heart. After a brief conversation in which she was clearly getting more and more frustrated, she hung up.

"What did he say?"

"He's coming by later, but as you heard me tell him, I'm not going to be here."

"Jenny, this is more important than my case. It can wait."

"No, it can't," Jenny said resolutely. "I'm not letting this creep win and keeping myself locked up behind a bolted door. We're going hunting for a killer."

"Are you sure?"

"I'm positive," she said.

I insisted we take my car, and Jenny agreed. As we drove to the Crest Hotel, I tried to get her to talk about what was happening with her, but she didn't really respond, so I finally dropped it. The police might not be taking these threats seriously, but I was going to make certain that Zach did. He'd figure out what was going on, and we weren't going to leave Raleigh until he did.

IT FELT STRANGE BEING BACK IN THE HOTEL WHERE I'D found Derrick's body the day before. At least I wouldn't have to go into the conference room again. At the front desk, I asked the clerk, "Could you tell me what rooms Brady Sims and Sylvia Peters are in?"

The young woman behind the desk kept looking at me, and then she clearly made the connection. "I'm sorry, but we're not at liberty to give out that information."

I looked around, suddenly realizing that Jenny had disappeared. I knew she didn't mind conflict—she was a lawyer, for goodness' sake—but I wasn't going to let her desertion stop me. "They're both friends of mine," I said, stretching the truth to the point of breaking, but not really caring about doing it. I needed to speak to them both, and if that meant lying to get their room numbers, I was fine with that.

"Sorry. There's nothing I can do about it. Edmond, could you come here please?" She turned toward the office in back of her, and ten seconds later, a large dark man with a pasted-on smile joined her up front.

"Is there something I can do for you?"

She whispered something to him, and then faded into the back. "What seems to be the problem?" he asked, his smile a little less warm than it had been before.

"I just need a few room numbers. Honestly, I don't see what the big deal is."

"Ma'am, at this hotel, we protect the privacy of our guests."

I was about to argue when Jenny suddenly reappeared at my side. "Come on, there's no use fighting with them."

I wasn't about to move, though. "He won't even call their rooms for me. This is insane."

"Savannah, trust me on this, okay?"

I gave Edmond an icy look, and then let Jenny lead me away. "Why did you do that? I had him on the ropes."

"From the look of things, he wasn't about to budge. I think you were close to having a police escort out of the building."

"I've been thrown out of nicer places than this," I said.

"But that's what I've been trying to tell you. There's no need."

"Why not?"

"Your two fellow suspects are having breakfast together in the dining room. It might be nice if we joined them, don't you think?"

"Lead the way. So that's where you disappeared to before."

Jenny smiled. "Hey, it never hurts to know your surroundings."

She led me through the atrium and into the hotel's dining room. I didn't spot them at first, but then Jenny pointed to one side, and I saw them hiding behind a display of greenery. The table had been placed there for privacy, and my fellow columnists had taken advantage of it.

"Mind if we join you?" I asked as we approached them. They both looked startled to see us.

Brady said, "Not at all," at the same time that Sylvia said, "Yes, as a matter of fact, we do."

I chose to ignore Sylvia and accept Brady's invitation. "Excellent. I take it you have both seen the newspaper today."

"It's actionable," Sylvia said, "portraying us all as suspects in Derrick's murder. Why, we were dear friends. I never would have dreamed of hurting that sweet man."

I exchanged a quick glance with Brady, who'd seen her storm out when I had. Neither of us decided to contradict her.

"Actually," Jenny said, "you aren't mentioned as suspects, merely clients. The newspaper did nothing they can be sued over."

"And who exactly are you?" Sylvia asked with an arched eyebrow.

"I'm an attorney," Jenny said with her sweetest smile.

"So, you feel you need legal representation?" Sylvia asked me. "That would seem to imply guilt to me."

"She's my old college roommate," I said.

"I take issue with the word 'old,'" Jenny said.

"Former, is that better?"

"Much."

"Still, you found reason to bring her with you," Sylvia said.

"Sylvia, I don't like being in the bull's-eye of a murder investigation any more than you do. Jenny's here to help us clear our names."

Brady spoke for the first time. "You don't think we did it, either?"

"I haven't formed an opinion one way or the other," Jenny answered truthfully.

"The sooner we can clear our names, the better off

we'll be," I said. "Brady, where were you when Derrick was murdered?"

"I was sitting in my car. I'd just been cut loose from the only job I can do. Savannah, you saw me when I left there. I was in shock, and I didn't come out of it until I heard the police sirens."

I could very well believe that alibi. Then again, it was impossible to verify, so Brady had to stay a viable suspect.

"How about you, Sylvia?"

"I don't owe either one of you an explanation of my whereabouts," she answered snippily.

"No, but I'm sure the police have already asked you," Jenny said. "What is it going to hurt to tell us as well?"

She looked from Jenny to me, and then back at Jenny. "Not that it's any of your business, but I was in my room."

"At this hotel?"

"Yes," she admitted reluctantly. "I booked the room when Derrick insisted on this ridiculous meeting. He wasn't going to terminate our agreement, you know. My column was far too valuable for that to ever happen."

"I wonder what's going to happen to us now?" Brady asked. At that moment, his phone rang, and we all listened to his side of the conversation. "Yes. Of course. I understand." He looked surprised, and then added, "They're both here with me right now. We're in the hotel restaurant. Sure, we'll wait."

"What was that about?" Sylvia asked.

"It was Kelsey Hatcher. She needs to meet with us."

"Whatever for?" Sylvia asked. "She was Derrick's assistant, for goodness' sake."

"There's only one way we're going to find out," I said. "I for one am going to wait."

Sylvia didn't look pleased by the prospect, but she didn't leave, so I had to assume she was as curious as I was by the odd summoning.

While we waited for Kelsey to show up, I asked each of them, "Have either one of you ever heard of Mindi Mills?"

Brady looked at me blankly, but from Sylvia's reaction, I knew that I'd hit home. "Sorry, no idea," she said, which was clearly a lie.

"Sylvia, don't hold out on me," I said.

"Are you questioning my truthfulness?" she asked archly.

I was about to admit that was exactly what I was doing when Jenny answered before I could. "Not at all. But if there's a link to someone else that might refocus the police investigation, I'm sure you'd do everything in your power to make that happen. I know from experience that when the police start digging, they don't stop until they've uncovered everything there is to find, whether it applies to their investigation or not."

Sylvia seemed to take that in, and then reluctantly admitted, "I may have heard the name a time or two, but I hate to spread malicious rumors, especially when it involves the dead."

"I'd say this supersedes someone's reputation, wouldn't you?"

Sylvia nodded reluctantly. "It is my understanding that Derrick was less than faithful to his current wife. Apparently, Mindi was Derrick's mistress."

"When did you hear that?" Brady asked her. The news clearly hit him harder than I expected it should. "I don't believe it."

"Do you know Mindi?" I asked him.

Brady shook his head, and then reluctantly nodded slightly. "We were at a few events together in the past, but I wouldn't really say that I know her. I just can't believe that she'd have anything to do with Derrick."

Sylvia looked at him with a mixture of pity and tolerance. "Dear sweet Brady, always one to think the best of people. I'm sorry to disillusion you, but often the nicer ones are the folks who end up disappointing us."

"I'm not simpleminded, Sylvia. I just don't think that there's anything wrong with giving people the benefit of the doubt." He turned to me and asked, "How do you feel about the world, Savannah?"

"I suppose I fall somewhere in the middle. I like to think the best of people, but I always try to watch out for their bad sides, too."

"Very diplomatic of you. I wonder what our lawyer has to say on the topic?"

Jenny smiled at her, but there wasn't a great deal of warmth in it. "I prefer to keep my options open, on every level you can imagine."

I wondered what exactly it was that she meant by that, but I didn't have a chance to ask. Kelsey Hatcher walked toward the table, but it took me a second to recognize her. While her hair had been pulled back and a bit mousy before, now it was newly colored and styled. Gone was the simple outfit, too. She now wore a charcoal gray suit and sported sharp black flats; in her hand was a black leather briefcase.

I walked up to her before she reached the table. "Kelsey? You look so different," I said, relieved that she wasn't screaming at me today. It took me a second before I realized how my comment must have sounded to her.

"Do you like it?" she asked.

"You look marvelous," I said, and I meant every word of it.

"Thank you. That means a great deal to me. Listen, I'm sorry about the way I acted yesterday. I kind of lost my head."

"It's perfectly understandable," I said.

"I'm so glad you feel that way. I'd love it if you'd wish me luck today."

"What's this about?"

"I'd rather wait and say in front of everyone, if you don't mind."

"Go right ahead." I followed her to the table, and took my seat. Jenny shot me a questioning look with her eyes, but I shook my head. There were no previews this morning, for either one of us.

"Thank you all for waiting for me. First of all, I'd like to say that I'm sure we're all still in shock and mourning over Derrick's loss." She paused for a single moment, and then quickly continued. "But I'm certain he'd want us all to carry on in his memory."

"Excuse me, but I have a question," Sylvia asked.

"Certainly."

"We were terminated yesterday. Pardon me for asking, but what has changed since then?"

"With Derrick's demise, all contracts have been reinstated and the sale to the Harrison group has been terminated."

A look of disbelief exploded on Brady's face. "Is this on the level?"

"Trust me, I've been in meetings all morning. I had to take a rather firm stand with them, but the contracts spell it out clearly enough."

"That's wonderful news," Brady said. "Thank you, Kelsey. I don't know what to say."

"Let's refrain from extending congratulations just yet, Brady," Sylvia said.

"I agree," I said. "Where do we stand now?"

"Derrick's company holds your contracts, and I've been named its interim operating officer. You'll answer to me, at least until everything is sorted out."

"That's quite a step up from assistant to managing editor," I said. "Congratulations."

"Thank you," Kelsey said, as she gathered her papers together. "Now, if you'll excuse me, I've got work to do."

She stood, and then, almost as an afterthought, added, "I'll need new columns from all three of you by nine a.m. tomorrow. You can fax them to me at this number," and she handed out brand-new business cards with her name and contact information embossed on it.

After she was gone, Sylvia rubbed the business card with a fingertip. "That didn't take long, did it? She must have had these made up weeks ago."

"I don't know. They could have been a rush job."

"You're certainly entitled to believe it, but I refuse to," Sylvia said. "Well, it seems that the tide has indeed turned. If you'll excuse me, I have a column to write."

"I'd better get busy myself," Brady said as he stood.

After they collected their checks and paid them, Jenny looked at me and said, "That was interesting."

"I was surprised when you didn't say anything."

"It wasn't my meeting," she said.

"I know that, but surely you have an opinion about what just happened. Come on, spill."

"I think Kelsey Hatcher has more motive than the rest of you to have killed Derrick Duncan."

I nodded. "I was just thinking the same thing. She certainly changed a great deal in one day."

"I wonder," Jenny said.

"Trust me, you didn't see her before. Yesterday she was this mousy little assistant, and now she walks in here like she owns the place, giving orders left and right."

"I'd like to see that contract," Jenny said.

"Mine's in Asheville, sorry."

"I wonder how it's worded, exactly."

"I wish I could help. What do you think about the revelation about Mindi Mills?"

"It doesn't surprise me one bit, based on what I've heard about Derrick Duncan's life so far."

I looked around the dining room. "There's no use hanging around here anymore. We've gotten all we're going to out of those two."

"Three you mean. Kelsey's as viable a suspect as the other two."

"Three," I agreed. "But I've got a problem now."

"You sure do," Jenny said. "You've got a puzzle to create."

"I'm not worried about that," I said.

"Maybe you should. Tell you what. Let's go back to my place. You can come up with a new puzzle, and I can catch up on paperwork. Then we can put our heads together after we knock all of that out and start doing a little more digging."

I wasn't thrilled about the idea, but I knew Jenny was right. With Kelsey in charge, I didn't know what to expect. I'd come too close to losing my job to jeopardize it now.

I'd better get a puzzle together before the deadline.

Chapter 6

...

BACK AT JENNY'S, WE WERE BOTH CLEARLY RELIEVED TO find no more flowers or notes by her door, though neither one of us said anything about it. I wasn't going to just forget about it, but there was really nothing else I could do until Zach got back from Richmond. The second he returned, I planned to dump the entire thing in his lap. Jenny was too important to me—a sister I never had— and I wasn't going to let anything happen to her if I could help it.

"Would you like some coffee?" she said as we walked back inside her house.

"I'd love some sweet tea, if you've got it."

She smiled at me. "I made a batch day before yesterday."

"You are an angel."

I got my briefcase and pulled out some of the paper and the pencils that I love. "I feel guilty working here. What are you going to do?"

"Don't worry about me, Savannah. I've always got a backlog of paperwork on my computer."

"You shouldn't have to do that on your vacation."

Jenny laughed. "Trust me, none of this time is going to be counted as vacation. I'm going to be billing my hours the instant I get to work. Do you need anything before I get started?"

"No, I'm set."

"Then I'll leave you to it."

After she disappeared into her office, I started thinking about how brave she was being about her stalker. I wasn't sure how I'd handle it if I were in her shoes.

After a few hours, I had a puzzle ready, granted not a very complicated one, but I was satisfied with it. Now all I had left to write was my snippet for the day. Letting my mind wander, I tried to come up with a theme that would justify the simplicity of the puzzle. After a few minutes of pondering different possibilities, I wrote,

Puzzles can provide us with many more answers than the ones we seek on the grids we love to play. Many times the events in our lives present puzzling challenges to us, and it is only after we see the patterns within them that their solutions become clear. As you work this puzzle, try to bear that in mind, and look for the patterns in the world around you. You might just be astounded by what you find.

And that was it. I looked at what I'd done, made a few tweaks on the snippet, and then I was ready to send it to Kelsey.

The only problem was that I didn't have my fax with me, and I'd purposefully left my computer at home. How on earth could I have known that I would need it?

Maybe Jenny had one. I walked down the hall and tapped gently on her door. I'd learned when we'd been roommates that if she was engrossed in what she was doing, the small taps wouldn't interrupt her train of thought, but if she wasn't deep into something serious, she'd hear me and respond.

After a moment, I heard her say, "Yes?"

"Sorry to bother you, but do you have a fax machine by any chance?"

"Hang on." Thirty seconds later she opened the door. I could see that she'd been crying, and though she probably would have liked me to ignore it, I couldn't do it. "You're really rattled, aren't you?"

She nodded. "I'm trying not to let it get to me, but it's hard."

I decided to tell her that I was calling in reinforcements. "We're telling Zach the second he gets back from Richmond."

Jenny shook her head. "Savannah, he's got enough on his mind getting you out of this murder investigation. I'm sure he doesn't have time to deal with this."

"That's where you're wrong. He'll be happy to do it."

She started to protest, and then finally nodded. "It would really help my peace of mind if he could help put a stop to this."

"Trust me, he'll find this guy."

"I hope you're right." She wiped away another errant tear, and then said, "My fax is over here. It's one of those combination units. I couldn't live without it."

"How does it work?"

She took the puzzle and snippet from me, and the card Kelsey had given me. "We'll have this sent in no time."

"Excellent," I said. "What should we do after that? Do you have much more work to do?"

"I've always got something on my plate," she said. "But there's nothing that won't wait. What did you have in mind?"

I started to say something when we both heard someone pounding on the front door. Jenny dove into her closet and grabbed a tennis racket.

I asked, "It's an odd time to want to play, isn't it?"

"Hey, I don't have a baseball bat, so it's going to have to do. You know how I feel about guns."

"Come on, let's see who's at the door."

We walked out into the hallway together, and the banging on the door continued as we approached.

Jenny was going into her backswing when I called out, "Who is it?"

"It's Zach. The doorbell must be broken. Let me in."

Jenny lowered her racket, and I opened the door with relief.

Zach knew instantly that something was going on. "What happened? Did I miss something?"

"Someone's been stalking Jenny," I blurted out.

Zach's brow furrowed as he walked in. "Tell me about it."

We sat together on the couch as Jenny recounted what had happened so far, all the way up to the most recent note and roses she'd just gotten.

When she was finished, Jenny said, "I feel foolish when I lay it out like that."

"You shouldn't. You have every right to worry. I can't believe Murphy hasn't done more to catch this guy."

"How do you fight something like this?" Jenny said.

"I have a few ideas. Let me check something first."

He walked out the door, looked down at the doorbell,

and then retrieved his pocketknife. After a few moments working on it, he pulled out a sliver of wood. "Someone jammed a toothpick into the doorbell so it wouldn't work. He's getting more aggressive, isn't he?"

"He seems to be," I said. "Can you do something about it?"

Zach touched my shoulder lightly. "I can do a lot of things about it. Don't worry. We'll get him."

"Why do I suddenly feel so relieved?" Jenny asked. "Nothing's really changed."

"You're wrong. Zach's on the case now. That makes all the difference in the world."

"Jenny's right, you know," Zach said. "I haven't done anything yet."

"But you will," I said. "Don't sell yourself short. How was your trip to Richmond? Did you learn anything?"

"As a matter of fact, I did. I had a chance to look into Frank Lassiter's life a little."

"What did you find out?"

"Their real estate partnership went rotten at exactly the right time for Derrick Duncan, and it's nearly ruined Lassiter."

"What happened?" I asked.

"Evidently Derrick was even trickier in land development than he was in newspaper syndication. He convinced Lassiter that one of their big deals was a lemon, and Derrick bought him out at twenty cents on the dollar. Funny thing was, two weeks later, Derrick tripled the initial investment and Lassiter was left with next to nothing."

"When did that happen?" Jenny asked.

"The deal closed three days ago," Zach said.

"Does Lassiter have an alibi for the time of the murder?"

Zach smiled at her. "He claims he was on the Outer Banks, but he can't prove it one way or the other." The

North Carolina Outer Banks was a developed set of is-
lands on the coast that still offered stretches of empty sand
dunes and lonely stretches of ocean. It was easy enough
to imagine getting lost there.

"But he could have just as easily been in Raleigh,"
I said.

"Oh, yes. He's pretty familiar with the place. This is
where he got his start, so I'm guessing he's still got some
connections in town."

"You need to tell Murphy everything you found out,"
Jenny said.

"We talked on my way back here. He's heading to
Richmond later today to confirm it all for himself."

"At least he's doing something," I said.

"It's not easy running an investigation when there
are so many people who wanted the victim dead," Zach
replied.

"We've got another name to add ourselves," I said.
"Evidently, Derrick was having an affair with Mindi Mills.
That's why she made Murphy's list."

"So then we add her name, and Cary Duncan's, too.
Maybe it would be easier listing the folks who didn't want
to see him come to harm."

"Hold that thought," I said as my telephone rang.
"Hello?"

"Savannah, this is Kelsey Hatcher."

"Hi, Kelsey. It's a nice courtesy, but you don't have to
call to tell me you've received a puzzle every time I send
one to you." I could see that it was going to take me a
little time to break her in.

"That's not why I'm calling. I'm afraid it didn't work
for me."

"Hang on a second," I said, and then covered the
mouthpiece of my phone. "Jenny, is your fax working?"

She nodded. "I use it all the time."

I uncovered the mouthpiece again. "Sorry, Kelsey, there must have been a glitch with the phone line. I'll send it to you again," I promised, and hung up.

My phone instantly rang again. Honestly, what more could the woman want? "Yes?"

"You didn't let me finish. I received it the first time, but that's not the problem."

"Then what is?"

In a sharp voice, she said, "There's no complexity to it. Our buyers have been complaining about your easy puzzles for months. You've got to do something a little more challenging, I'm afraid."

"I don't redo puzzles," I said, taking the warmth out of my voice as well. I'd hoped we would have a longer honeymoon, but if she was going to start being difficult from the start, then I was going to have to follow suit.

"According to page four of your contract, section seven, subparagraph two, when the syndicator requests a revision or alternate puzzle, you are to comply within twenty-four hours, or risk termination of the contract, with prejudice. I hate to be a stickler about it, but you signed it, did you not?"

"We both know I did, but Derrick, as much as he fussed at me about doing easier problems, never had the gall to bounce one of my puzzles."

"I can't address the past. Consider this official notice that your puzzle dated with today's date has been deemed unacceptable. It is up to you to comply with the terms you agreed to, Savannah. Honestly, do we really have to drag the lawyers into this? How hard could it be to make another puzzle?"

"If you think it's that easy, by all means, go ahead and do one yourself."

"As we both know, that's not in my area of responsibility. Have a new puzzle to me by this time tomorrow, Savannah."

She didn't even wait for me to say anything else.

Zach took one look at me and said, "I've seen those storm clouds before. Bad news?"

"Kelsey Hatcher just ordered me to supply her with another puzzle, one more complex, in twenty-four hours, if you can believe that, or she said she was going to cancel my contract and sue me for damages."

Jenny shook her head. "I told you to let me look that contract over before you signed it."

"Are you kidding me? I would have done anything to see that first puzzle published. I was afraid to show the contract to you. You probably wouldn't have let me sign it, and then where would I be?"

"Where are you now?" she asked.

"In need of a new puzzle, apparently," I said. "Sorry I can't work on this with you two, but I've got work to do. Work I've already done once, if you can believe that."

Zach rubbed my shoulder gently. "Sorry, Savannah. It looks like you're trapped."

"I just hope she gets this power trip out of her system. I'm not going to keep doing two puzzles for the price of one for very long."

I CREATED THE PUZZLE, THOUGH IT TOOK ME FOREVER TO DO it, and by the time I was finished, I was in no mood to write a cheerful and upbeat snippet.

I ended up writing,

Power is a precarious thing. It can build up confidence in some folks even as it destroys common sense in others. When power goes to someone's head, disaster is a likely result. The wise use power to nudge, not to bludgeon, and realize that there are consequences to most actions.

I took the snippet into the living room, where I found my husband and my best friend in deep conversation. "Can I read you two something?"

"Absolutely," Zach said.

Jenny nodded as well, so I recited my snippet. After I was finished, I asked, "Did I go too far?"

Zach frowned as he said, "Not if your goal was to alienate Kelsey Hatcher. If that's what you were going for, I think you've probably succeeded admirably. I know you're not happy with her orders, but is this the right way to go about protesting?"

"Do you honestly think she's going to read it? Even if she does, I'm not all that certain she's bright enough to realize I'm taking a shot at her."

Jenny shrugged. "It's not actionable as it stands."

"Are you saying that I should make it more direct?"

She shook her head. "I never said that. I'd send it, if I were you. What's the worst thing that can happen, she makes you write it over? You can always sanitize it then."

Zach smiled. "You two must have been a pair of holy terrors in college."

"We were angels," I protested.

"Unless provoked," Jenny added.

"True. All bets were off then."

Zach laughed. "I'm just glad I'm on both of your good sides. Savannah, why don't you go fax that new puzzle? Jenny and I have been brainstorming, and we've come up with a new plan of action."

"Don't make me wait to find out," I said. "What do you have in mind?"

"Fax first, and then talk," Zach said.

I reluctantly agreed, if only to send the new puzzle and snippet in before I lost my nerve. Two could play it that way, and if Kelsey was going to give me grief, I planned to give it right back to her.

I sent the puzzle, not sure I'd even hear from her. I could sympathize with the editors, and my readers, but I had a lot going on at the moment. I honestly believed that it was important to mix easier puzzles in with the more difficult ones to give first-time folks a chance, but that wasn't my true rationale at the moment. I'd do better when things settled down, but for now, the puzzles I was submitting would just have to do.

I wanted to get back to my husband and my best friend and see what the two of them had come up with.

"It's taken care of," I said as I rejoined them.

"That was quick," Zach said.

"I know everyone wants more complex puzzles, and I love this job too much to disappoint them lightly, but I've got to focus on this right now. As soon as things settle down, I'll give everyone some real brainteasers. Now, what do you two evil geniuses have in mind?"

"We're going to go buy a little surveillance equipment," Jenny said.

"Excellent. Who exactly are we going to spy on?"

Zach explained, "Jenny's stalker is getting bolder, and I think that's going to be his downfall. There's a place in town where I can get some small cameras, and we're going to hook them up to Jenny's DVD player and record what happens. I've got a feeling we'll catch this guy in twenty-four hours."

"I hope so," Jenny said. "This is getting creepier by the minute. I'm really glad you two are staying with me for a while."

"We'll hang around as long as you need us," I said.

"At least one of us, anyway," Zach added.

"She needs us," I said. "That takes precedence over everything else."

"Not everything," Zach said. "We still have to go after Derrick's murderer, and I'm not going to let myself be distracted completely from that."

"Zachary Stone, I thought you didn't like it when people interfered with police business."

My husband grinned at me. "That was when I was on the force. As things stand now, I believe Murphy could use a little nudge, and I'm not afraid to be the one to give it to him."

"We're going to work on both cases," I said firmly. "They're equally important."

Zach nodded. "Let's take care of the cameras, and then we'll start interviewing suspects for Derrick's murder. It's going to all work out in the end."

I wasn't sure if he actually believed it or not, but just hearing him say it was enough for me.

When my telephone rang three minutes later, I wasn't sure what to expect.

That didn't make things any easier when I heard who was on the other end of the line.

Chapter 7

...

"**H**ELLO, KELSEY," I SAID.

"Hello, Savannah. There now, that wasn't so hard, was it?"

Trying to keep my temper in check, I said, "I still don't think it was necessary. It's impossible to get new people to try my puzzles if I don't throw in an easy one every now and then. If they're all too hard to solve, nobody's going to want to work them, and then where will we be?"

There was a pause on the other end, and then she said, "You know what? You're right."

"I'm sorry, there must be something wrong with our connection. What did you just say?"

"I said you were right, and you heard me the first time. Listen, I'm sorry about the way I acted earlier. I thought I had to do business the way Derrick did, and I might have gotten a little carried away."

"Might have?" I asked.

She laughed fully that time. "Okay, I admit it; I got carried away. The whole thing about power corrupting, and absolute power corrupting absolutely has a ring of truth to it, doesn't it?"

"It certainly can."

"Don't think for one second that I didn't realize your little snippet was aimed directly at me. I nearly called you and demanded another puzzle, but then I realized that you were probably right."

"So, I can keep doing easy puzzles?"

"As long as there is a healthy mix with harder ones," she said. "I'll keep your first submission here, and we'll go with that one next time. We both need to find a balance here, Savannah."

Kelsey was making sense, and she had given some real ground, so it was time for me to be a little more gracious than I'd been so far. "I'm more than happy to work with you until we do," I said.

After I hung up, Zach asked, "What was that all about?"

"Apparently I was wrong about Kelsey," I said. "She apologized after reading my snippet. We might just be able to work things out after all."

"Some harmony in your work might not be a bad thing," Zach said.

Jenny stood and clapped her hands. "Now that we've settled all that, why don't we go get these cameras Zach keeps raving about?"

"I'm ready," he said.

As we walked out and locked the front door, I glanced over to see if Charlie was still standing guard, but he was nowhere to be seen. That could explain how the stranger had slipped onto Jenny's porch to make his deposit without Charlie seeing him. Apparently the man wasn't there every minute of every day, which was actually something of a relief.

As we walked to Zach's rental car, I had a sudden thought. "We should go next door."

"Why?"

"Jenny has a neighbor who likes to watch what's happening on the street, especially over here. Maybe he's seen something."

Jenny said, "Trust me, Charlie keeps me apprised of all the neighborhood happenings, like who's walking their dog and who doesn't mow their lawn often enough."

"Maybe Savannah's right," Zach said. "It wouldn't hurt to talk with him before we go."

I pretended to clean out my ears. "Did I actually hear you say that?"

"Hey, I admit it all the time when you're right."

"Rarely," I said with a smile.

Jenny put a hand on Zach's arm. "Maybe Savannah and I should talk to him without you."

"Why? I'll be civil."

Jenny looked at him. "I know you think so, but there's a lot of cop left in you, no matter how the circumstances may have changed. You're likely to scare the poor man half to death. Why don't you wait in the car? We can handle Charlie ourselves."

"Okay," Zach said grudgingly, "but if you need help, remember, I'm just a shout away."

As we walked up Charlie's front steps, I said, "You handled that quite well. Almost as good as I could have."

"I get paid to make people see my point of view, remember? I didn't want to say anything so direct to Zach, but he can be intimidating, whether he knows it or not."

"You don't have to tell me, I married the guy." As we glanced up toward Charlie's house, I thought I saw the curtains move on the second floor. "Do you think he'll come out?"

"With just us out here? I'd have to believe so. We're not nearly as imposing as your husband."

"No, our talents lie in other directions. Should I let you do the talking?"

Jenny thought about that for a moment or two, and then she nodded. "It might be for the best. Do you mind?"

"Of course not, but I'm not promising I won't jump in if I think of something."

She laughed, a sound I missed when we were apart. "Savannah, you wouldn't be you if you did."

Jenny barely had to knock on the front door before Charlie threw it open. "I happened to glance out the window, and I saw you coming. Is there something I can do for you, Jennifer, I mean Jenny?"

"I've told you a thousand times, Charlie, it's Jenny."

"I know. I'm trying, really I am."

"There are only three men in the world who have ever called me Jennifer, but I'll let it slide."

"Who are the other two?" Charlie asked, clearly interested in her answer.

She started to tell him, I could see it in her eyes, and then she waved her hand in the air. "It's not important. What really matters is whether you've seen someone leave something by my front door lately."

"The UPS man came by two days ago," Charlie volunteered. "Didn't you get the package he left?"

"Yes, it was an autographed book I ordered from Poisoned Pen in Arizona," she admitted. "Have you seen anyone else hanging around the place?"

"No, no one who didn't belong," he said. "I'm assuming you don't mean your friend here, or the man staying with you now."

He hadn't missed that much. "I'm Savannah Stone," I said as I offered my hand, "and that man is my husband, Zach."

Did Charlie seem a little relieved to know that Zach was with me? I couldn't really tell, and I'd been looking for a reaction.

"Sorry, I forgot to introduce you," Jenny said.

"You work too hard," Charlie said.

"How could you possibly know that?" I asked.

"I see lights coming on late at night when she gets home," he explained. Realizing how that must have sounded, he quickly added, "My TV room faces Jenny's front porch. I can't help noticing when the lights come on."

"It's fine, Charlie. If you see something odd, would you do me a favor and call me? You've got my cell phone number, don't you?"

"I don't think so," he said.

She reached into her pocket, pulled out a business card, and then scrawled her number on the back of it. "There you go."

I added, "But just call if it's suspicious."

Jenny must have realized what she might be letting herself in for. "That's right. You know me, I'm working all of the time."

"Don't worry about a thing. You can trust me. I'll be your eyes here," he said. Inside, we could hear his telephone ringing.

"We should be going," I said.

Charlie answered quickly, "It's fine. The machine can get it."

Jenny said, "We do really need to be going. Thanks, Charlie."

"What are neighbors for?" he asked.

As we were leaving, I said, "That was odd."

"Charlie's a bit of an acquired taste," Jenny said. "But he's not that bad once you get to know him."

"I'm not talking about his behavior," I said. "He kept calling you Jennifer. Don't tell me you didn't notice."

"Of course I noticed. He's been doing it since I first moved in. It's just his way."

"Who are the other two men who call you Jennifer?"

She frowned, and then said, "I should learn when to keep my mouth shut, shouldn't I?"

"It wouldn't be a bad trait for a lawyer to have," I admitted. "Who are they?"

"You've met one of them," she said. "Shawn always used to call me Jennifer before we broke up."

"And who was the other man?"

"I don't want to talk about it," she said abruptly. "It didn't end well."

"All the more reason to tell me," I said.

"If you must know, it's another lawyer from the firm. We dated a few times just before I went out with Shawn, but nothing ever developed between us. He wasn't exactly thrilled when I turned him down."

"I need to meet this man."

"Honestly, Savannah, just let it go."

"I can't do that, and you know it," I said as we got in Zach's car, an oversized SUV.

"What are you two talking about?"

Jenny started to tell him when I beat her to it. "There are three men in her life who call her Jennifer, but she doesn't think that it's significant, even given the notes she's been getting."

"It could be the most important clue we've gotten so far. I need names," Zach said as he took out the small notebook he always carried with him.

"I really don't think any of them are involved."

"Be that as it may, we're not going anywhere until I get those names."

She sighed, and then finally said, "Shawn Murphy's one of them, Charlie's another, and Mason Glade is the third."

Zach nodded. "I know the first two, at least indirectly. Who's the last one you mentioned?"

"He's from the office. He's a partner in the firm where I work."

"A man she used to date," I added.

"I was getting around to that," she admitted.

"It's so much more efficient this way though, isn't it?"

Zach frowned, and then instead of starting the car, he opened his door and said, "I'll be right back."

Before either one of us could stop him, he started up Charlie's steps. I wondered if the man would even open the door when my husband approached, but he did. After a brief conversation, Zach came back, scowling about something.

"He had a cake in the oven," Zach said. "I'll have to speak with him later."

Jenny put a hand on his arm. "Zach, trust me. He's harmless."

"He could be," my husband said. "But seven women thought the same thing about the Slasher, and look where it got them, all on slabs at the morgue."

"Fine, I won't try to stop you, but in the meantime, can we go get these security cameras so we can get on with our lives?" I asked.

"We're on our way," Zach said as he started the car and drove off.

I wasn't sure which side of the argument I agreed with, and no one asked. Until I had more evidence, I was going to assume that everyone we talked to was up to something. It might not be the healthiest way to look at the world, but it was the only way I was going to find a killer and now, a stalker, too.

"**WHERE EXACTLY IS IT THAT WE ARE GOING, ZACH?**" Jenny asked as we drove into Raleigh.

"I know a place where we can get what we need."

Jenny's voice made it clear that she was skeptical about his selection as she looked out the window. "I usually don't go to this section of town."

"You're with me," he said. "You'll be fine. I can't find what we need on Edenton Street, you know?"

"Trust him," I told Jenny. "He knows what he's doing."

Jenny nodded. "I don't have much choice, do I?"

Zach glanced at me and said, "Thanks for that vote of confidence."

"It isn't misplaced, is it?"

He laughed. "Savannah, have I ever gotten you into so much trouble I couldn't get you out of it again?"

I took longer to think about it than he clearly would have preferred, but I finally replied, "No, but you have to admit that we've had some close calls in the past."

"Think about it. How many times was it because of me, and how many times were you the reason we were in the jam in the first place?"

"What can I say; I like life to be interesting."

Zach parked the car in front of an older building on the outskirts of town, a dark redbrick façade with high windows and no real signage out front.

"Where exactly are we?" Jenny asked.

"If you have to ask, you won't ever know." He turned off the engine and handed the keys to me.

"What are these for?"

"You put them in the ignition," he said with a grin, "and they make the car go."

I gently slapped his arm. "Why are you giving them to me?"

"It might be better if I go in alone. If the three of us walk in together, we're going to pay double what this guy is going to charge if it's just me."

I looked at the building, and then at Jenny. "I'm going to leave it up to you."

She said softly, "If it's all the same to you, I'd rather wait out here."

"Then that's what we'll do." I turned to my husband and added, "Be careful."

"It's not dangerous. I promise."

I kissed him on the cheek anyway, and he disappeared into the building after ringing a buzzer and waiting for a full minute to be let inside. I didn't like the look of the place, but I had to trust that Zach knew what he was doing. Otherwise I would never be able to sleep at night.

While we waited, I asked Jenny, "So, what else have you been up to since we got together the last time? Any scandalous stories you feel like sharing?"

"No, I lead a pretty quiet life these days. You have more excitement than I do, I'll bet."

"Are you kidding me?" I asked as I looked around outside. "I mostly sit around the cottage making puzzles and trying to keep up with my garden. I've put raised beds in, and we're growing all kinds of things, but it's not exactly front-page news."

"I don't know, it sounds pretty exciting to me—" Jenny broke off what she was saying, and then grabbed my shoulder and said, "Duck."

I didn't even ask why as I slumped down in the front seat. "Why are we hiding?" I whispered.

"Do you remember Mason Glade, that partner I told you about from my firm just now?"

"The one you used to date?"

Jenny pointed to a man walking out of the building my husband had just entered. There were two heavy bags in his hands, and he wore a nice suit and shoes that gleamed from their shine as he walked away from our car.

"That's him," she said. "It's Mason."

I started to open my door, and Jenny protested, "Where do you think you are going?"

"I'm going to follow him," I said. "I figured that much would be obvious."

"Savannah, get back in here," she called out, but it was too late. I wanted to catch Mason before he had a chance to get away, and a second later, I heard Jenny's door shut behind me.

"If he sees me, I have no idea what I'm going to say," Jenny said as we trailed the partner from her firm.

"We have as much right to be here as he does," I said. "We don't owe him any explanations."

"You don't know Mason. He'll demand to know."

"Then we'll tell him you were showing a friend from out of town the big city," I said. From the way Mason hurried down the street, I had a feeling we weren't going to have to tell him anything. A herd of buffaloes could be following him and I doubted that he'd notice.

He turned the corner, and Jenny put a hand on my arm. "Hold back a second."

"We'll lose him if we do," I answered, pulling free from her. As we turned the corner, my worst fears were confirmed. Mason was nowhere in sight.

"Where did he go?" Jenny asked as we both looked wildly around.

"Maybe he wasn't as oblivious as we thought he was," I said. "He must have spotted us following him and ditched us the first chance he got."

"I can't see Mason being able to do that, even if he noticed us, which I doubt."

"Well, he's not here, is he?"

Jenny shook her head. "Sorry. I didn't mean to lose him."

"It's okay. I would love to know what he bought in there, though."

I turned around and headed back to the shop.

Jenny asked, "Are we going back to the car?"

"No, ma'am. We're going into the shop and asking the owner what Mason bought from him."

She looked at me as if I'd lost my mind. "And what makes you think he'll tell us?"

"We won't know unless we ask," I said.

Back in front of the shop, I looked for the buzzer that my husband had used to summon someone to the door. My finger was poised above it when, much to my surprise, the door opened.

It was Zach, and he had a bag that matched the pair we'd seen Mason carrying out of the shop.

"I thought you two were going to wait in the car?" Zach asked us.

"We were, but then we saw Jenny's ex-boyfriend and fellow law partner walk out of the shop with two bags like those."

Zach shook his head. "Don't tell me. You decided to follow him."

I admitted as much. "We lost him, though. That's why we need to get inside. We have to ask the owner what he just sold Mason."

"You can't do that," Zach said.

"Why not? What would it hurt?"

"You haven't met Skinny Tony," Zach said. "Not only would he not tell you what you want to know, but he could take it personally. Besides, it's not important."

"What do you mean, it's not important," I said. "This could have something to do with Jenny. We need to know what he just bought."

"That's what I've been trying to tell you. Tony won't tell you, but I can. I saw him bag it all up."

"Well, don't keep me waiting. What did he buy?" I asked.

Zach looked around, and then said, "First we get into the car, then we start driving, and after that, we'll have plenty of time to talk."

I looked around, too. There were several men on the street, dressed in scruffy clothes and most of them needing a shave. "You're not worried, are you?"

"Savannah, there are times when calculated risks make sense, and times when it's just stupid to make yourself a target."

"I'm convinced," Jenny said as she hurried into the back of the rental car.

"Coming?" Zach asked.

"You know I am," I said.

As we drove away, I noticed a few of the men watching us. Had they been paying such a close vigil while Jenny and I had been trailing Mason? I'd broken one of my husband's cardinal rules. I hadn't been aware of my surroundings at all times, and the people around me. If I was going to insist on investigating Derrick's murder I was going to have to do better.

The tension in Zach's shoulders eased considerably once we were on our way. He glanced at Jenny in the rearview mirror and asked, "What kind of work does Mason do for your firm?"

"Mostly he works our corporate accounts," she said.

"No divorce cases?"

"No, nothing like that. We're more of a boutique firm.

We don't handle anything that could be considered even a little bit lurid."

Zach shook his head. "Then it doesn't make sense."

"Why? Don't keep us in suspense. What did he buy?"

Zach studied Jenny for another few seconds, and then said, "He got some long-range listening devices. They'd be perfect for eavesdropping, but I don't know why he'd need it if he's just practicing corporate law."

"I know," I said. "He wants to hear what Jenny's doing in her house."

"Ew, that's just creepy," she said.

"Maybe so, but if he's stalking you, he's not exactly Prince Charming, now is he?"

"I just can't believe Mason's the one," Jenny said.

"There are a hundred different reasons he could be buying that equipment, and only one of them concerns Jenny," Zach said. "We need more information before we start trying to come to any conclusions."

"And how exactly are we supposed to get that information?" Jenny asked.

"We use the cameras I just bought, and then we see if we can catch a glimpse of who's after you. I have one thought," he added, "but I'm willing to bet you aren't going to like it."

"What's that?" she asked.

"You two move into a hotel while I stay out there and watch your place."

"Forget it," Jenny said. "If I run, he wins. I'm staying right where I am."

Zach glanced over at me. "Savannah, talk to her."

"Okay." I turned around in my seat and said, "Good for you."

"That's not what I meant," Zach said.

"I know, but it's the best I can do. She's right, you know. If she leaves her own home, this loser wins."

"There's no use arguing with either one of you, is there?"

I looked at Jenny. "Not me. How about you?"

"My mind's made up."

Zach sighed, and then said, "Then I guess I'll just have to do the best I can. Let's get back to Jenny's so I can install these cameras. Maybe they'll show us something."

Chapter 8

∎∎∎

ZACH HAD THE CAMERAS INSTALLED IN NO TIME, AND even though I knew where he'd placed them, they weren't that easy to spot once he was finished.

"You did a good job, honey," I said.

"I've done this a time or two in the past," he said as he made a few adjustments. He called inside to Jenny, "Start the DVD player."

"Got it," she said.

We walked out to the sidewalk, and then Zach approached the porch from every possible direction.

I said, "Aren't you worried about warning Charlie about what we're doing? I know he doesn't seem like that likely a suspect, but he calls her Jennifer."

Zach shrugged. "I think we're safe enough. His car's not in the driveway. Didn't you notice that as we drove up?"

"Of course I did," I said, lying through my teeth. "I was just testing you, and you passed with flying colors."

At that moment, we saw Charlie drive up, and as Zach waved to him, he said, "Testing time is over. Let's go see what we've got."

Once we were inside, Jenny hit the stop button on her DVD recorder, and after hitting play, we watched as Zach and I left the porch, and then he approached it from several different directions. "There's a small gap from the motion detection to the taping, but unless you want to spend a great deal more money, it's going to have to do."

"It's perfect," Jenny said. "I feel better already."

"You know this won't stop anyone from coming up to your front porch. The only thing it does is give us a record of it."

"That's more than we had before." Jenny reset the DVD player, and then she said, "Now that we've worked on my problem, what are we going to do about Derrick Duncan?"

"Let me make a few telephone calls," Zach said. He got out his cell phone and as he began to dial, he walked back outside. I hated when he did that, since it meant that I couldn't listen in to his side of the conversation, but he needed privacy when he talked so he could speak freely.

"There's got to be something we can do in the meantime," Jenny said.

"Don't worry. If Zach runs into a dead end, I have a few ideas of my own."

He came back inside three minutes later, scowling.

"What happened?" I asked.

"Nothing. It doesn't matter."

"Zach, what happened? Talk to me." My husband had a way of clamming up when news wasn't to his liking, and I'd seen it enough in the past to be able to recognize it with no problem now.

"I checked our messages at home," he finally admitted.

"What's so bad about that?" A sudden, dark thought came to me. "Nothing happened to either one of my uncles, did it?"

He raised one eyebrow as he looked at me. "What? No, they're fine, at least as far as I know."

"Then what is it? Trust me, nothing you can say is going to be able to touch what my imagination can provide, and you know it."

"That's true enough. It's about a job."

I smiled at him. "What's wrong with that? I thought you were eager to get another consulting job."

"It's not that kind of job," he said. "Savannah, you remember Greg Starks, don't you?"

"Sure, he's the sheriff in Asheville. Hang on a second. He didn't have the nerve to call you for another consultation, did he? The last time you helped him out, your pay 'got lost' in the mail for six months until I started raising a fuss about it at City Hall. I told him you weren't going to work for him ever again, and I meant it."

"Apparently Greg delayed more checks than mine. They just fired him for embezzling from his department."

"Then why is he calling you about a job?" Something clicked at that moment. "Does he seriously want to come work for you? I can't believe you'd even consider it. You can't afford to take anyone on, and you and I both know you can't trust him."

"Savannah, if you'd let me finish, I could tell you what is going on, instead of you just guessing."

Jenny started to smile, and I asked her, "What's so funny?"

"Nothing. Absolutely nothing whatsoever."

"Good." I turned back to Zach. "Go ahead," I ordered my husband. "I'm listening."

"The mayor called the house looking for me. He wants me to take the job."

"Hang on a second," I said. "He knows about your heart, right?"

"There's nothing wrong with my heart," Zach said forcefully. While it was true that technically he could have gone back to work after the shooting, his doctors hadn't recommended it.

"You're retired, remember?"

"Savannah, people come out of retirement all of the time," he said.

"And they usually pay for it, don't they? What are you going to do?"

"I have no idea," he said.

Zach headed for the front door and then added, "I need to take a drive."

"You're just going to walk out? Can't we even talk about it?"

He stopped and looked at me. "Savannah, I need to figure out what I want to do myself before we have any conversations about it one way or the other."

Almost as an afterthought, he bent over and kissed my forehead. "I'll see you later."

After he was gone, I looked at Jenny and asked, "What just happened?"

"Give him a break, Savannah. He needs some time to think before you discuss it. That's not a bad thing, is it?"

I frowned as I bit back tears. "It's not a good thing, either. Trust me. If he's thinking about it, then there's a chance he'll take the job."

Jenny touched my arm lightly. "He said you'd discuss it. Give him a chance to wrap his head around it."

"I really don't have much choice, do I?" A few tears had escaped down my cheeks, and I dabbed them away.

"Well in the meantime, we're not going to just sit around here waiting for him to come back," Jenny said with renewed fire in her eyes.

"What do you propose we do?"

"We're going to go interview our suspects," she said as she grabbed her car keys.

I knew Jenny was right. I might not be able to do anything about my husband at the moment, but that didn't mean I couldn't start going after Derrick's killer myself. Whatever happened with Zach would work out for the best; I had a strong faith that was true, but with Derrick, I wasn't so sure.

He'd been murdered in cold blood, and the police had me near the top of the suspect list. If I was going to get myself out from under that cloud of suspicion, I was going to have to do something about it.

"LET'S GO BACK TO THE CREST," I TOLD JENNY AS WE GOT into her car.

"We should talk to Brady and Sylvia again."

"I'm sure we will, but I want a little more ammunition before I do. What I'd really like to see is the suite where Derrick was staying."

She glanced over at me. "How do you know that it's a suite?"

"Trust me; Derrick had no problem pampering himself, especially if he could write it off on his taxes. That's just the kind of guy he was."

"I still don't understand how we're going to get into the suite."

I thought about it. "We could bribe a maid."

"No thank you. I can't afford any black marks on my record, and if we pay somebody off, I'm sure it will come back to haunt me later. How about your uncle? Surely he would know someone he could call to help us."

"He's out of reach right now." Then I had a sudden

thought. While it was true that Uncle Barton was unavailable, I knew one of his top men.

As Jenny drove I dialed Garrett's number and heard him answer on the first ring.

"Savannah, how nice to hear from you. I'm sorry, but your uncle is still away."

"You're the one I need to talk to," I said. Garrett ran one of my uncle's hotels, the Belmont in Charlotte, and he did his job very well.

"You know that I'm happy to be of service, if I can," he said.

"I need a contact at the MCS Crest Hotel in Raleigh. Can you help me?"

He didn't even hesitate as he replied, "Ask for Benjamin Lowe. I'll call him now, so he'll be expecting to hear from you."

"How on earth did you come up with something so quickly, Garrett?"

"I'd love to tell you that I've got some kind of magical directory at my fingertips, but Benjamin and I were at a conference together last year in Greensboro. He's the assistant manager there, so you'll be in good hands."

"Thanks, Garrett. You're a lifesaver."

"When are you going to visit us again, Savannah? You've been missed."

I thought about the luxury accommodations, and the view of Charlotte I'd enjoyed when I'd stayed there last, and began to wonder the same thing. "If we get a chance, we'll come by soon."

"Excellent," he said.

After we hung up, Jenny said, "Wow, so that's what it's like to know people."

"Come on, you know people."

She shook her head. "I know some folks around the

edges, but not with those kinds of resources, at least not yet. Who knew you would ever turn out to be such a mover and a shaker?"

"It's my uncle, not me," I said as we pulled up to the hotel, got out of Jenny's car, and walked up to the front desk.

A dapper young man with a trim mustache was waiting for us. "Are you Savannah Stone, by any chance?"

I admitted that I was, and he extended a hand. "I'm Benjamin Lowe. How may I be of assistance to you?"

"So, you've already spoken with Garrett. That was fast, even by his standards."

He smiled, and I saw a perfect set of gleaming white teeth. "Let's just say that I'm in his debt, and I'm happy to be able to reduce the burden in any way I can. I must warn you, though, that I won't breach the confidentiality of our guests, but anything else I can do for you, know that I'm at your service."

"I need to see Derrick Duncan's room. I'm willing to bet it's a suite on the top floor."

Benjamin frowned. "I'm not certain the police have released their hold on that suite yet." He turned to one of the young women behind the desk, asked for her keyboard, and then began tapping something into the computer system as he looked at the screen. "I'm truly sorry, but that room won't be available for occupancy for another six hours." He tapped a few more keys, and then swiped a golden-hued card from a nearby stack.

As we walked toward the elevator, Benjamin said softly, "I trust you will leave things there as undisturbed as possible."

"I promise," I said. "I'm curious, though. Am I to understand that you aren't willing to breach a guest's privacy, but you don't have any problem with disobeying the police?"

"What troubles you about it? We've held the suite as a courtesy only. I don't have to tell you that it's not a crime scene, since Mr. Duncan was murdered in one of our conference rooms, not his suite. I've been told that his widow will be by later to pick up his belongings. From what I've been told, the police have finished that part of their investigation, so there's nothing you can really disturb. Still, I wouldn't want it bandied about that I'd allowed you free access to someone else's room."

"You can trust me," I said.

"I'm sure of it. Garrett was quite emphatic about that point."

"Well, please accept my thanks."

"If it is ever my pleasure to serve you again, do not hesitate to ask."

We got onto the elevator, and started our ride to the penthouse level. Jenny had been quiet during most of the conversation, preferring to observe rather than directly participate. "I don't know what Garrett's got on Benjamin, but it must be something."

"I'd rather not know, to be honest with you. I'm just glad he has a contact that can help us."

"Is it right what we're doing here? I feel a little odd snooping around a dead man's room."

"Jenny, if you're uncomfortable doing it, I'd be glad to meet you back in the lobby after I'm finished."

"You wouldn't mind?"

"Of course not. It's probably better that we give you some deniability about this, anyway. I'll snoop around a little, and then I'll be back before you know it. Would you like to meet in the lobby, or should I look for you in the restaurant?"

"You're being awfully understanding about this," Jenny said.

"You've got a lot more to lose than I do if we're

caught," I said. The elevator opened on the top floor, and I walked out.

To my surprise, Jenny stepped out as well.

"I thought you were going back downstairs."

"I've changed my mind," she said suddenly. "I'm not about to leave all of the fun for you. I can't let that happen, now can I?"

I looked into her eyes and saw that she meant it. "I guess not. Let's go do a little digging."

EITHER SOMEONE HAD TOSSED THE PLACE AFTER DERRICK died, or he was a born slob. I was willing to bet it was the latter, given his general personal appearance. There were dirty dishes on the floor by the door, and magazines and newspapers were strewn out all over the place. Clothes had been ditched haphazardly, and I had to wonder how long it had been since a maid had stepped one foot into the room.

"Are you kidding me?" Jenny asked as she stared in disbelief.

"Sorry, but it's too late to back out now."

As Jenny surveyed the room, she asked, "How can anyone live like this?"

"I don't like it any more than you do, but we don't have much time. Let's dig in and see what we can find."

Jenny frowned, and then took a deep breath. "Okay, if you can do it, I can, too. I just wish I had some gloves."

"Or a biohazard suit," I added as I looked around. "Do you want the living room or the bedroom?"

"Could the other room really be any worse than this is?"

"We could always flip a coin," I offered.

"No, I'll take the bedroom."

"Are you sure?"

"Yes. No. Yes. Forget it. I can't stand the thought of what I might find in there. You take the other room, but you have to do the bathroom, too. Agreed?"

Since I was lucky to be getting any help at all, I could hardly refuse her offer. "It's a deal."

I started for the other room when she said, "Hey, wait a second. You gave in too easily just now."

"Just chalk it up to my easygoing nature," I said.

"I would, but we both know that you don't have one," Jenny said.

"I'll trade back. Just say the word."

She thought about that for a few moments, and then said, "We'll keep things the way they are."

"Sounds good."

I left before she could change her mind again. It wasn't like Jenny to be so wishy-washy, but then again, I'd never asked her to help me search a dead man's room before and put her career in danger, so maybe it was exactly like her, given the circumstances.

If it was any consolation, the bedroom was even worse than the living room had been.

The only thing I could figure was that Derrick must have been living there more than a few days. Did that mean there was trouble in Paradise? I opened the closet door and saw that he hadn't been staying there alone. A woman's clothes were hung neatly inside, and from the look at one of the labels, it was a thin woman at that, a size 2, if the dress I pulled out was any indication.

Did the clothing belong to his wife, or Mindi Mills? If it all belonged to his mistress, then where was his wife? Had the police even spoken with her yet? I wished I could pick up my phone and call Zach, but he was off somewhere thinking and brooding, and I knew he hated to be disturbed whenever he did that. I knew he would take my feelings into account when he pondered his decision, but it was my life, too. I'd just grown accustomed to the idea that he was out of the line of fire these days, though his consulting job put him in harm's way enough as it was. Working as Asheville's sheriff would be dangerous, though not as hazardous as running the Charlotte force had been.

As I searched, I kept thinking about my husband, and the wonderfully strange journey our marriage had become.

A thought suddenly occurred to me as I looked around the cluttered room. Where was Derrick's planner? He didn't believe in modern technology, clinging to old ways long past their obsolescence, and while other folks had upgraded to PalmPilots and BlackBerries long ago, Derrick had faithfully bought planners every new January to run his life by. Where could this year's edition be?

Maybe Jenny had better luck than I did. I walked back into the living room and found her sitting on the couch.

"Have you had any luck finding a yearly planner?"

"Like the kind we used in school?"

"Yes, but a little nicer," I said.

"No, I haven't seen anything like that. I did find these," she said as she held out her hand. In her palm was a set of keys.

"They must have been Derrick's," I said as I took them from her. "No car keys here, though." I held one up. "This is probably a house or apartment key, and this looks like it goes to a mailbox. What's this one for?"

Jenny shrugged. "I'd say it might belong to some kind of safe. Did he have one?"

"I'd be shocked if he didn't," I said. "How did the police miss these?"

"They were hidden in one of his shoes," she said. "There was a sock tucked in hiding it, and I was trying to be thorough, so I pulled it out. Do you think they are important?"

"They could be. What I'd really like to get my hands on is his planner. There must be some kind of clue hiding in there. He put his entire life in that thing."

"Even his affair?" Jenny asked. "If it's true, could he have been that stupid? His wife would surely have found out."

"Found out what?" a voice behind us said.

I wasn't expecting anyone to interrupt us, and I had purposely locked the door behind us, but someone had still managed to get in. She was a heavyset brunette that had help from Miss Clairol, and when she was younger, she'd probably been labeled cuddly and cute. Now she was simply overweight trying to fit into expensive-looking clothes that barely managed to contain her.

"I'm sorry, can I help you?" I asked in my most professional voice.

"I was about to ask the same."

"And you are?"

She looked at me with one raised eyebrow. "I'm Cary Duncan, and I'm calling Hotel Security and having you thrown out of my husband's room this instant."

Chapter 9

...

"**T**HERE'S NO NEED FOR THAT," I SAID AS I CROSSED THE room and extended my hand. "My name is Savannah Stone. I'm so sorry for your loss."

She hesitated a moment before dialing and looked at me curiously. "You're the puzzle woman?"

"Yes, I suppose you could call me that. I created puzzles for your husband," I said. "He will truly be missed." Maybe not by me, but surely by someone. I hated stretching the elastic of the truth to the breaking point, but I didn't want to get Benjamin in trouble any more than I wanted to give Cary Duncan a chance to add to her possible suspicion of me.

"That still doesn't explain what you're doing here," she said.

I was at a loss for an explanation when Jenny spoke up. "We were looking for you."

"I find that hard to believe," Cary said.

I did myself, if the truth were told. Had she heard that I'd found her husband's body, and that I was one of the police's prime suspects? No, she couldn't have. If she had, I had a feeling she wouldn't be as cordial as she was being at the moment. Still, I didn't know what to say in defense of our presence there.

Jenny offered her a reassuring smile. "It's true. We wanted to offer our services to you in this difficult time."

"And you are?"

Jenny offered a hand and introduced herself, adding, "I'm one of Savannah's dearest and oldest friends." She didn't mention that she was a lawyer as well, and I certainly wasn't about to bring it up.

"Go on," Cary said.

"Savannah, having the big heart that she does, thought this might be too painful for you to deal with, so we came by to offer to take care of this suite for you and return your husband's clothes and such without putting you through the arduous process of packing them away."

"It *has* been a shock to my system," Cary said. She pretended to dab an imaginary tear, and then said, "Savannah, I never thought you two were that close."

"We worked together a long time," I said. "He got me my first deal." And tried to screw me in the process, I considered adding, but knew better.

"That's true," she said as she surveyed the living room. "My husband was too important to bother with simple things like housekeeping. It was a sign of his genius, you know."

Then he must have been another Einstein, I thought as I glanced around.

She sniffed a few times, and then said, "I'm sorry, I can't deal with this. I'd appreciate your help."

"We're glad to do it," I said. "Where should we bring

the bags when we're finished? Are you staying at the Crest Hotel?"

"No, I'm at the Brunswick," she said. "I couldn't bear to stay here, not after what happened."

"Did you just get into town?" I asked.

She nodded. "An hour ago. The police are going to tell me exactly what happened. So far, all I know is that he was found murdered in one of the conference rooms downstairs. Someone used a knife on him." She shuddered at the thought. At least that confirmed that she hadn't heard my name mentioned in connection with his murder, but I doubted it would take Detective Murphy long to bring it up. We had a limited window of opportunity, and Jenny and I had to take full advantage of it. "Why don't you go back to your hotel, and we'll be there soon. You really should rest."

She looked around once more, and then nodded. "That sounds good. Thank you."

When she was gone, I dead-bolted the door behind her and smiled at Jenny. "Wow, that was close. Way to think fast."

"It gives us the perfect excuse to finish our snooping, doesn't it?"

I nodded. "I thought she might have heard that I was the one who found Derrick's body."

Jenny shook her head. "I was pretty sure we were in the clear when she didn't attack you the second she found out who you were."

"Yes, that was a pretty big clue. I've got another one for you."

"What? Did you find something in the bedroom?"

"Come with me," I said as I led her into the other room.

She looked around, and then said, "It's at least as messy as the living room."

"True, but that's not why we're here. Look in the closet."

She did as I asked, glanced in, and then asked, "Does this mean Cary was lying to us? Had she been staying here all along?"

"Pull out one of the dresses and look at it."

Jenny did, and an instant later after examining a cute little black dress, she said, "There's no way Cary Duncan could have squeezed into this, not on her best day."

I nodded. "Someone else was staying here with Duncan, and if I had to bet, I'd say it was Mindi Mills."

Jenny looked stricken. "She's going to know what her husband was up to. How awful."

"I'd say when she starts unpacking and sees these clothes, she's going to have a pretty good idea that they belong to someone else, and unless Derrick was a cross-dresser who could squeeze himself into something this small, there was a pretty good chance her husband was seeing someone on the side."

"We can't tell her," Jenny said. "It's just not right."

"We offered to clean the place up and deliver the clothes to her at the Brunswick," I reminded her.

"Yes, Derrick's things. We didn't say a word about his mistress's clothes."

I looked at Jenny a second before I spoke. "Jen, how on earth are you so sensitive about this type of stuff and still working as a lawyer?"

"They made a special exception for me, and remember, we don't do domestic cases," she said as she started collecting the smaller clothes.

"What are you going to do with them?"

"I can't just throw them away," she said.

I took a plastic bag from the top shelf, one reserved for dry-cleaning, and began folding the dresses so they'd fit.

"They'll wrinkle that way," Jenny said.

"Do you have any better ideas? We could always do what I suggested and mix them in with Derrick's clothes."

"No, that's fine," she said. We added shoes and some things from the drawers that clearly belonged to the mystery woman.

"Jenny, we don't know for a fact that these belong to Mindi," I said.

"Do you honestly think that he had TWO mistresses on the side?"

"I would guess that it was highly unlikely, but I suppose it's a possibility. There's one good way to find out, though."

"How do you propose we do that?"

"It's simple," I said as I tied a knot in the top of the bag to secure it. "We ask Mindi ourselves."

"I'm not about to disagree with your logic," she said, "but I can't wait to hear how you're going to bring it up."

"I'll think of something," I said. "In the meantime, let's get the two suitcases down from the top shelf and start packing up Derrick's things."

"It should make it easier to search the place that way," she agreed.

As I pulled the suitcases down, I instantly realized that they were heavier than I'd expected them to be.

There was something inside each one of them, but I didn't have a clue what it could be.

"These things weigh a ton," I said as I threw them onto the bed. "What did he keep in them, rocks?"

"Maybe they're stuffed with bars of gold," Jenny said.

"Derrick wasn't a pirate. Well, not the kind you mean, anyway."

Nothing could have surprised me more when I opened the first one and saw what was really hidden inside.

* * *

"**W**HAT IS IT?" JENNY ASKED AS SHE TRIED TO LOOK past me into the opened suitcase.

I pulled out a telephone book, and then another, and another, and another still. "It's full of phone books."

She opened the other suitcase and found the same thing. "There are more phone books in here."

"Where are they from? Are they all for Raleigh?" I asked as I looked at the books in front of me. Mine were all from the Triangle of Raleigh, Durham, and Chapel Hill.

"All from this area," she said as she lifted one telephone book up and fanned the pages. Nothing fluttered out, though I'd been hoping it might have been jammed with hundred dollar bills, or clues, or something other than what we got.

I checked a couple of the ones from the suitcase I had, but there wasn't anything there, either. "How odd. Why would he do something like that? It's got to mean something, unless he's just into stealing telephone directories wherever he stays."

Jenny frowned, and then said, "I've got an idea, but it's kind of far-fetched."

"If it helps explain this, I'm willing to listen."

"What if there was something in these bags, something pretty heavy. If someone took what was stored there, they might want to leave behind something of similar weight to fool Derrick into thinking all was right with the world."

I shrugged. "I suppose it's possible, but if he was checking his luggage anyway, why wouldn't he just open the suitcase up to see for himself?"

"You've got a point. I just don't get it."

"Neither do I, but there might be something here that we're missing. Let's find a box or something stout to put these in, and we'll put Derrick's clothes back into his suitcases after we search them."

"I found a heavy box in the other room we can use," Jenny said.

"Then grab it and let's get busy."

BY THE TIME WE HAD DERRICK'S CLOTHES PACKED INTO his suitcases, the suite was actually beginning to look fairly decent, though the trash cans were all full. In all the time we'd been working, we'd found the keys, the telephone books, and a stack of papers that on first glance didn't make a great deal of sense.

What we didn't find was Derrick's planner.

That was the oddest thing of all. I knew from personal experience that he never went anywhere without it. Could it be holding the key to what had happened to him?

We wouldn't know until we found it.

A thought occurred to me as we made a final sweep around the rooms before releasing the suite back to Benjamin.

Could the police have Derrick's planner themselves?

I wanted to call Zach so he could check for me, but we were having communication problems at the moment. I couldn't call Detective Murphy either, but for very different reasons. I had a feeling that if he knew what Jenny and I were up to, he wouldn't approve.

It was just one more question I was going to have to file away.

For now, there wasn't much I could do about it.

DID YOU FIND ANYTHING ELSE?" I ASKED JENNY AS I walked out of the bedroom with the suitcases. She'd taken the clothes we presumed belonged to Mindi Mills, and I deposited the suitcases beside the bag near the door.

"Nothing," she said. "I'm afraid I'm not much of a detective."

"I think you're doing a great job. You found the keys, didn't you? That's more than I can say."

"I'm sure you would have found them if you'd looked at Derrick's shoes first instead of me," she said, but I could tell she looked a little pleased by my praise.

"Don't bet on it. I just wish I knew what they unlocked."

"We could always ask Cary," she said.

"Maybe if we get desperate, but for right now, let's just keep it between the two of us."

Jenny looked at me with a slight bit of concern in her eyes. "Do you mean we should keep the fact that we found them from Zach, too?"

"Of course not. If I talk to him again, I'll be sure to mention it."

Jenny shook her head. "If you talk to him? Savannah, you two will work this out."

"I know, but that man can be so stubborn sometimes."

At that comment, Jenny started laughing. I looked at her for a second, and then asked, "What's so funny?"

"If anybody knows what stubborn looks like, it would be you."

I chuckled softly myself. "I'd like to dispute that, but we both know that I can't."

My phone started quacking, and I couldn't help but smile. "That would be my husband," I said.

"Would you like some privacy?" Jenny asked as she stepped away. "I'll go in the bedroom and wait."

"You're fine," I told her, and then answered, "Stone Investigations," in my best, most professional voice.

"Sometimes I wonder if you're not the better detective in the family at that. What have you and Jenny been up to?"

"More than I can say over the phone," I answered.

"Then why don't we get together and discuss it," he said.

"Have you made up your mind about what you're going to do?" I asked, trying to remember to breathe as I did.

"Savannah, there won't be any decisions made until we both discuss this and come to an agreement."

"And what if we can't?" I asked, my voice suddenly growing softer.

"Then I turn them down without discussion. You're more important to me than any job. You know that, don't you?"

"Of course I do," I said. "But it's still good to hear every now and then."

"I'll try to do better," he said. "Are you two still at Jenny's?"

"No, sir," I said, my mood suddenly lightened. "We've been busy since you left. At the moment, we're in Derrick's suite at the Crest Hotel. We just finished searching the place for clues, and we found a few things that are pretty interesting."

"Savannah, have you lost your mind? You can't interfere with an active police investigation like that."

I took a deep breath, and then asked, "Are you through scolding me?"

"For now," he said grudgingly.

"The police released his room hours ago, and we got Cary Duncan's blessing to search the suite."

He whistled. "How'd you manage that?"

I didn't want to tell him the truth, but I didn't see that I had much choice. "She caught us searching the place, so Jenny convinced her that we were there to help her take care of Derrick's belongings so she wouldn't have to deal with everything herself. Soon enough, she's going to know that I'm the one who found him, and honestly, how much of a leap is it for her to figure out that I'm a suspect in his murder?"

"I don't like Cary knowing that you're involved so deeply in this," Zach said.

"I'm not thrilled about it either, but she is going to find out sooner or later. I had to take a calculated risk. Besides, if I get into any real trouble, Jenny can bail me out."

Zach laughed at that, a sound I never grew tired of. "If I'm ever in a jam, I think I want Jenny representing me. You're in good hands, Savannah."

"I couldn't agree with you more," I said. "We're about to deliver Derrick's things to his widow. Would you care to join us?"

"Try and stop me. Where is she staying?"

"She's at the Brunswick," I said. "Would you like us to wait for you in the lobby?"

"I'll be there before you will," he said. As he was about to hang up, he added, "I really do love you. You know that, don't you?"

"Right back at you," I said.

After I hung up, I called out to Jenny, "It's safe to come out now."

She walked out, and without waiting for me to say a word, Jenny said, "Good, you two made up."

"How can you tell?"

"There's a smile you don't bring out enough, one that lights up your eyes. You're displaying it right now."

"You always were great at reading me. We're going to return these things to Cary at the Brunswick Hotel. Zach's going to meet us in the lobby."

"Sounds good," she said.

As I opened the door to the suite, a young woman with platinum blonde hair and a figure nearly as artificial was hovering just outside.

"My key doesn't work anymore," she said. "Who are you?"

"We're friends of Derrick," I said, truly stretching the truth beyond its breaking point. "And you are?"

She didn't answer, instead pointing at the bags near the door. "Those belong to Derrick. Are you trying to tell me that he's okay with you waltzing in here and taking his things?"

"He doesn't have much to say about it anymore," I said.

"Why not? What's going on here?"

"You haven't heard?" I asked.

"Heard what?" The suspicion was even stronger in her voice and eyes now. "If he thinks he's dumping me for one of you, he's sadly mistaken."

"You're Mindi, aren't you?"

"Not that it's any of your business, but I am. I'm still waiting to hear who you are."

"That's not important," I said. "When's the last time you saw Derrick?"

"Three days ago," she said. "I had to leave town, but he knew I was coming back. I'm getting tired of this. Tell me who you are and what you're doing here, or I'm going to call the police."

"Mindi, I don't know how to tell you this," I said, "but I'm afraid I've got some bad news for you. Derrick's dead."

She looked as though she'd been hit between the eyes with a sledgehammer. One second she was standing there talking to us, and the next, she was plummeting to the floor in a dead faint.

As Jenny and I rushed to her, my old roommate said, "Man, you've got a lot to learn about giving someone bad news."

"What should I have said?"

"I'm not sure, but I'm guessing there was a better way of handling it than just blurting it out like that."

"I'll get some water," I said.

Jenny nodded as she knelt down. "She's out cold. It should wake her up."

"I'm not getting it for her. I'm thirsty."

"Not funny, Savannah. She took it really hard, didn't she?"

"It appeared that way, didn't it?" I got water from the sink in one of the hotel glasses and flicked some onto Mindi's face. It took more than a few sprinkles to wake her, and when she finally came around, she asked, "Is it true? Is he gone?"

"I'm sorry, but I'm afraid he is," Jenny said as we helped Mindi up.

We walked her to the couch, and as she sat down, I handed her the rest of the water. "Drink this. It will help."

She gulped the water down, and then said, "Thank you." After taking a deep breath, she asked, "How did he die?"

"Someone stabbed him with a steak knife," I said. I didn't feel the need to add that the police believed that I was the one who'd done it.

"So Cary finally killed him," Mindi said, her voice suddenly dead.

"What do you mean?" I asked.

"She's been threatening him for ages, and when he asked her for a divorce, she said she'd give him one over her dead body. I just never thought she'd kill him instead of setting him free." As she looked around the suite, she asked, "Who cleaned up in here?"

"We did," Jenny admitted.

Mindi got up and hurried to the closet in the other room. When she threw open the door, we all saw the lonely little hotel hangers with steel balls welded to their necks, an antitheft device that was probably pretty effective, since the hangers were useless without the receiving brackets that allowed them to work. "My things. Do the police have them?"

"No, we've got them in the other room," I said.

Mindi looked around the bedroom as we walked out into the living room, and it didn't appear to be a casual glance. She was searching for something, something that was clearly missing.

"Did you leave something else behind?" I asked her.

"No, just my clothes," she said.

Jenny retrieved the dry cleaning bag and handed it to her. "Sorry, we didn't have anyplace else to put your things."

"It's fine," she said absently. "Can I have his suitcases? There are some things of sentimental value in there."

"I'm sorry, but Cary asked for them. We're doing this for her."

Mindi bit her lower lip, and then said, "At least let me get his favorite shoes. I got them for him after our first date."

"Again, we can't help you," I said.

Jenny took her arm and led her out the door as I collected the suitcases. She told Mindi, "If you'd like to ask Cary, you're more than welcome to, but she trusted us to do this, and we don't have any choice. We gave our word."

"I understand," Mindi said.

It was clear that she was more interested in the suitcases than she was in us, and I was beginning to worry that she was going to take them anyway, but Mindi finally turned toward the elevators. "Are you two coming?"

Jenny started to tell her that we were when I touched her arm lightly. "You go ahead. We have a few more things to do here first," I said.

She frowned, and then nodded in acceptance. "Fine. Good-bye, then."

"Good-bye," we said, and closed the door behind her.

"What was that all about?" Jenny asked me once we were alone again in the hotel suite.

"Did you see the way she looked at those suitcases? I wouldn't put it past her to mug us for them on the way to your car, and I don't think there's anything sentimental about her motives."

"She wants those keys," Jenny said.

"You got it on your first try. I'm going to call Zach and have him meet us up here. I'd feel better having him with us when we leave."

"Do you honestly think that Mindi could be dangerous?"

"I don't want to underestimate her," I admitted. "Don't forget, someone's already dead, someone close to her."

I dialed Zach's number, and when he answered, I said, "I can't explain, but it would be great if you could meet us in Derrick's suite in the penthouse."

"What's going on? Did something happen?" The concern in my husband's voice was easy to hear.

"No, but I'd feel better if you were with us," I admitted.

"Then say no more. Lock the door, and don't let anyone in until I get there. Understood?"

"We're not under siege," I said.

"Your gut's telling you that you two might be in danger, and that's all I need to hear," he said. "I'll see you soon."

As we waited, I worried that I'd alarmed my husband for nothing, but I knew I wouldn't relax until he was there with us.

I was about to tell Jenny that I might be overreacting when there was a heavy pounding on the door, and from the sound of it, I doubted that Mindi Mills could make such a racket.

It appeared that someone else was paying us a call.

Chapter 10

...

"**W**HO'S THERE?" I ASKED AS I TRIED TO LOOK OUT THE door's peephole. The view was blocked, and all I saw was darkness on the other side when I tried to look through it.

A muffled voice said, "Delivery," and whoever was on the other side tried the handle.

"You can leave it at the front desk," I said.

Jenny whispered, "What's going on?"

"I don't know, but I don't like it," I said softly.

"You have to sign for it," the voice said in a low tone. I couldn't honestly tell if it was a man or a woman. Whoever was speaking didn't want me to know either.

"Slide the paper under the door," I ordered. As I did, I told Jenny, "Call the front desk, ask for Benjamin, and have them send Hotel Security up here right now."

She nodded, and I held my breath waiting for a reply.

When there was no answer, I counted to ten, and then looked out the peephole again. It was now clear, but I couldn't see anyone standing there. I started to undo the chain when Jenny grabbed my arm.

"What are you doing?"

"I want to see who's out there," I said.

"Too bad," she said as she put her hand on mine. "We're waiting for reinforcements."

One minute later, there was another knock at the door, and when I looked outside, Benjamin was standing there.

I opened the door, and he came in. "I was at the front desk when you called. What happened?"

"It's probably nothing," I said, "but someone just tried to get me to open the door, claiming there was a delivery."

"The deliveries all come through the front desk," he said. "No one should have access otherwise."

"When I couldn't see out the peephole, we called you."

He leaned forward, checked the peephole, and then said, "There's nothing wrong with it."

"Not now," I said, feeling a little impatient with him, "but someone was blocking it earlier."

"I'll have my men check the stairs," he said, and then he spoke softly into a walkie-talkie unit.

As he did so, the elevator opened and Zach walked out. He looked up and down the hallway before coming in, and there was a look of concern on his face as he spoke. "What just happened?"

"Someone tried to trick their way into the suite," I admitted, "but Jenny and I were too smart for them."

He conferred with Benjamin after he introduced himself, and the two of them went to the stairwell.

"This door's been propped open with a book of matches," Zach said.

"But there's no smoking in the hotel," Benjamin said.

"That's the least of our worries," Zach said. He carefully

extracted the matchbook with his handkerchief. "I'm going to ask Murphy to run this for prints."

"Do you honestly think he'll do it for you?" Jenny asked.

"He might, out of professional courtesy. Anyway, there's only one way to find out."

Zach made a quick call, and I thanked Benjamin for coming upstairs.

"There's no need to thank me," he said. "Garrett was most specific in his instructions."

"Well, I'll let him know what a good job you've done taking care of us," I said. "We're finished here."

He nodded, and then spied the suitcases. "Are you taking those with you as well?"

"We're returning them to the widow, at her request," I said, and Jenny nodded her verification.

"Very well," Benjamin said. He hesitated, and then added delicately, "Is that . . . everything?"

I knew instantly what he was asking. Apparently I wasn't the only one who'd noticed the discrepancy between the dress sizes of what was hanging in the closet and Cary Duncan. "The dresses have been returned to their rightful owner as well," I said.

"Then I am in your debt," he said. "You've saved me from having a very awkward conversation."

"I'm happy to help," I said, not admitting that I'd done it for a selfish reason of my own.

"If there's anything else I can do for you, you have my card," he said.

"Thanks."

We all stepped out into the corridor, and I locked the door behind us, and then handed Benjamin the electronic key. Before I could protest, he retrieved the suitcases, and Zach grabbed the box full of telephone books.

"What do you have in here, bricks?" he asked as he started to open the top of the box.

"Don't be silly," I said as I put my hand on top of his. "I'll be happy to carry it if it's too much for you to handle."

"I've got it," he said as he shot me a quizzical look. I chose to ignore it, at least for the moment.

Once we were in the lobby, Jenny and I each took a suitcase, and Benjamin walked us to the front door. After he was gone, Zach couldn't wait to open the box, and there was no reason to stop him then.

He flipped it open, found one telephone book after another, and then said, "I'm sure there's a perfectly good reason the three of us are stealing phone books from a hotel."

"There is," I said.

"Would you care to share it with me?"

I just laughed. "It will have to wait until we get to the Brunswick Hotel."

He shrugged. "Okay, I can stand not knowing that long. I'll see you both there."

The next stop was the Brunswick Hotel. I couldn't wait to get rid of the suitcases filled with Derrick's clothes. It hadn't bothered me searching them and packing them up, but for some reason, having them in my car was making me a little skittish.

It's hard to say what makes most people's minds work the way they do.

And that goes double for mine.

WHEN WE GOT TO THE BRUNSWICK, I CHECKED AT THE front desk for Cary's room number. Zach and Jenny had stayed back so Cary wouldn't feel like we were ganging up on her.

The clerk punched a few numbers into his computer,

and then said, "I'm sorry, but Ms. Duncan has left notice that she is not to be disturbed."

"I understand," I said, "but she's expecting me. I have some of her late husband's things."

"You must be Ms. Stone," he said.

I decided to let the Ms. slide this time. "I am."

He nodded as he tapped a few more keys. "In that case, I have specific instructions for you."

He smiled slightly as he said, "You are to leave Mr. Duncan's things with our bag check service, and then return with the receipt and give it to me. She asked me to thank you for your assistance in this most difficult time."

"Are you serious? That's it?" I asked.

"I'm afraid it's out of my hands." He didn't look all that upset saying no to me. Some people looked for ways to make things happen, while others delighted in throwing up roadblocks whenever the opportunity availed itself.

I walked back to Jenny and Zach, and my husband hit the up button before I could say anything.

"There's no reason to take the elevator," I said.

"Why? I didn't think there were any guest rooms on the main floor."

"It appears that Cary has decided not to speak with us again, and there's not much we can do about it."

Zach looked surprised by the statement. "What's going on?"

"She wants us to check these bags, and then give the clerk the claim ticket. It doesn't look like there's a chance we're going to be able to have another face-to-face conversation with her today."

"We'll see about that."

I grabbed my husband's arm as he started for the front desk. "Zach, you're not a cop anymore, and you don't have any standing in this case."

"We know that," he said softly, "but I'm guessing this guy doesn't."

"It's okay. We'll talk to her later."

"Why wait? You two did her a service, no matter what your motives were, and she could at least have the decency to thank you in person."

"Jenny? What do you think?" I asked.

"Don't drag me into this. I'm staying out of it."

"Come on, you've got the tiebreaking vote. What's it going to be?"

Jenny frowned, and then pointed to a corner of the lobby and said, "Let's go over there. We can discuss it where no one's watching us."

I looked over to see that the clerk was indeed following us with keen interest. We moved to the edge of his sight line, and I said, "Go on. Let's hear what you've got to say."

"I'll tell you, but you're not going to like it."

Zach crowed. "Excellent. I knew you were the most sensible one around here."

"Not exactly."

"You can't be on both our sides," I said.

"I'm not. I don't think you should talk to her, but not for the reason you might think."

"Go on," I said. "I'm always willing to listen to what you have to say."

She took a deep breath, and then said, "Guys, you know I love you both, but I'm beginning to have some doubts about how active I should be in this investigation of yours. Savannah, I'm your attorney of record, so it might be good if I left myself some room to wiggle if the police find out what you're up to, which trust me, they are going to, sooner or later. Murphy is a good cop, no matter what I think of him as a person. You two are just visiting Raleigh, but I have to work with these people after you're gone. Maybe I should take a little less active role in the investigation from here on out."

"She's right," I said as I looked at Zach.

"No doubt about it," he agreed.

Jenny said, "Hang on. I'm not saying I don't want to help at all. You both know that, don't you?"

I hugged her. "Of course we do. I've got an idea. Why don't you take that vacation you've been planning?"

"I'm not leaving town until your name is cleared," she said emphatically.

"You could always go back to the office, then," I suggested.

"Are you trying to get rid of me?"

Zach grinned. "You know better than that. You're right about getting too close to what we're doing, though."

She crinkled her nose with her frown. "I'd go crazy relaxing, you both know me better than that. I think I'll go into work after all. There's always something I can do there. Besides, this stalker has been worrying me so much lately that I haven't been able to focus on my work. That way, too, if I hang around and you need me, I'm just a telephone call away."

"That sounds like a good plan," I said.

Zach grinned. "We'll see you at your place tonight, then."

Jenny hugged me, and then embraced my husband.

On impulse, I asked, "Would you mind taking that box of phone books with you? I'm not done with them yet, and we've got our hands full with these suitcases."

"Sure, I'd be glad to," she said as she hefted them up and walked across the lobby and out the door.

After she was gone, Zach asked, "Okay, what should we do now?"

"Let me ask you something first. Are you certain you're okay with Jenny taking a backseat in our investigation?"

"To be honest with you, I was a little worried about her being so actively involved myself. This is absolutely for the best." He paused, and then grinned at me. "Besides, we work better as a team, just the two of us. We always have."

"Agreed." I stared at the bags still at our feet.

My husband must have been reading my mind. "What are we going to do with these suitcases? I'm not thrilled about the idea of letting them go just yet, especially when we've been commanded to surrender them."

I thought about it, and then said, "If you're game, I have an idea."

His smile lit up his entire face. "Just try me."

FOLLOW MY LEAD," I SAID AS I PICKED UP ONE OF THE suitcases and started walking across the lobby where Jenny had just gone. As soon as I knew the clerk had seen me, I nodded to Zach, who followed me with the other one. It was clear that the clerk was wondering what we were up to. Instead of walking to the bag check station as I'd been instructed, I started for the exit. I was curious to see what the clerk would do, and the worst thing that could happen was that we retained possession of Derrick's clothes. If Cary wanted them back, and I had a suspicion that she did, she'd have to come with us.

We nearly made it to the door before someone called out behind us, "Ms. Stone. Wait."

"It's Mrs.," I said when he caught up with us.

"Mrs. Stone," he corrected himself. "I believe I told you that you were supposed to check those bags with our service."

"Sorry, but I don't respond well to orders. You can ask him if you don't believe me," I added as I pointed to Zach.

"She hasn't so far, but I keep hoping," my husband answered amiably.

The clerk looked at me as if I'd lost my mind. "But you heard Mrs. Duncan's wishes on the matter."

"I heard what you said just fine."

He looked a little relieved by this information. "Then you're going in the wrong direction. Our claim service is over there."

"I know perfectly well where it is. I just choose not to go there."

Now he really looked confused. I winked at Zach, who remained silent as he winked back at me.

"Then where are you going?"

"I don't see how that's any of your business. Mrs. Duncan's wishes are not my orders. We had an agreement, and if she is choosing to alter it, I have the right not to accept her new terms. Please tell her that if she'd like her husband's suitcases back, she knows how to reach me." I doubted very much if Cary had the slightest clue where I was staying while I was in Raleigh, but I didn't think it would come to that.

"Would you indulge me for two minutes before you leave?" he asked.

I turned to my husband. "What do you think, Zach?"

"It's your call," he said.

"Two minutes," I said.

"Thank you so much," the clerk said as he scurried back to his desk.

After he was out of earshot, Zach said, "I've got to hand it to you. That was inspired."

"I have my moments," I said.

"Are you watching the clock?"

I shook my head. "I can't imagine that I'll have to." I looked back at the desk and saw the clerk walking rapidly toward us. For a moment, I had a devilish impulse to run away, the suitcases in tow, but I fought it and waited for his return.

"She'll see you now," he said, the poor man nearly out of breath.

"Very good. The room number?"

"One-two-two-one," he said.

"Thank you."

"Thank you," he said. He stood there waiting until Zach and I took the suitcases and walked toward the elevator instead of the exit. What was the clerk planning to do if we made a run for it, tackle us both? He might be able to bring me down, but I would have paid good money to watch him try to keep my husband from doing anything he really wanted to do.

When we got on the elevator, Zach pushed 12, and as soon as the doors closed, we burst out laughing. It was brief, but extremely satisfying, and when we stopped, my husband kissed me.

"Thank you, kind sir," I said.

"Thank you. Sometimes I forget just how much fun it can be hanging around with you."

"Then I'll try to keep reminding you." The elevator was fast approaching the twelfth floor, and I asked Zach, "Any ideas on how we should handle her?"

"Are you kidding? I'm just planning to follow your lead."

"Fine. We'll play it by ear, then."

Cary was waiting in the hallway when the door opened, and she looked surprised to see my husband carrying Derrick's other suitcase. "Savannah, why on earth did you feel the need to bring a bodyguard with you to my room?"

"He's no bodyguard," I said. "He's my husband."

Zach offered his free hand, and she took it, albeit a little reluctantly at first. My husband can be intimidating on his best day, but when he wants to, he can be pretty charming as well.

"Please, come in," she said as she stepped aside. We

walked in, and I was amazed by how elegant the Brunswick's rooms were. While Derrick's hotel was cookie-cutter in its looks and layout, this place appeared to be taken from someone's living room. Someone who was wealthy and had excellent taste, I might add. The furniture wasn't a chain knockoff, but looked to be custom-made for the space, and the walls were covered with original art that seemed to enhance the room's elegance.

"Would you like to go through these while we're here?" I asked.

"No, of course not. Just put them over there. I'm afraid Derrick's tastes did not match mine. He chose not to pay attention to his wardrobe, so I stopped caring about what he wore." She must have realized how that sounded, because she quickly added, "I can't tell you how much I'm going to miss him."

"I'm sure," I said.

Zach asked, "I hate to bother you, but is there any chance I could use your restroom?"

She hesitated, and then pointed to a door that led into the bedroom. "Of course."

Once he was gone, I asked, "Cary, how have you and Derrick been getting along lately?" She started to cloud up, so I quickly added, "I was one of his biggest fans, but believe me, I know how difficult he could be at times."

Cary nodded, but without too much vigor. "He was an artist in his own right, and we must make allowances for creative people. They seem to be wired differently than we are."

If Derrick could draw a picture of the sun with a stick in the mud, I would have been surprised. Many words came to mind when I tried to describe the man, but "artistic" wasn't one of them. "So, things were tense for you?"

"Of course not," she said. "Savannah, what are you trying to say?"

"I'm not saying anything. I'm just making conversation," I said.

She didn't buy it for a moment, and I didn't know any way to convince her otherwise. "Then let's change the subject, shall we?"

"That's fine with me. I must say, I was a little surprised to hear that Kelsey Hatcher was taking over the Duncan Empire."

Calling it an empire was a joke, but Cary seemed to like the notion. "Kelsey is quite capable. I convinced Derrick to hire her, you know. Her talents were being wasted where she was before."

"And where was that?"

Cary started to say something, and then obviously thought better of it. "She's well suited to run things. I trust you and the others are cooperating during this transition period."

It wasn't a question, so I decided not to answer it.

Zach came out, and said, "Cary, I've got a great idea. Why don't you join us for a late lunch?"

I looked at my husband, wondering what on earth he was up to, but it was time for me to back his play. "Please do. It might be exactly what you need."

"Thank you, but no, I'll have to refuse."

"Are you sure?" Zach asked, somehow managing to look crestfallen from the news.

"Positive." She glanced at her watch, and then said, "I don't mean to be rude, but there are a thousand arrangements I need to deal with. Thank you again for taking care of things for me at the suite."

"Glad to help," I said as she walked us out the door and to the elevator. As the doors closed, I could still see her watching us, offering a halfhearted wave at the last second.

As Zach and I rode down, I asked, "What did you find?"

"Excuse me?"

"Zach, I know you were snooping around. What did you find?"

He shrugged. "She's alone, no doubt about it. I checked the closets, the luggage, and the vanity in the bathroom. There's no sign of anyone being there but her."

"So it was a dead end."

"Not exactly," he replied. The elevator opened into the lobby, and he pulled me to one side, beside a massive tree planted in a dark gray pot.

"What are we doing?"

"Lower your voice," he said. "I got a glimpse at the notepad on the desk by the bed, and I saw that she has an appointment in a few minutes. Why don't we wait to see who comes along?"

"You're tricky," I said.

"I prefer to think of it as being clever," he replied. We stood there in the shadows of the tree's leaves when I saw a familiar face coming toward the elevator. I grabbed Zach's arm and pointed to the man, carrying a bouquet of flowers in one hand.

He punched an elevator button, and after a few seconds' wait, got on.

I pulled Zach out and watched as the floor numbers lit up.

"Who was that?" Zach asked.

"Hang on one second," I said as I continued watching. A few seconds later the elevator stopped, and I saw that it had reached the twelfth floor.

"I don't believe it," I said.

"Savannah Stone, if you don't tell me right now who that was, I'm walking out of here."

"It was Brady Sims. He worked for Derrick writing the Wuzzle World puzzles."

"And now he's visiting the widow," Zach said. "It doesn't

necessarily mean anything, you know. He could be here to pay his respects."

"He could be, but I doubt it. Did those flowers look like something you'd give to a grieving woman?"

"You're asking me? Seriously?"

"Trust me, they're not. They looked more like courting flowers."

"I don't know," Zach said. "It's a reach."

"Maybe, but it's not one we can afford to ignore."

My husband nodded. "Then Brady moves up a few spots on our suspect list."

"As long as I keep moving down, I'm fine with that."

I tried to imagine Brady and Cary together, but I just couldn't wrap my head around it.

Love made up some stranger matches than that, though. I saw it nearly every day.

But it certainly was something we needed to investigate.

Chapter 11

...

"**W**HAT SHOULD WE DO?" I ASKED ZACH. "SHOULD WE stay here until he comes back down so we can talk to him?"

"It's hard to say how long that might be," he answered. As he looked around the lobby, he added, "Besides, we're a little conspicuous standing here, even with this tree blocking us from view."

"We could always go to the restaurant and get something to eat while we're waiting."

"Come on, Savannah. Surely we can find someplace better than that," he said as he glanced at the formal dining room that was connected to the lobby. I was certain that the men in suits offered the reason for his hesitation. Zach didn't like to go anywhere that he had to dress up for, particularly to eat. It was all I could do to get him to take me out to a fancy restaurant on our anniversary every year.

"I'm sure they have a jacket you can borrow."

"No thanks. I say we leave Brady and Cary to their tryst, or whatever it is, and go talk to another suspect."

"I'm good with that," I said, giving in. "Which one do you want to go after next?"

"Well, since Brady and Cary are busy upstairs, and Sylvia's at the other hotel, that leaves Mindi and Frank Lassiter at the top of our list."

"I can't believe we have five suspects already without even trying."

"Six," Zach said.

"Who did we miss?"

"Kelsey Hatcher. I keep asking myself, who had the most to gain by Derrick's murder, and Kelsey's name keeps popping up."

"She is in charge now, isn't she? That's quite a step up, from assistant to editor and syndicator. Cary must trust her an awful lot. Or Kelsey must have something pretty damaging on Cary."

"Who's being cynical now?"

"More like realistic," I said. "You didn't see Kelsey when she called us all together. It was pretty clear the power has already gone to her head."

"I thought you two made up?"

"For now," I admitted, "but I can see some rocky times ahead. There was an edge to her before that she's trying to hide now, but she's not what she seems."

"To be, rather than to seem," Zach quoted.

"Yeah, and mountaineers are always free," I answered.

"What's that got to do with anything?"

"I figured if we're quoting state mottos, I'd throw out a few of my own. You gave me North Carolina, and I replied with one from West Virginia."

Zach looked into my eyes. "Savannah, I'm not in the mood for any foolishness."

I couldn't keep from laughing. "Boy, did you ever marry the wrong woman, then."

He tried to look stern, but his visage suddenly broke into a smile. "I think I did pretty well for myself, thank you very much."

"You're very welcome," I replied.

The clerk must have been watching us the entire time we'd been standing in his lobby. "Was there something else you needed?" he asked as he approached us.

"No, we're good," I said with a smile.

"Very well," he replied as he backed up a few steps.

I tugged on Zach's arm. "Come on, we're clearly making the man nervous."

"We have that effect on folks sometimes, don't we?"

I looked up at my powerful husband. "I think they're more intimidated by you than me."

"Don't kid yourself. I know some hardened criminals who'd rather take me on than you."

"Now you're just trying too hard."

I led him out of the hotel, and we got into the rental. As I started the ignition, I said, "We never really decided what we were going to do next, did we?"

"Is there a place around here I could make a few telephone calls? I hate to be where anyone else can hear me."

"How about right here in the car? Or did you want me to leave, too?"

"Of course not." He opened his cell phone, and then said, "I'm having a hard time getting a signal in here anyway."

"I have an idea," I said. "It's on the way to the other hotel, too, if that helps."

"I'm in your hands."

As I drove through town, I said, "This is a place where you should have plenty of privacy, and the views are pretty spectacular, too."

"You've got me curious. Any hints?"

"We'll be there in a second," I said. I took the last turn, and wondered for a minute if I'd gotten it right. The neighborhood we drove through was a little sketchy, but a few minutes later, I saw the sign I'd been looking for.

"We're here," I said as I pulled into the parking lot.

Zach looked at the train tracks and the benches. "Where exactly is here?"

"It's Pullen Park," I said. "Jenny brought me here the last time I visited. They have the coolest carousel in the world here."

"We don't have time to ride, Savannah."

"Come on. We can at least go look at it."

Zach nodded, and we walked down the path of gray brown interlocking pavers. The view, once obscured by bushes, now presented a large lake of beautiful water. There were paddleboats docked close to us, though none were out on the water at the moment. Several ducks were sitting on the wooden docks, as if waiting patiently for their turns to ride.

"Everything's closed," Zach said.

"I don't understand," I said. "The carousel has to be open."

As we walked toward the round building, I saw shutters closed at every opening.

A man was working nearby, replacing the trash bags from one of the garbage cans. "Excuse me? Is it closed?"

He nodded. "They had to do some repairs. Don't worry, it'll be back open in a few days."

"Thanks," I said.

"Is the train running?"

He shook his head. "Sorry, you just missed the last ride."

Zach shrugged. "Hey, you tried."

"Perfect. At least the statues should still be there, unless they've hauled them off somewhere for cleaning."

"What statues are you talking about?"

I didn't say a word. I just grabbed his hand and led him to the place I remembered from my last visit.

To my delight, they were still there.

I watched Zach as he rounded the corner, and an immediate grin came up on his face. "Savannah, how cool is that?"

It was a bronze statue of Andy and Opie Taylor, father and son, from *The Andy Griffith Show*, a North Carolina love letter to the rest of the world. They each had a fishing pole, and the two held hands as Opie looked adoringly up at his father, while Andy looked lovingly at his son. Growing up, my husband had loved the show, and whenever he saw a rerun channel surfing, he always paused on it.

"That is one of the neatest things I've ever seen in my life."

"Go on, I'll take your picture with them with my camera phone."

He looked a little embarrassed by the suggestion. "Savannah, have you lost your mind?"

"Think of it this way, Zach. When are you ever going to get the chance to do this again?"

He frowned for a second, and then grinned. "Why not?"

After I got a shot of him standing in front of the duo, he shook his head in disbelief, though the smile was still clear on his face. "We're not going to be able to show that to anyone, you know that, don't you?"

"We don't have to. Isn't it enough to know that it exists?"

I kissed his cheek, and he surprised me by wrapping me up in his arms. "I love you."

"More than Andy?" I said.

"Andy, Barney, Opie, and Aunt Bea, too."

"Wow, I feel special."

Zach kissed me again, this time more soundly, and then he released me. "Now if you'll excuse me, I've got some calls to make."

My husband walked over toward the water, and I moved nearby where I could see the lake myself. It was beautiful, a serene vision just minutes from downtown Raleigh, and I silently thanked the park's designer for preserving something so special so close.

I don't know how long I took it all in, but Zach came back and broke into my thoughts. "Savannah, did you hear me?"

"Sorry, I was thinking about something else," I said. "What did you say?"

"We've got a meeting, and we need to get across town in ten minutes to make it in time."

"Then we'd better get going," I said as I started back to the parking lot.

"Don't you even want to know who we're seeing?" he asked.

"I figure you'll tell me eventually."

"I spoke with Derrick's former business partner, Frank Lassiter. He's in town at the police's request, and he wants to talk to me."

"Not us?"

"I don't think he'll mind if you tag along, too."

"Well, I've had warmer invitations, but I've had worse ones over the years, too, haven't I?"

"Probably even from me."

"Where are we meeting?" I asked.

"We need to head over to Edenton Street. We're going to talk to him on the grounds of the State Capitol."

* * *

AS WE DROVE THE SHORT DISTANCE TO THE CAPITOL, I asked Zach, "How did you manage to get him to meet us?"

"He feels like the police are going to railroad him for this, and he wants someone with some influence on his side."

"And you know someone like that?"

He grinned at me. "I'm talking about me."

"How did he get the impression you had some pull in Raleigh?"

"Well," Zach said as he rubbed his chin, "I may have misled him a little on that. After I identified myself as the former Charlotte chief of police, I told him I had an interest in Derrick's homicide case, which is strictly true. He asked me a few questions, I answered them honestly, and he agreed to this meeting."

"Can I be there, too?"

"Yes, but it's best if you don't say anything."

I looked over at my husband to see if he was serious. "You're kidding, right?"

"Normally I would never dream of asking you to do that, Savannah, and you know it, but I want your reactions to his answers."

"Does he even know I'm your wife?"

Zach hesitated a long time before he answered. "I'm not planning on telling him, and you shouldn't, either."

"Let me get this straight. You want me to lie to him?"

"Of course not," he said as I pulled up into an empty parking spot on Edenton Street. "Just don't volunteer any information."

"I suppose I can do that," I said.

Before I opened my door, I reached into the backseat and grabbed a clipboard I stowed there when I wanted to work on a puzzle.

"What's that for?" Zach asked.

"Camouflage. People think you're official if you keep your mouth shut and carry a clipboard around."

"Where did you learn that?"

"I read it in a mystery novel, if you must know, but it sounds like it could be true, doesn't it?"

"I suppose it's worth a shot," Zach said.

We got out of the car and walked over to a large marble memorial that sported a bronze woman on top. "Where is he?"

"He said he'd be by the small cannons," Zach said.

"They're over this way," I said as I took a left.

"How do you know that?"

"I came here right after Derrick fired me, remember?"

"I thought you said you went to the museum."

I pointed across the street. "That's where I ended up."

We found a pair of small cannons where I remembered them, and there was a heavyset older man in a three-piece suit waiting there, glancing at his watch.

My husband approached him, and I took a few steps back. Zach identified himself, and the man said in a gravelly voice, "I'm Lassiter."

He looked at me, obviously expecting me to provide my name, but I just stood there, nodded, and then glanced down at my clipboard, as if there was something there more fascinating than a puzzle that was only partially completed.

"Before we get started, I need to know a few things," Zach said.

"Fire away. I've got nothing to hide."

"When was the last time you saw Derrick Duncan alive?" Zach asked.

"In Richmond, the day before he was killed," Lassiter said. "And I can prove it."

I couldn't help myself. I'd promised Zach to keep

quiet, but the gear between my mouth and my brain clearly weren't working. "How could you possibly prove that?"

"There were witnesses," the man said. "Who are you, anyway?"

"An associate who sometimes forgets herself," my husband replied. "She does make a good point, though."

"I've got witnesses," Lassiter said, starting to get aggravated with both of us.

"You have witnesses who saw you together the day before he was murdered, but that doesn't prove that you didn't see him again later," Zach said, and I smiled slightly. He'd gotten my point, even if Lassiter hadn't.

"He was murdered here, right? I've never been to Raleigh before, so it would have been tough for me to kill him."

"That's true," Zach said. "But again, it's hard to prove that you've never been somewhere before, too."

"What is this? I thought you were going to help me."

"I can't do anything until I find out more about you and your situation."

"I'm not the one anyone should be looking at. There are a boatload of people with more motive and opportunity than I ever had."

"Would you care to explain?"

"Sure I would. Like I told that detective Murphy, Cary Duncan had five hundred thousand reasons to want the man dead. Derrick told me that she took out a life insurance policy on him six months ago. He said he was worth more to her dead than alive. That's an odd thing to brag about, wouldn't you say?"

"Did they have problems?"

"Let me ask you something. Are you married?"

To his credit, he didn't look at me as he answered. "Sometimes it feels like I have been all my life."

"Then you know."

"Know what?" Zach asked a second before I could.

"There's not a couple I've ever known who didn't want to kill each other at least a dozen times over the course of a marriage, and that includes the ones who get along."

I was about to answer that when Zach shot me a warning look. "She had to have had more of a reason than that."

Lassiter raised one eyebrow as he said, "How about a little piece of fluff on the side?"

"Derrick was cheating on his wife?"

"Some gal named Mindi," Lassiter said with a smile. "That's not all, though. I happen to know that Cary wasn't sitting at home being faithful when Duncan was out kicking it up."

"She was having affairs, too?"

"Oh, yes. Sometimes I wondered why they even bothered to stay married. The worst part of it was, from what I heard around town, she was stepping out with somebody Derrick knew."

"It wouldn't be you, would it, Mr. Lassiter?" I asked.

Lassiter looked at me with the same expression that Zach had on his face. It said simply, Have you completely lost your mind?

"Lady, I don't know who you are, but you're out of line."

"Perhaps it would be better if you waited in the car," Zach said.

"I'll shut up," I promised, though all three of us knew there was no chance that was going to ever happen.

"You don't have to. I'm leaving," Lassiter said as he started to walk away.

"We're not finished here," Zach said.

"That's where you're wrong. Listen, if you want to be somebody's advocate, you might want to try believing them when they're telling you the truth."

After he was gone, I prepared myself for a barrage from Zach, but he just shook his head and walked back to the car. I felt worse than I would have if he'd chewed me out.

"I'm sorry," I said as I caught up with him. "I didn't mean to push him. I should have kept my mouth shut like I'd promised."

I couldn't see Zach's face, but when he glanced over at me, I could see that he was grinning.

"What are you smiling about?"

He ordered, "Keep walking. You might not realize it, but Lassiter is still watching us. I want him to think that I'm upset with you. It might get us another angle inside, if we play it right."

"You're not mad?"

"I'd have been disappointed if you hadn't started goading him when you did," Zach admitted. "Savannah, did you honestly think I believed for one second that you could listen to me interview someone without interjecting? Give me a little credit, will you?"

"I'm not sure that's a compliment," I said.

"It wasn't meant to be. I figured you'd make a crack or two, and I wanted to see his reaction to you. I had a feeling that he was indeed having an affair with Cary Duncan, but you disproved that."

"How so?" I asked as we got back to the car.

"Lassiter's not all that fond of strong women, if his reaction to you is any indication. Can you imagine him putting up with Cary Duncan? One of the main questions about him was if he were capable of an affair with her, and I'd have to say no at the moment."

"He could have been acting," I said.

"Not the way he was looking at you. I've got a feeling Lassiter likes women who don't talk back. That doesn't mean he's off the hook, though. If he lost the kind of money we've heard he did, that was reason enough to kill Duncan."

"So why didn't you ask him about that?"

"There wasn't time," Zach said. "I thought it would take longer for us to make him mad than it did."

"Then at least I'm sorry about that," I said.

"Don't sweat it, Savannah. There are other ways of finding that out. At least we accomplished something."

"What's next, then?"

He glanced at his watch, and then said, "I think it's time we sat down and had a chat with Mindi Mills. She seems to be at the edge of all of this, don't you think?"

"Why would she kill him? She doesn't stand to gain by Derrick's death."

"Maybe she killed him for another reason," Zach said.

"True. If he were dumping her, it might give her motive. How do we find that out, though? I shouldn't have let her go when I had the chance."

"Don't be too hard on yourself. We'll track her down and talk to her, then see how she reacts to our questions. How does that sound?"

"It depends."

"On what?"

"Do I get to participate this time, or am I just going to be a puppet for you again?"

Zach hugged me before we got into the car. "Savannah, my dear sweet wife, you are a great many things, some of them so frustrating I want to howl at the moon, but anyone's puppet, you are not."

"Good, at least you admit that. We're a team, you know."

"Trust me, I'm well aware of it."

As I drove back to the Crest Hotel, I kept wondering about all of the people in Duncan's life who had a reason to want him dead. It made me wonder how a man could alienate himself so thoroughly from the people around him. Had he known how little he'd been loved? Had he even cared? It was hard to believe that he did, knowing the man as I had. He'd aggravated me a thousand times since we began working together, but I'd never disliked him enough to kill him.

It was clear that I was in the minority there, though.

Chapter 12

...

THE FRONT DESK HAD NO PROBLEM TELLING US THAT Mindi Mills was in room 1918. I would have suspected that Benjamin had something to do with it if they'd known I was the one asking.

"I'm beginning to wonder about the security here," I said as we rode the elevator upstairs.

"What, with Derrick's murder and all?"

"Sure, there's that, too, but they just gave me the room number without a fight."

"Just count your blessings she's not staying at the Brunswick."

"If she was, I'd just find a way to get Benjamin to tell me."

Zach laughed. "So, apparently the security level is about the same, if you know how to work the system."

"You've got a point."

As the elevator doors opened, we could hear yelling the second we got off on the nineteenth floor.

"What do you suppose that's all about?" Zach asked.

"Hang on a second." We paused in the hallway, and I could make out Cary's voice, though it was quite a bit louder than it had been the last time we'd spoken.

"That's Cary Duncan," I told Zach.

"How'd she get over here that fast?"

I looked at my watch. "We were at the park for nearly an hour. She had plenty of time to ditch Brady and come over here."

Zach started creeping closer to the bend in the corridor, and I followed. We could start to make out words now, and they were rough ones at that.

"You shrew. How dare you?" That was clearly Cary.

Another woman's voice, this one nearly an octave higher, replied, "I wouldn't have been with him if you'd taken care of him better yourself."

"A harem of women wouldn't have satisfied that old goat. If you think you're getting away with this, you are sorely mistaken."

There was a real sense of outrage in the other woman's voice as she said, "You've got some nerve. You're the one who killed him. Everyone knows it."

"Maybe in your feeble little world," Cary shouted.

The elevator door opened back down the hallway, and two members of Hotel Security got out.

Zach made a decision quickly, and moved toward the battling women before he consulted me. That was fine. If he had a plan to make this work in our favor, I was all for it.

"Cary, Mindi, Hotel Security is on its way," he said as he reached them. "Unless you both want to go to jail for disturbing the peace, follow my lead."

Was he kidding? This was his plan?

To my amazement, both women nodded.

As the security pair rounded the corner, Zach said in a loud voice, "I told you that television was too loud before. Thanks for turning it down."

"No problem," Mindi said with a rise in inflection.

"We'll see you later, then," Zach said as he ushered Mindi into her room and quickly returned to the hallway.

Cary looked dumbfounded as Zach took her arm. "We need to go. We're late for our meeting."

"Of course we are," Cary replied.

"Is there a problem here?" the lead security man asked.

"Just a television turned up a little too loud. Sorry about the commotion."

One man looked at the other, and it was clear that neither was fooled by Zach's story, but some kind of silent conversation went on between them, and the older man finally shrugged. "Just tell her to keep it down from now on."

"It's taken care of," Zach said.

After the men left, Cary said, "Not that I'm ungrateful, but how did you happen to be here?"

"We were looking for a friend staying at the hotel," I lied. "When we heard the commotion, we decided to see what was going on. Zach stepped in so there wouldn't be any more trouble."

"You didn't have to do that."

"I figured you'd been through enough already," my husband replied. "I'd hate to give the police another reason to question you."

Cary shuddered noticeably at that comment. "How right you are. If I can ever repay you, all you need do is ask."

"I might just take you up on that," Zach said.

Cary barely looked in my direction as she headed for the elevator herself.

Once she was gone, I asked Zach, "Are you serious? That story honestly worked on everyone?"

He shrugged. "Savannah, Hotel Security just wanted the problem to go away. I found a way to let them ignore it in good conscience, and that was enough for the moment. If Cary and Mindi go at it again, it's going to be on their heads, not mine."

"Nice save, Zach."

"I do what I can."

He knocked on Mindi's door, and she answered, cowering behind it as though she was afraid to come out. "Yes?"

"I didn't have a chance to introduce myself before," my husband said smoothly. "I'm Zach Stone, and you've already met my wife, Savannah. May we come in?"

To my amazement, she nodded and stepped aside. "Of course. Thank you for coming to my rescue. It's hard to tell how ugly that could have gotten if you hadn't stepped in when you did. Hi, Savannah. You've got quite a husband there."

"I was glad to help," Zach said, and I was amazed he didn't throw in a "Shucks, it was nothing" while he was at it.

I looked around the room and was surprised to see that it was as neat as could be. It was hard to believe that Mindi had been able to stand cohabiting with Derrick after seeing what a slob he could be.

After she closed the door to her modest room, Mindi said, "I'm not afraid to say it; that woman frightens me."

"I know what you mean," I said. "She was really blasting away at you."

"Normally, I hate confrontation," Mindi said, "but I couldn't just stand there and listen to her abuse. It's not called for in polite society."

Neither is sleeping with another woman's husband, I said in my head. I wasn't there to point fingers, though.

Zach and I were looking for clues. "Do you believe what you said to her?"

"What's that?" Mindi asked, looking slightly confused.

"You told Cary that everyone knows she killed her husband."

"Isn't it obvious?" Mindi asked. "She's getting a fat insurance settlement, from what I've heard." Mindi began to whimper softly, and then she added, "She didn't even love him."

"And you did," I said softly, not making it a question, but rather a statement.

"It's true. I did."

"Listen, I hate to bring this up, but we need to know. Was there anyone else in Derrick's life?"

"You mean romantically?" she asked as she looked at me quizzically.

"That's exactly what I mean," I said.

"He'd never be unfaithful," she said. "Derrick loved me."

"And yet he was still married to Cary," Zach said. "That must have infuriated you."

Mindi didn't rise to the bait. "They had an arrangement. She didn't care if he slept with me, as long as we were discreet."

"Did Cary tell you that?" Zach asked.

"No, Derrick did, and I believed him."

Zach just shook his head, and she asked, "What are you trying to say?"

"If he really loved you, he would have left his wife, wouldn't he?"

For a split second, Mindi hesitated, and then began crying with such force that I was certain someone from Security would be back.

I tried to calm her down, but she just pointed to the door and shrieked, "Leave this instant."

We had no choice but to comply, and as Zach and I walked to the elevator, I said, "Smooth, Zach, really smooth."

"Those tears were a little too convenient, weren't they?"

I looked at him. "You noticed that pause before she busted loose, too?"

"Hey, I was once a trained detective, remember?"

I shook my head, though I couldn't hide my smile. "She got out what she wanted to say, and once you started pressuring her, she kind of conveniently fell apart."

"It didn't work though, did it?"

"What should we do now, tackle the other writers under Derrick's thumb, or go after Kelsey Hatcher?"

His stomach rumbled, and Zach asked, "Is there any chance we can get a bite to eat? I saw a hamburger joint on the corner. We wouldn't even have to drive to it, so we can keep our space in the hotel parking lot."

"Fine, I know how you get when you're hungry," I said. "Let's go eat, and then we'll tackle the rest of them."

A FTER A QUICK MEAL, WE WENT BACK TO THE HOTEL TO finish our second round of interviews.

Zach asked, "Can we stop off at the car for a second?"

"Sure, what did you forget?"

"Nothing. I just want to get another pen." He'd taken notes about what had happened so far during our lunch, and his pen had slowly failed him.

"I have one in my purse that you can use."

As we walked back past the car, I noticed that it was sitting lower than it had before. Was it sinking into the pavement of the hotel's parking lot?

Zach must have noticed it the same time I did. "Hang back a second, Savannah."

He reached into his jacket and pulled out his gun. "I didn't even know you were carrying that."

"It's a new holster," he said. "You should go inside."

"I'm not leaving you out here by yourself."

"Savannah, stop arguing with me."

"Then stop ordering me to do things you know I have no intention of doing," I said.

He shook his head in disgust, but he quit trying to drive me away. If anything happened, I was going to be there for it, no matter what. The not knowing was the worst part about it.

I'd learned that lesson the hard way.

Zach moved back to the rental car, his gaze taking in our surroundings with laserlike precision. Once he was satisfied no one was around, he reholstered his gun. "It's all right."

I joined him, and we examined the car together. All four tires had been slashed. There was no patching that could fix it, no hope for them at all.

"The question is," Zach asked, "was this random, or was it directed at one of us?"

I noticed a note on the back windshield wiper. At first I'd taken it for just another menu that littered some of the other cars around us, but as I reached for it, I saw that someone had written on it with a black marker. The note said simply, STOP DIGGING, OR DIE.

"What do you make of that?" I asked Zach as he read it over my shoulder.

"You probably ruined any prints that were on it."

"Hey, I held it by the edges."

"Maybe that's good enough." He took the note from me using one corner of his handkerchief, a faded old bandana that he always carried around with him. "It looks like we hit a nerve somewhere."

"Yes, but where?"

I studied the note. "I can't tell if it's in a woman's hand, or a man."

"That's kind of the point of block printing," Zach said. He opened the car door and put the note on my seat.

"We need to call a tow truck," I said.

"Four new tires aren't going to be cheap," Zach replied. "We're going to have to pay for them, too. I didn't get any extra insurance on it."

"So we'll pay whatever it takes. It beats running around on rims. At least we're getting closer."

He shook his head. "I don't see that. It feels like we've antagonized most of our suspects with the same amount of grief. How do we know what we're getting to?"

"That's a point," I said. I looked at the tires again, and then added, "Then that means that all of this was for nothing."

He hugged me. "I wouldn't say that. I think it's a call to start pushing harder and see what happens."

I pointed to the note in the seat. "That means nothing to you, does it?"

"Savannah, we've both been threatened before. The only way we can lose is to give up, and I know neither one of us is about to do that. Now, let's see about getting those new tires."

"We're calling the police first, aren't we?"

Zach nodded. "As soon as I call a tow truck, I'll call Murphy. How much do you want to bet on who gets here first?"

"I've waited on two tow trucks before. No bet."

DETECTIVE MURPHY SHOWED UP SEVEN MINUTES AFTER Zach called him. I'd been expecting speed, but nothing this fast.

"Were you just around the corner?" I asked.

"I was having a late lunch at my desk," he said. I remembered from my previous visit that the police station was just a few blocks away from the hotel where we were at the moment.

He took the note, sealed it in a clear plastic bag, and then looked at it again. "The message is pretty clear. You're not going to take the advice though, are you?"

Zach shrugged. "Would you, if you were in my position?"

Murphy did something that surprised me. He smiled. "Officially, I have to say that what you're doing is dangerous, and could undermine an ongoing investigation."

"And off the record?" Zach asked.

Murphy just shrugged, really all the answer my husband needed. As we stood there, a flatbed tow truck pulled up. "This for you?"

"It's tough to drive in this condition," Zach said.

Murphy nodded, and then said, "Have him take it to Lakeland Tire and use my name. You'll get a good price."

"Thanks."

He nodded, saluted with two fingers, and then left.

"What was that about?" I asked. "That's not the same man I spoke to the day Derrick was murdered."

"Sure it was."

"You couldn't tell by his behavior today."

Zach frowned. "Savannah, we didn't know each other then. He gets what we're trying to do, though he can't officially endorse it. As long as we keep him up to speed, he's not going to have a real problem with us digging around the edges."

"You got all of that how, exactly?"

"We speak the same language."

"Cop, you mean."

"Sure," Zach admitted. "We might not be on the same

force, but we've both seen a lot of the same things. That counts for something, even these days."

"I'm just glad you're on my side," I said.

"There's nowhere else I want to be," he said.

After the tow truck driver loaded my car up, he asked, "Where we going?"

"Lakeland," Zach said. He turned to me and added, "Savannah, why don't I take care of this myself? There's no need for both of us to be bored while we get new tires for this thing. Will you be all right without me?"

"Zach, I can take care of myself," I said as I touched his hand lightly. "There are plenty of people around for safety's sake, and I don't plan on taking any chances."

"We never mean to, though, do we?" he asked.

"Go on, I'll be fine. Besides, there isn't enough room there for me in the truck anyway." My husband enjoyed taking care of the maintenance of automobiles, and I generally didn't mind letting him.

"If you're sure."

"Absolutely certain."

My husband climbed up into the passenger seat of the truck, rolled down the windows, and then said, "Don't do anything crazy while I'm gone, do you hear?"

"Me? Crazy?"

"You know it," he said.

"I'm not making any more promises I can't keep."

Zack just shook his head and laughed as the tow truck pulled away. I had a few hours to burn while he was getting us new tires for the rental car, but that didn't mean I had to sit around waiting.

There were people of interest I could talk to, with or without my husband by my side, and I was going to do just that.

Chapter 13

• • •

THAT SHOULD MAKE MY MESSAGE CLEAR. IT WAS A REAL thrill slashing that nosy woman's tires. I was amazed at just how easy it had been to destroy all four of them without getting caught.

One instant they were intact, and the next they were so much useless rubbish.

I'm not a creature of violence by nature, but I am beginning to enjoy the feel of a knife in my hands.

I feel powerful, almost unstoppable, and it wouldn't be wise for anyone to cross me.

If she and that husband of hers don't take my advice, they are going to pay the ultimate penalty.

I cleaned the knife again, feeling the hard, cold steel slip between the folds of my towel.

There is a cost associated with every action, a penalty that has to be paid for every offense.

And I am naming myself the ultimate arbiter.
They've been warned.
Now it is in their hands.
I can't be held responsible for my actions if they choose
to ignore my promise of what will happen next.

Chapter 14

...

As I STEPPED BACK INTO THE LOBBY, MY CELL PHONE rang. It was a number I didn't recognize, so I answered tentatively, "Hello?"

"Savannah, it's Kelsey."

"Hi, Kelsey. What can I do for you?"

"I'm afraid it's your puzzle. I'm sorry to say that it's not quite what the papers wanted."

I wasn't about to stand for that. "Kelsey, I already did a new one, remember? You can't expect me to keep making puzzles until they find one they like."

"My hands are tied here, Savannah. I need it in two hours. Thanks for understanding."

I was about to tell her I didn't understand, or accept that, at all, when she actually hung up on me.

"Oh, no, you didn't just do that," I said out loud. I dialed star 69, and her voice came back on. "Hello?"

"It's Savannah," I said.

"I thought we had that cleared up," she said.

"You did, I didn't. I need to see you. Are you still at the Crest?"

She hesitated, and then said, "I don't see what that has to do with anything. You're not going to be able to change my mind."

And then she hung up on me again! My blood was boiling when I felt someone tap me on the shoulder.

"Savannah? Are you all right?"

It was Sylvia Peters, the Bridge Queen herself. "I just got off the telephone with Kelsey."

The woman arched one eyebrow. "She's dreadful, isn't she?"

"Is she making you rewrite your columns, too?"

Sylvia looked confused. "No, of course she isn't. Hold on, you just said, 'too.' She's actually making you resubmit your work like some kind of neophyte? I wouldn't put up with that if I were you."

"I'm not, but she won't even take a meeting with me to discuss it. What a wretched little weasel she's turning out to be."

Sylvia grinned, and I asked her heatedly, "Is there something you find funny in all of this?"

"I know her room number," Sylvia said.

"Tell me."

She hesitated, and then said, "I don't suppose there's any chance I can talk you out of this, is there?"

"No chance whatsoever."

Sylvia shrugged. "Well then, I tried. She's in one-two-two-four. Good luck."

I waved back to her as I rushed toward the elevators. Kelsey might think she was going to muscle me again, but she was sadly mistaken.

I got to her room and knocked on the door.

There was no reply.

"Kelsey, I know you're in there."

"Savannah?" she asked through the closed door. "Is that you?"

"In the flesh. We need to talk."

"I don't think so," Kelsey said. "I've said all I need to say."

I pounded again. "Then you can listen while I talk."

"There's no way I'm opening this door while you're so agitated."

I tried to take a few deep breaths to calm myself. She was right. It wouldn't do to start shouting and threatening. I'd already done that once in the past few days, and look where it had gotten me, on top of the police's prime suspect list.

"Okay, I'm better now," I said a minute later. "Could I please come in?"

She hesitated longer than I would have liked, but after thirty seconds, the door opened.

Before I could say a word, Kelsey said, "If we can keep the conversation civil, I'd be happy to hear your concerns."

I started to snap at her again, but then realized that would get Security up here. I focused on remaining calm. "Kelsey, surely you can see that it's not fair to keep rejecting my puzzles and giving me shorter and shorter deadlines."

"I understand your predicament, but one of our biggest newspapers called me two minutes after I faxed your puzzle to them and they turned it down."

"It was Cragen, wasn't it?"

She hesitated, and then said, "Yes, as a matter of fact, it was. How did you know that?"

"He turns one down every month as a matter of form. Trust me, he doesn't even read the snippet, let alone work the puzzle. Did anyone else complain about it?"

"No," she admitted reluctantly, "but we can't afford to lose his paper as a client."

"Trust me, you won't. Do you still have the easier puzzle I sent you?"

Kelsey nodded. "Of course, but I still don't think it's strong enough to go to the newspapers, especially while we're transitioning into a new management organization."

"Send it to him," I said.

"Savannah, weren't you listening?"

I stared hard at her, but fought to keep a friendly expression. "Kelsey, take my word for it. He'll run the easy one, and then for the next puzzle, send him the one he bounced today."

She looked shocked by the idea. "But he'll just reject it again."

"If he does, I'll write another one just for him. But if he doesn't, I want a promise from you."

Kelsey looked clearly uncomfortable by the request, but finally, she asked, "What would that be?"

"If I'm right, stop bouncing my puzzles, at least without giving me a fair chance to explain myself before you do."

"Yes, I can understand how that could be aggravating." She added, "Would you excuse me for a second?"

Was she going to start crying? I hadn't meant to be so rough on her. "Absolutely. I'll wait right here."

She disappeared into the bathroom, and I walked around the room, admiring the view from her window. When I glanced at the chair, I saw something poking out from under one of the pillows. It looked like a yellow sticky note, and when I lifted the cushion up, I found Derrick's planner! There were handfuls of yellow notes bristling out from it like quills on an angry porcupine, with the exception of a single lime green note. This might just hold a clue that would lead to figuring out who had killed him. Why was Kelsey hiding it? I could understand why she'd want it, since it had Derrick's plans and notes all through it. I started leafing through it when the bathroom door opened. It was too late to put it back where I'd found it, so I shoved it into my bag, hoping she wouldn't notice its absence.

Her makeup had been freshened when she reappeared. "Savannah, I hope you'll forgive me. I'm new at this, and it's turning out to have a pretty steep learning curve."

"It's all right to ask questions," I said.

"That's one thing I don't have the luxury of doing. I should explain why I didn't want to see you earlier. I haven't had a minute to myself all day. It's been a string of malcontents coming through my door since nine o'clock this morning, and I'm at the end of my rope."

"Who's been here?"

"Who hasn't? First there was Brady Sims, then Sylvia Peters, and then Cary came by with some man named Lassiter."

"What did they want?" I asked, not being able to see those as a team, unless they were actually having an affair after all.

"They were asking questions about Derrick's businesses that I didn't have the answers to."

At least I wasn't the only one she'd suspect of the theft.

"Well in that case, I've taken up enough of your time," I said as I headed for the door. The sooner I could dig into that planner, the better chance I'd have of seeing if it had any clues that Zach and I could use.

I had one hand on the doorknob when Kelsey said, "Stop. Something's wrong."

It was clear that I was busted.

How in the world was I going to be able to explain this?

"What's wrong?" I asked Kelsey as I turned around.

"Something's missing," she said.

"You'll have to give me a better clue than that."

"Derrick's planner," Kelsey said, and I felt the bottom go out from under me. "It was right here."

"Right where?"

"Under the cushion of this chair."

I wasn't sure how I was going to get out of this, but I wasn't ready to confess that I'd taken it just yet. I had one chance to muddy the waters, and I was going to take it. "When's the last time you saw it?"

She frowned, and then admitted, "It was last night. I was going through a few of his notes for the week, and I jammed it under there when Mindi Mills came to the door with some story about missing Derrick so much."

"Mindi was in here, too?"

"For a minute. I got her a cup of water, and then she left."

"Did you look at the planner after that?"

Kelsey paused for a second and then said, "No, I sort of forgot about it. I had so many other things to do, you understand."

"So then, it could have been Mindi, Brady, Sylvia, Cary, or Lassiter that took it," I said, carefully leaving my own name off the suspect list.

"I suppose you're right, but why would any of them want it?"

"Could there be something incriminating somewhere in the pages and notes?" I asked.

"I don't think so, but then again, anything is possible."

"Maybe it will turn up," I said as reassuringly as I could.

"I hope so. I'd be lost without it."

"I'll keep my fingers crossed," I said, and promised myself that I'd find a way to get Derrick's planner back to her once I was finished with it. If she needed it, it was wrong of me to keep her from it, but for now, I didn't have any choice.

I finally got outside into the corridor, and Kelsey actually smiled at me as I left, something that made me feel that much dirtier about taking the planner, and then diverting suspicion away from myself at the expense of the other people on my list.

As I started down the hallway, a voice called out behind me. "Savannah? Did you get the results you were hoping for?"

"As a matter of fact, I did. I'm glad I ran into you again, I had a few questions to ask you," I said as I turned and faced her.

Sylvia looked at me skeptically. "Why exactly do you want to talk to me?"

"Do you honestly want to have this conversation in the hallway?"

"It suits me," she said.

That was odd. I wondered what she might be hiding in her room. Or perhaps whom? Could Brady be in there, cowering behind the drapes? No, I had a hard enough time believing that Brady was fooling around with Cary Duncan. The idea that he was also having an affair with Sylvia Peters was just too much to believe.

"To be honest with you, I'm asking everyone where they were when Derrick was murdered," I said. I hadn't yet, but it made sense to do it now. The killer knew Zach and I were investigating, so the time for being coy about it was over. My husband believed that whenever you are attacked, you step up the assault, and I couldn't think of any other way to handle it.

She looked bemused by my question. "I told you before that I was in my room when he was murdered, and I was alone. Are you honestly asking me for an alibi?"

"Yes, I am," I said, holding my ground. "And you've got to do better than that."

"It happens to be the truth."

I shrugged. "Suit yourself. I just thought you might like to get your name off of everyone's suspect list."

"You really should leave detective work for the detectives."

"My husband was the chief of police for a major metropolitan city," I snapped.

"The key word there being 'was,'" she said.

"That doesn't make his accomplishments any less impressive."

"No, I'm willing to grant you that point, but it does bring into question his standing in this investigation."

"Sylvia, it's obvious, isn't it? He's working to clear my name."

"By throwing me to the wolves instead? I understand his motives, but you'll forgive me if I choose not to supply any rope for my own hanging." She pivoted and went back into her room, and as much as I tried to see if anyone else was there, my line of vision was limited to the square of carpet in front of the door, which at the time was sadly bare.

Well, that had accomplished a whole lot of nothing. Maybe I should let Zach ask the hard questions. After all, he'd trained for many years to do it. I had a knack for seeing patterns—it was part of the reason I was so good at making puzzles. But what were the patterns here? So far, all I saw was a jumbled mess, chaos instead of order.

I needed a key to figure things out further.

And at that moment, I remembered something that Jenny and I had found in Derrick's room. The ring of keys was still in the bottom of my bag. I wondered what Zach would make of them, and the planner I'd so rashly taken from Kelsey's room.

I wasn't sure if he'd be pleased with me, or disappointed, but one thing was certain. I was bringing new facts to light, and with a case as murky as this one, any illumination had to help.

I HAD A LOT OF NEW RAW DATA, BUT SO FAR, NO REAL INFORMATION. It was time to go somewhere and see exactly what it was I had, so I went downstairs, even going as far as heading to the parking garage when I remembered that Zach still had our rental car.

I dialed Jenny's number, hoping she was in her office.

She picked up on the fourth ring, just as I was getting ready to hang up and try to come up with another plan.

"Hey there," I said. "Any chance you're around?"

"I'm just finishing something up in my office. I was going to head back home, but I'm flexible. Is there something you'd like to do?"

"Truthfully, I was hoping to get a ride with you back to your place."

"What's wrong with the rental car?"

I didn't really want to get into it at the moment, but it was a question that deserved an answer. "Someone slashed all four of the tires," I admitted.

"That's terrible," Jenny said. She lowered her voice as she asked, "Was it tied to the case?"

"I certainly hope so," I said.

"That's kind of an odd answer, isn't it?"

"Think of it this way. At least we're making some progress if we've scared the killer into taking such a bold step. There was a note written on the back of a Chinese takeout menu."

"I can't wait to hear what it said."

"Why don't I tell you when you pick me up? I'm at the Crest Hotel."

She paused, and then said, "Tell me now."

"'Stop digging or die,'" I quoted.

"Hey, I was just asking. There's no need to get melodramatic about everything."

"No, that's what the note said. 'Stop digging or die.'"

There was silence on the other end of the phone, and Jenny finally broke it by asking, "Is there any possibility you're going to listen to that advice?"

"Come on, you know me better than that. And even if I wanted to, do you think there's a chance on earth that Zach's going to be bullied off anything?"

"No, I wouldn't think so."

"So, we press on. Now, about that ride."

"I'll be there in five minutes," she said. "And Savannah, try not to get into any trouble between now and then."

"Hey, I'm not making any promises."

As I waited for Jenny, it took every ounce of willpower I had not to take out Derrick's planner and start digging into it, but I had no idea who might be watching me, and I couldn't afford to let anyone know that I'd taken it. I'd tell Zach of course, that went without saying, and Jenny had a stake in knowing as well, but that was it.

Good to her word, Jenny showed up four minutes later. As she pulled into the garage, I was waiting at the door. Once I was safely in the front seat and buckled up, I said, "You wouldn't believe what I did."

"Should I hear about it?" she asked.

"I don't know. I can tell you, but then I can't take it back, can I?"

"On second thought, maybe we'd better not talk about what you've been up to."

"Okay, I can buy that," I said. "How was your day?"

She laughed. "I got some work done, but only after I convinced two of my partners that my vacation has been put on hold." She smiled at me as she added, "They were under the impression that I still worked for them, not with them."

"I'm sure you did your best to set them straight."

"Oh, I believe they got the message."

When we pulled up to her driveway, I noticed that there wasn't any activity next door at Charlie's place. Where was Jenny's own Neighborhood Watch Program? Maybe making another cake, like he'd told Zach he'd been doing. As we approached the front steps, Jenny pointed to the sidewalk.

Just out of camera range, someone had left a stuffed animal, a golden teddy bear with sad brown eyes.

And there was a letter opener plunged into its chest.

Was this a warning for Jenny, or for me?

Chapter 15

■ ■ ■

JENNY LEANED DOWN TO PICK IT UP WHEN I GRABBED her arm.

"Don't touch it," I snapped.

"Why? Do you think it could be booby-trapped?"

"No, but there might be prints on it. I need to call Zach."

He picked up on the first ring. "Hey, Savannah. We're now in possession of four new tires. It's got to be cheaper than what the rental place would have charged us. I've got to tell you, Murphy may have his faults, but I like his tire guy."

"That's great. How close are you to Jenny's house?"

He sounded confused as he said, "I thought I was picking you up at the Crest?"

"Plans have changed. Get here as soon as you can."

"Did something happen?" he asked, his voice shifting into police mode.

"We found a pretty mean little calling card on Jenny's sidewalk. The only problem is that I can't tell if it's for her, or us."

"Don't touch anything. I'll be right there."

After I hung up, I said, "Zach is on his way." I started to lean over the teddy bear when Jenny reminded me, "Hey, you told me not to touch it."

"I'm not about to," I said as I got closer. "What's that under him, though?"

She looked with me, and then finally said, "It looks like there's some kind of note."

I took a pen from my bag and moved toward the bear.

"Savannah, what are you doing?"

"I want to see what it says," I answered.

"No. We're going to go back to my car and wait for your husband."

"Since when did you become so interested in following the rules?"

"Since I have so much to lose," she said.

I shrugged, and we walked back to her car to wait on Zach.

In nine minutes, he pulled up in front of her house, the new tires squealing as he stopped.

"Hey, those are brand-new," I said as he jumped out of my car.

"Then there's tread to spare. Do you think the rental place is even going to notice that we replaced the tires? What's going on?"

I pointed to the skewered bear. "Someone's trying to warn one of us, but we can't figure out who."

Zach nodded, looked at the bear, and then took out his cell phone.

"You're not calling Detective Murphy about the teddy bear, are you?"

"Not yet," he said. As he lined up his telephone, I suddenly knew what he was doing. "You're taking a picture for the record, aren't you?"

"What can it hurt?" After he got his shot, he took his borrowed pen and nudged the teddy bear onto his side. Taking his bandana out, Zach gently pulled out the note from underneath it, and then laid the bear back down.

Jenny and I looked at it at the same time he did. It said in block letters,

DON'T BREAK MY HEART, JENNIFER.

"It's for you," I said as I turned to Jenny.

"Wonderful. It's a shame whoever did it didn't give us the courtesy of appearing on camera."

"How do we know he didn't?" Zach asked. "We need to check the DVD."

"Should I get the bear?" I asked as he started toward the house.

"Leave it right where it is," he ordered, and I could see how he'd commanded a room full of cops. There was an air of unquestioning authority in his voice that made me want to obey. In our marriage, it was something I generally did my best to ignore, but this time, I decided he was right. Zach was a world better at handling evidence, while I tended to be better at putting seemingly unrelated pieces together until there was a complete picture. We were the perfect complement of each other.

Zach placed the note on Jenny's table, and two minutes later, came back with the bear. It was almost sweet the way he'd wrapped his bandana under it to carry it.

I felt really bad for the bear.

And worse for Jenny.

She looked pretty shaken up by this latest discovery. "This is serious now, isn't it?"

Zach nodded. "I won't lie to you, this isn't a good sign."

Way to sugarcoat it, I thought.

But he was right.

We looked at the DVD, but the only trespass it had captured was a neighborhood cat running across the frame.

"He's smart," I said.

"A little too smart, if you ask me."

"What do you mean?"

"It's pretty clear that he spotted my cameras. Why else leave the bear on the sidewalk?"

"You did a masterful job of hiding the cameras," I said.

"I think so, too. To spot them, you almost had to know that they were there."

"Do you mean like if someone saw you looking at them at the store?" Jenny asked.

Zach nodded. "Mason Glade."

"Hang on a second," I said. "Let's not jump to conclusions. There's someone else who might be able to spot a camera. Say someone with a cop's eye for detail?"

"Murphy," Jenny said. She stared at the bear, and then said, "Yes, he could have done this."

"Does that take Charlie off our list? He wasn't at the store, and he certainly doesn't have a cop's eye for detail. He couldn't have seen you plant them, he was gone, remember?"

"Sure," Zach said, "but could he have been watching us from the corner before he came home? Did anyone notice anything?"

None of us had. After a moment, I said, "Then we're right back where we started from."

"Maybe not," Zach said. He gently removed the letter opener, as if operating on a real patient. After examining the blade, he set it aside and started looking at the bear.

"This wasn't cheap," he finally said.

"All the more reason not to butcher it," Jenny said.

"That's not what I'm getting at. There's a good chance a grown man bought it. We need pictures of the three of them so we can show some toy store owners in town."

"I've got photos of Mason and Murphy from when we were together," Jenny said. "Charlie might be a problem."

"Let's see what you've got."

She retrieved a shoebox from her bedroom and opened the lid. Inside were an assortment of photographs, talismans, and other small reminders of lost loves. Jenny was a nester, and that was a good thing at the moment. After she pulled out two reasonable photos of her former boyfriends, she said, "Hang on. I have to have a picture of Charlie somewhere."

She frowned, and then went to one of the bookcases. Jenny took a photo album out, started leafing through the pages, and then suddenly stopped. "Is this good enough?"

We both peered over her shoulder and saw a photo of a block party, clearly taken out front. It showed Charlie smiling for the camera, and Zach said, "It's perfect. Now we're cooking. Tomorrow, we'll start looking for that teddy bear's mates."

"In the meantime, there are some things I need to discuss with you," I said to Zach.

"Understood," Zach said.

"So, where do we begin? With the keys we found earlier?" Jenny asked.

I'd been about to pull out the planner, but that could wait. "Sure," I said as I retrieved them from my jacket pocket.

I handed them to Zach, and as he took them, he asked, "Where did you find these?"

"Jenny found them while we were searching Derrick's hotel room."

"And you didn't think to turn them over to his wife?"

I recognized that tone of voice, and I wasn't in any mood to hear it, especially from my husband. "Zach, we weren't about to give her what could be an important clue. If we decide they aren't going to help us, we can 'find' them someplace else."

"Okay," he said, trying to appease me. "Let's have a look."

He went through the keys, and saw a house key, a dead bolt key, a key to a cylinder lock, and another one that said, "Security."

"This one's for a safe," he said. "I wonder where it is at the moment."

"My guess is Richmond," I said. "Should we all go check it out?"

He scowled a little as he said, "I've already been there. I've got a hunch it's a dead end."

"Why?" I asked. "It could be holding a thousand things that Derrick was hiding, and one of them might have gotten him murdered."

"Take it easy," Zach said. "If he'd been killed in Richmond, I'd tend to agree. But think about it. Why kill him in another state, hours from where any evidence might be? Don't you think it would have made more sense to kill him in Richmond, take the keys, and then get whatever the murderer wanted out of the safe before anyone knew Derrick was dead?"

Jenny nodded. "That's probably true, but what if it was spur-of-the-moment? Stabbing him with a steak knife he was going to need for his meal doesn't exactly shout premeditation."

"That's a good point," Zach said. "But at the very least, the killer should have taken the keys. Where exactly were they?"

"Tucked into the toe of one of his shoes with a sock disguising it. You'd have to know it was there to find it."

Zach nodded. "Okay, maybe there is something of value there, but we can't break into his house in Richmond and search for it." He spun the key-ring around his index finger. "And we can't exactly ask Cary where it is without giving away the fact that we found the keys in the first place. All of that is supposing that the safe is at his home and not his business or somewhere else we don't know about."

"So, it's a dead end," I said, deflated that what we thought had been important really wasn't all that significant.

"I wouldn't say that, but it's not going to help us at the moment."

I nodded, and then reached into my bag as I said, "This may or may not be of any immediate use either, but I'm pretty sure it's going to be important." I retrieved the planner, and Jenny asked, "Where did you find it?"

"Kelsey had it in her hotel room," I said. "It was stuffed under the cushion of one of the chairs."

"And you just walked out the door with it? She's going to realize you stole it sooner or later, Savannah."

"Take it easy," I said as my husband started pacing around the room. "She noticed it was gone before I even left."

"Is that supposed to make me feel better? What did you do?"

"I deflected suspicion onto anyone else who'd been in her room since she'd seen it last. Trust me; the only person she doesn't suspect at the moment is me."

Zach still wasn't pleased with what I had to say, and Jenny decided to intercede. "Regardless of how she came about getting this, shouldn't we look at it and see if it's any help figuring out who murdered Derrick? Doesn't that serve the more important need, instead of trying to establish who actually has an ownership claim to the planner?"

"You're talking to me like a lawyer," Zach said. "Stop it."

She grinned at him. "Sorry, I can't help myself." Jenny turned and looked at me. "So, what does it have in it?"

"I haven't had a chance to even crack it open yet," I admitted.

"Don't tell me you were waiting for me, because I'm not going to buy it," Zach said.

"Let's just say that the opportunity hadn't presented itself yet."

I opened the planner, and Zach said, "Skip to the last day of his life. I want to see who his last appointment was with."

I did as he asked, and then said, "It's not important."

"Sure it is. That could easily be the name of the killer."

Jenny shook her head. "Zach, isn't it obvious that Savannah's name is probably the last one written there?"

"Oh, of course," he said. "I didn't consider that. Savannah, did he have any appointments later that evening? Is anybody down for dinner?"

I scanned the page. "No, I don't see anything." I looked at one of the many sticky notes protruding from the book. "Hang on a second. Here's something interesting."

I looked at the note and saw that Derrick had dated it for the day of his murder. It was so last-minute that he hadn't even taken the time to record it in his planner, but it was there nonetheless.

From the look of things, Derrick had a late appointment with Sylvia Peters. I wonder if keeping it had killed him.

"That doesn't make any sense," I said. "I saw Sylvia when she left Derrick at the hotel, and she practically threatened him with bodily harm. Why would he agree to meet her later? Derrick was a lot of things, but he wasn't stupid."

"Maybe she had something else to offer," Jenny said.

"You've seen Sylvia. I doubt Derrick would succumb to her charms, even if he didn't already have a wife and a mistress."

"Ewww, thanks for that visual. That's not what I meant. Could she have threatened him with something to keep her column syndicated? Do you think she'd be capable of it?"

I thought about it, and then nodded. "She's got a dark edge to her, there's no doubt about it. I'm not sure she'd kill him, though."

"Think about it," Zach said. "You told me yourself that Derrick threatened every one of his clients with the non-compete agreements he forced you all to sign. If Sylvia couldn't work anywhere else, and Derrick was firing her, it was like he was holding a gun to her head."

"Then we need to talk to Sylvia and see if she actually kept that appointment," I said.

"Hang on a second," Zach said. "There's no reason to jump to conclusions until we've looked through the rest of the planner. There could be a dozen clues here about who might have killed Derrick."

"Okay, fine, be the logical one."

He took the planner from me and started leafing through it. "How did he ever get anything done with all of these notes attached?"

"It must have worked for him," Jenny said.

"Well, I don't know how we're going to keep it all straight and still return it in some kind of order later."

"Would a copy of it help?" Jenny asked.

"Absolutely. Do you know any copy centers open at night?"

"I've got one in my office."

Zach said, "I'm sure you do, but I don't want to go back into town just to copy this thing."

"No, the office in my spare bedroom. I can make a copy for you in ten minutes."

"That's a deal. Can you set the exposure to a darker level? Some of these notes were done in pencil, and they're starting to smudge."

"Leave it to me," Jenny said as she took the planner and disappeared back into one of her spare bedrooms.

"She's really excited about this," I said.

"I suppose it can be fun, if you're not the one in the sights of the investigating detective."

"Do you think Murphy honestly believes I killed Derrick?"

Zach sighed as he stretched. "Savannah, he's playing this one close to the vest, and I don't blame him. It's got to be tough having another cop looking over his shoulder all of the time."

I looked at my husband a moment before speaking. "That's how you think of yourself, isn't it?"

"What, as a cop? I was one for a long time."

"You want to take the Asheville job, don't you?"

He shook his head as he stared out the window. "I told you, I haven't figured out what I want to do yet, and I'm just not ready to discuss it."

I walked over to him and hugged him. "Sometimes I forget how much what you used to do is still a part of you." Suddenly I knew the right thing to say. "Zach, do whatever you think is right about the job offer. You have my blessing either way."

He pulled back from the hug and frowned at me.

"What did I say?" I asked.

"Savannah, we'll make this decision together, and we'll both live with the consequences. I'm not going to shoulder it alone. Do you understand?"

"Of course I do. I was just trying to help."

"Well, you're not, at least not by giving in. I need us to hammer this out together. We're a team, remember?"

"Got it."

I noticed that Jenny had come out of the bedroom. "If this is a bad time, I can give you two some privacy."

I was about to answer when Zach beat me to it. "Everything's fine. That was fast."

"I believe in getting the best, and my copier is no exception."

Zach took the original, while Jenny handed the copied pages to me. I saw that the penciled notations were now crisper than they'd been on the original documents.

"Hang on a second, this one stuck to my copy." I looked at the lime green note and saw in printed block letters, THIS IS YOUR LAST WARNING.

"Did you see where this was in the planner?" I asked.

"No, I didn't even notice it as I was making copies," Jenny said. After she and Zach read it, she asked, "Was he threatening someone?"

"Maybe," Zach said. "Or somebody was threatening him." He scratched his chin, and then added, "But I have to admit, I have no idea what it means."

"What should we do now?"

"Before we start digging into all of this, we need to figure out how to get it back to Kelsey without her knowing we had it."

"That's going to be tough," I said. "She knows it's gone, so I can't exactly slip it back under the cushion of her chair."

"No, but you could leave it at the desk for her."

Jenny asked, "Wouldn't she ask who dropped it off? We don't want to implicate Savannah in the theft."

"Don't worry. I'll find someone to do it for us."

"How are you going to do that?" I asked.

He grinned at us both. "Leave that to me."

I started flipping through the pages Jenny had copied for us. "A lot of these notes are for Kelsey."

Zach scanned as well, as Jenny asked, "Are they orders?"

"Most of them. There are a couple he hadn't delivered yet stuck to the back of the planner," Zach said. "Here's something odd. Jenny, did you happen to tear one of the notes while you were making the copies?"

"No, I'm sure of it. Why?"

"This one says, 'Fire,' but the rest of it is missing."

"That's no mystery," I explained. "He fired Brady and Sylvia after I got there for my meeting, so it could have easily been for one, or even both of them."

"True," Zach said as he kept looking at the planner. "He had to be a tough man to work for."

"You don't know the half of it," I said.

Zach grinned at me. "I'm not talking about you. How do you think Kelsey managed to put up with it?"

"She wasn't with him very long," I said. "Who knows how long she would have lasted."

"Well, she certainly ended up all right, didn't she?"

"What do you mean?" Jenny asked.

"I keep thinking about who had something concrete to gain by his death, not just having a contract saved."

"Hey, it's a bigger deal than you think. Losing your source of income and not being able to get another job for five years is huge."

"So is murder," Zach said. "But we shouldn't forget that Cary is the one who really benefits. I'm sure Kelsey wasn't expecting to take over for him, and I doubt Sylvia or Brady knew their firings would be canceled with his murder. What could Mindi have gained? She lost her meal ticket. That leaves Cary."

"There are more reasons for murder than money," I said. "Love is another factor."

Jenny nodded. "If Derrick was dumping Mindi, she had a motive."

He countered, "And if he was dumping Cary for Mindi, she'd have an emotional and financial motive to want to see him dead, too."

"So, are you saying we forget all about the others and focus on Cary Duncan?"

He shook his head as he walked to the window. "No, we still need to see if Sylvia actually met with Derrick after you left, but you have to admit, Cary has some good reasons to want Derrick dead. It makes her the prime suspect, as far as I'm concerned."

"Hey," I said, "as long as it's not me, I'm fine with it. Jenny?"

"It's something to consider," she said. "I don't want us to forget Frank Lassiter. He lost a great deal of money, and while he wasn't going to get any of it back, he could have killed Derrick as a way of getting revenge."

Zach threw his hands into the air. "That's the problem with this situation. We have reasons to suspect everyone who ever came into Derrick Duncan's life, but that's not getting us any closer to finding the killer."

I nodded. "I know it's frustrating, not being able to officially question our suspects or check out alibis, but we have to do whatever we can to figure this out."

"Sorry, I didn't mean to raise my voice." He looked at us in turn, and then asked, "Do either of you masterminds have an idea how we can start eliminating suspects?"

Jenny just shrugged, but I had an idea. "Why don't we use the same approach we tried on Frank Lassiter?"

"Tell him we're on his side?" Zach asked. "That was a tough sale, remember?"

"No offense," I said, "but you have a way of intimidating people and not realizing it. Why don't you let me try?"

"On your own? Out of the question," he snapped. "Besides, *you're* the one who aggravated him the first time we spoke."

"Zach, it's my neck on the line. Let me handle this my way."

"I could go with her when she talks to them," Jenny volunteered.

"You need to keep a low profile with the police, remember?"

She picked up the planner. "They couldn't even find

this, could they? I don't think you're getting a fair shake. I'm in, all the way."

"Great," I said.

Zach just scowled. "What am I supposed to be doing in the meantime while you two are out interrogating witnesses?"

"Sweetheart, there are other ways you can help." I hugged him, which he resisted at first, but then allowed. After I pulled away, I added, "You can find out who Jenny's stalker is. That's as important to us as finding Derrick's killer."

"I don't know if this is such a good idea," he said.

"Give us one day. We'll brace our suspects tomorrow and try to enlist them openly in our cause. If any of them refuse, we'll keep them on our suspect list, but who knows, someone might volunteer some information just to get us off their backs."

"Will you both at least be careful?"

"I promise we will," I said, just as the front doorbell rang.

ARE YOU EXPECTING ANYONE?" ZACH ASKED AS HE MOVED toward the door.

"Not really. Why?" Jenny asked as her face went pale. "Do you think it's my stalker?"

"If it is, he picked the wrong night to show himself," Zach replied. I moved toward him, and he said, "Savannah, you and Jenny need to wait for me in the back bedroom."

"No," we both said as the doorbell rang again.

"Stop arguing and do it."

Jenny started to move, but I stood fast. "I'm not going. Now, are you going to answer the door, or should I?"

"Woman, you're pushing me too far."

"Then answer the door."

I wasn't sure who was there, but I wasn't about to let my husband face them alone.

I certainly wasn't expecting the visitor we got.

Detective Murphy was standing there when Zach carefully opened the door, and from the grim look on his face, he wasn't there to bring us good news.

Chapter 16

...

"**D**ETECTIVE," ZACH SAID, AS I TRIED TO HIDE THE PLANner and the copy Jenny had made from him.

"We need to talk," Murphy said.

"Come on in."

Zach moved aside, and I gathered everything together and looked around for a place to put it. Jenny was watching me, and it appeared that she was going to try to provide me with a diversion so I could accomplish it.

"Hello, Shawn," she said as she moved toward him.

"Hello," he said. "I don't mean to be rude, but this doesn't concern you. Maybe you'd like to take a walk around the block while we chat."

"I'm fine right here, but thanks for asking. It's been a while since you've been here, hasn't it?"

He glanced around. "I guess so." He must have spotted

the opened teddy bear on the dining room table. "What are you doing, a teddy bear autopsy?"

"It's from my stalker," she said, blurting it out. "He's getting bolder every minute, since you haven't been able to catch him."

The shocked look on his face was all I needed to hide the planner and the copy under a newspaper. What was she doing? He was one of our three suspects, and now she was confiding in him?

"Talk to me."

Jenny looked over at me, and then she said, "We're handling it."

Murphy walked toward her, and from the look in his eyes, it was clear that he'd forgotten Zach and I were even there. "Jennifer, this is no time to try to be brave."

"Shawn, I've asked for help, remember? And yet he keeps coming after me. What's it going to take to stop him? Does he have to actually assault me, or do something even worse?"

There was a look of pure frustration on his face. "I can't keep an officer on you around the clock. Give me something to work with, and I might be able to help."

"We have suspects," Jenny said, and it was all I could do not to put my hand over her mouth. What was she thinking? Did she really expect Shawn Murphy to help us, especially when he could be her stalker?

"Who do you think might have done it?"

Zach said, "We haven't narrowed it down that much yet to give you any names."

"Bull. You have a list, don't you?"

Jenny said, "We can do better than that. We have pictures."

She handed him the folder, and I wondered what she was doing. "That's the wrong one," I said as I tried to grab it. Had she forgotten that Murphy's photograph was there as well?

The detective was too quick for me, though. He snatched it away, and then looked at the photographs. When he got to his own, he looked at her with a puzzled expression. "What's this?"

"You're on our list," Jenny said, not afraid to meet his gaze.

"Jennifer, you've got to be kidding."

"There you go, you just added to the case against you. Every note and reference to me calls me Jennifer, just like you used to do."

He shook his head. "You don't really think I'd do this to you, do you?"

"You have to admit that you took it hard when we broke up," she maintained.

"Sure, it stung, but I've moved on. I've even got a new girlfriend now."

"You do?"

He nodded as he reached into his back pocket. I saw Zach's hand go to his jacket, and the move wasn't lost on Murphy, either.

"Take it easy. I'm just getting my wallet out," the detective said.

He gingerly removed it, and then showed Jenny a photo of him with another woman.

Jenny looked at it, and then said, "This is Nancy Waters."

"Do you know her?" I asked.

"She's one of the police dispatchers."

Murphy shrugged. "I figured she'd know something about cops, so it might make things a little easier. We started dating two weeks after you and I broke up."

"Why haven't I heard anything about it?" Jenny asked.

"Hey, Raleigh's not exactly Mayberry," he said. "It would

probably amaze you to learn about some of the things that go on." He tapped the folder. "I'll keep this, if you don't mind."

"We were going to show it to some of the premium toy stores around town," Zach said. "Someone might recognize one of them."

"It's worth a shot. May I take the bear as well?"

Zach looked at Jenny, who nodded slightly. "Fine."

"Good enough. I'll start looking into this tomorrow."

"Detective," I said. "You never said what brought you here in the first place. Something's wrong, isn't it?"

"What makes you ask that?" he said as he stared intently at me.

"It's pretty clear that you didn't drop in for a social call. When Zach answered the door, I saw that look on your face. Something bad happened tonight, didn't it?"

"I'm afraid it did," he admitted. "Someone tried to kill Kelsey Hatcher this evening."

"**W**HAT HAPPENED?" ZACH ASKED.
"She was walking to a restaurant and someone shoved her from a crowd into traffic. If the guy beside her hadn't noticed, she would have been hit dead-on by a bus."

"Did anyone see who shoved her?" I asked.

"That's the problem. Nobody admits to seeing anything," he said. "By the time we got there, some of the crowd had dispersed, so there was no way we could even interview all of the suspects."

"And you think this is related to Derrick's death," Zach said.

Murphy scratched his ear. "I don't believe in coincidences."

"Neither do I," Zach quickly agreed.

"How's she doing?" Jenny asked him.

"She's shaken up, but physically, she's fine. I can't help wondering why someone would want to get rid of her."

"Why are you looking at me when you say that?" I asked him.

He didn't let up for one second. "I understand you two have already had a few clashes since she's taken over."

"Where did you hear that from?"

He shrugged. "Does it really matter? All I need to know is if it's true."

"You don't have to answer that," Jenny said as she put a hand on my shoulder.

"I appreciate that, but I've got nothing to hide."

Zach said, "Maybe you should listen to Jenny."

"No," I said loudly. "I'm not hiding behind my lawyer, especially when I didn't do anything wrong."

"It's your funeral," Jenny said.

I turned to Murphy. "In any new relationship, business or otherwise, there's a period of time where the people involved have to work out how they relate to each other."

He pulled out his notebook and jotted something down. "So, that would be yes."

"Murphy," Jenny said with a warning tone in her voice.

"Hey, I'm just asking questions."

Zach stepped between them. "Then stop putting your own spin on the answers. Next question."

Murphy stared at him a second, and then looked back at me. "Here's an easy one. Did you see Kelsey Hatcher at any point today?"

I was about to answer when Jenny said, "Whoa. That's enough."

"We could do this in my office, if you'd rather," Murphy said.

"My client and I need to confer. If you want to bully

her into going downtown, I'll simply advise her not to speak with you at all. Is that clear?"

Murphy shrugged, and then closed his notebook.

I wasn't sure exactly what was happening. "Does that mean I'm coming with you?"

He shook his head. "I don't see the point of wasting your time or mine. Once I have more information, I'll want to speak with you again."

"Not without me being present," Jenny said.

"And me," Zach added.

Murphy smiled a quick, wry grin. "You win. For now."

As he started for the door, his mood suddenly changed. "Jennifer, until I can run down a few leads, don't take any chances. It would be good if you had someone with you at all times."

"You're not worried about me, are you?" she said.

"It just makes sense not to take any chances." Murphy looked at Zach and said, "You'll look out for her, right?"

"You can count on it. Let me know as soon as you hear anything about the bear."

"Will do."

After he was gone, I asked Jenny, "Why wouldn't you let me answer his question? I'm sure someone had to have seen me with Kelsey today."

"Don't assume anything."

"I was there," I insisted.

"Did you shove her in front of a bus?"

I looked at her as though she'd just lost her mind. "Of course I didn't."

"Then don't make Murphy's job of railroading you any easier than it has to be."

I looked at Zach. "And what's with you? You were actually nice to him there at the end."

"It was about a different case. We all know I have no official standing here. He's not obligated to tell me anything about what he finds out about Jenny's stalker. I need his goodwill on that one."

"And no one else sees a conflict between the two issues?"

Zach shook his head. "I don't. When you're a cop, you need to compartmentalize everything in your life. The two cases don't necessarily touch, but even if they did, I trust Murphy to do the right thing where Jenny's concerned."

I picked up his photograph, which he'd taken out of the folder Jenny had handed him. "I can't believe you actually told him we suspected him of stalking you."

"I didn't want him to catch you hiding Derrick's planner. I had to do something to create a diversion."

"Why didn't you knock a lamp off the table or something?"

Jenny touched the base of one of her lamps. "Are you kidding me? I love this lamp."

"You know what I mean. It could have been reckless telling him we're on to him."

Jenny shrugged. "Think about it. Did I say one word about the cameras Zach put in?"

I thought back over the conversation, and realized that subject hadn't come up. "No," I admitted.

"Then bringing him partially into the loop may make him slip, if he's the one who's been doing this, new girlfriend or not."

"You're taking an awfully big chance," I said.

"Like you're not?"

"That can't be helped," I said. I looked at my husband and asked, "Where does the attack on Kelsey leave us?"

"We keep doing what we're doing," he said finally. "Right now, it's all we can do."

"Then what's next?"

"After we get something to eat, I'd like to talk to Sylvia."

"You're off the interview team, remember?"

He looked hurt for a moment. "But Murphy's doing my job now."

"Sorry, I don't want anyone to be too scared to answer."

Zach seemed to think about that, and then he said, "The least I can do is drive you two around." He saw that I was about to protest when he added, "But I'll stay out of the way."

"Promise?"

"Of course I do," he said. "Jenny, are you ready to go?"

"I'm ready. Should we get something to eat on the way?"

"I'm not about to eat at the Crest Hotel," Zach said.

"Don't worry," I said laughing, "we'll find a place where you can eat without a jacket and tie."

W E GRABBED A QUICK BITE ON THE WAY, STOPPING OFF at a barbeque place Jenny loved. It was delicious, a real Eastern-style menu with a vinegar-based sauce that I thoroughly enjoyed. Zach loved the tomato-based Western recipe, but we got plenty of that at home. We all agreed that the hush puppies, little deep-fried corn-bread bombs, were some of the best we'd ever had, and the sweet tea was thick enough to have trouble pouring from the pitcher to the glass, a real requirement for North Carolina sweet iced tea.

After we ate, Zach said, "I'm almost too full to drive."

"You can take a nap in back of my car," I said. "I don't mind if you stay there when we go into the hotel."

"You and I both know that there's no way that's going to happen." He did take the backseat, while Jenny joined me up front.

"Are you honestly going to take a nap? We'll be there in ten minutes."

"No, but I might rest my eyes."

Two minutes after we left the restaurant, Jenny said, "Is he actually snoring back there?"

I grinned at her. "He can't be. You heard him. He's just resting his eyes."

"And every other part of him," she said. In a softer voice, she added, "You really got lucky finding him; you know that, don't you?"

"I like to think he got lucky finding me, too," I said.

"Of course he did. I just wish I could do it, too."

"Maybe if you stop working eighty-hour weeks, you'll be able to."

She shrugged. "There is that, isn't there?"

"It must limit your dating pool."

"You've seen the whole sum of my love life in the past three years. There have been exactly two men, either one of which is most likely stalking me at the moment."

I could tell Jenny was feeling morose about her dating life, but there was nothing I could do to help her. Maybe a change of topics would distract her from her thoughts.

"I wonder who pushed Kelsey," I said.

"I've been thinking about that myself. It's a clumsy way to try to kill someone, wouldn't you say?"

"What do you mean? Using a steak knife on Derrick wasn't exactly poetry."

"No, but at least it was pretty reasonable to believe that it would be effective. How hard must that shove have been?"

"I don't know," I said, "but there's something the two events have in common."

"What's that?"

"Most likely they were both done on impulse," I said. "That means our killer isn't a planner. He or she takes advantage of a situation and acts boldly when the opportunity affords itself."

"So they haven't been caught because they've been more lucky than methodical. How long can they keep taking risks like that?"

"I don't know," I admitted. "But we need to start thinking like the killer if we're going to have a prayer figuring out who it is."

"How do you do that?" Jenny asked.

"We need to ask Zach. He's known across the South for being able to put himself into a murderer's shoes."

Jenny shivered noticeably. "I can't imagine how creepy that must be for him."

"I wonder about that myself sometimes, but Zach finds a way to deal with it."

He stirred in back, and then sat up, rubbing his eyes. "Did someone mention my name?"

"Go back to sleep, Zach. We've got at least another ninety seconds before we get there."

"I told you, I was just resting my eyes. Now will someone tell me why my name was mentioned in conversation?"

Jenny said, "Savannah was just telling me how you can project yourself into a killer's shoes, and we were wondering if that's what we should be doing right now."

"It's not a bad idea, but we don't have a lot of information, do we?"

"That's not necessarily true," I said. "We know they act spontaneously, and that there's no hesitation to their movements. Don't most amateurs have to work up the nerve before they commit murder?"

"It depends on the crime. If they are in the heat of the moment, there's no planning at all. Those are the easiest killers to catch. The ones that plan carefully and act coldly are a little tougher to find."

"Do you agree that Derrick's murder and the attempt on Kelsey's life were unplanned?"

I glanced at him in the rearview mirror and saw him frowning as he stroked his chin. "They appear to be spur-of-the-moment," he finally conceded.

"So then, who do we know who isn't afraid to make

bold moves? We've already established that everyone on our list had a reason to kill Derrick, but who had the nerve to do it?"

"I'm not sure that's the best way to look at it. Savannah, some of the most outrageous killers I ever saw acted in the heat of the moment, almost transforming as they committed murders, and then they reverted back to their normal personalities."

"How does anyone ever get caught?" I asked in frustration.

He shrugged. "I can't speak for every circumstance, but in mine, it was mostly due to brilliant detective work."

I laughed out loud, and Jenny joined me.

From the backseat, Zach said, "Hey, it wasn't that funny."

"Yes it was," I said as we pulled into the Crest Hotel's parking lot again.

It was time to tackle our suspect list with our new "we're on your side" angle and see what we could uncover.

Chapter 17

...

"WHERE DO YOU THINK YOU'RE GOING?" I ASKED ZACH as Jenny and I got out of the car.

"I thought I'd hang out in the lobby, in case something interesting happened," he said.

"You're not going to talk to anyone though, remember?"

"Come on, Savannah. Surely you don't expect me to wait by the car and guard it, do you?"

"After what happened today, is that really such a bad idea?"

He gestured around. "Look, you're in a spot right by the door. Nobody's going to be crazy enough to try anything here. There are too many witnesses."

"That's been the MO of the killer so far, though, hasn't it?"

"I'm not staying here," he declared. "I'm either going

to wait in the lobby, or I'm coming with you two. Take your pick."

"The lobby," I said.

For one split second, he looked like a frustrated little boy. "Seriously? You're not going to let me come with you? Even if I promise to behave myself?"

"There's not really much chance of that, is there?" Still, I had a hard time saying no to him. "Tell you what. We'll tackle Brady and Sylvia, and when we talk to Cary, you can come along with us."

"That I can live with. How about Mindi and Lassiter?"

"We'll take Mindi alone, and you can come with us when we speak with Lassiter. After all, you've got a relationship with him already."

Jenny laughed. "Do you two haggle over every decision you make? It's like watching two good old boys from Georgia arguing over the price of a bale of hay and a peck of apples."

"Hey, it's what we do."

We walked into the lobby, and I pointed to a set of chairs out of the way. "You can wait for us over there."

He gave me a mock salute, and then picked up a *USA Today* newspaper before he sat down.

As Jenny and I rode the elevator up to Sylvia's room, Jenny said, "I can't believe he's really going to just sit there."

"Don't kid yourself. If he sees an opportunity to do something, he'll grab it with both hands. When Zach's working on something, he'd rather ask for forgiveness than permission."

We walked out of the elevator when it arrived at the right floor and headed to Sylvia's room.

I started to knock when I noticed that it was slightly ajar. Someone had put a telephone book in the opening to block the door, and I wondered what we were going to find on the other side.

"SYLVIA? ARE YOU IN THERE?" I ASKED AS I PUSHED THE door open.

Jenny grabbed my arm. "We should call Hotel Security, or at the very least, Zach."

"Not yet," I said. I took another step in, to be confronted by Sylvia.

"Is there something I can help you with, Savannah?"

I saw that her suitcase was packed and sitting on her bed. "Why is your door propped open?"

She grimaced. "Can't you feel it? The heating unit is stuck on high, and it's become a blast furnace in here. I'm going to insist that they move me to another room."

"Then you're not leaving?" I asked.

"I would like nothing better than to return home, but the police have asked me to stay, and I'm complying as a courtesy, at least for now." She glanced at Jenny and asked, "Are you still tagging along?"

"I am," Jenny said.

"As a friend of Savannah's, or her attorney?"

"Why can't it be a little bit of both?"

Sylvia didn't seem to care if Jenny was there or not. She looked sternly at me as she said, "I repeat, was there something I can help you with?"

It was clear that there was no use trying to pretend I was on Sylvia's side. It was time to take her head-on and see what she had to say for herself. "I heard that you had an appointment with Derrick after I left him the day he was murdered," I said.

"Where did you hear that?" she asked.

"Does it matter? I just need to know if it's true."

Sylvia had a face that was devoid of expression, and I

wondered if she'd been drawn to bridge because of it, or if she'd developed it over the years to help her play with a poker face. I suddenly realized that what she did must take a great deal of thought and planning, bidding and playing her cards to yield the most points. It was a methodical game, one that most likely wouldn't appeal to someone who took a lot of chances, at least that's how it looked from my perspective. I was looking for a gunslinger, not an accountant.

Finally, she admitted, "I had an appointment, but I chose not to show up for it. We were originally going to discuss a new column, but after the way he treated me, I was in no mood to work for him on another project."

"And you said you were here in your room the entire time, is that right?"

"I'm growing weary of the same questions over and over, Savannah."

"Just think about how I feel having to ask them. Did you hear about Kelsey Hatcher?"

Sylvia asked, "What about her? Don't tell me she's rejected another one of your little puzzles."

"Someone tried to kill her today."

That finally shook loose a little of Sylvia's iron expression. "Did they use a knife?"

"No, they tried to do it with a bus."

She looked puzzled by that. "How do you commit murder by bus?"

"It's a pretty effective weapon if you push your victim in front of one that's still moving," I said.

"I hadn't heard," she replied. "Is she all right?"

"A little shaky, but other than that, she's fine. When's the last time you saw her, Sylvia?"

"I don't know that it's any of your business, Savannah."

"Do you mind telling me where you were this afternoon?"

Sylvia frowned, and then admitted, "I was here, working on next week's column." It was clear she was upset by my questions, but I couldn't stop just yet.

"You seem to spend a great deal of time alone in your room," Jenny said. "It's tough to prove that you were here."

"I had a salad sent up from room service," she said. "Would I have been able to do that if I was out shoving people in front of buses? I waited an hour for it, if you can believe that."

I wasn't sure what I believed, but I did know that I was going to check up to see if Sylvia had ordered a salad as she claimed.

A maintenance man appeared at the door. "Do you have a problem with your room?"

"Not if I want to open a sauna," Sylvia said.

He nodded, refusing to rise to her baiting. "Don't sweat it. I'll have it fixed in no time."

"'No time' is what I've got. I'm demanding a new room."

He shrugged. "Lady, I can't help you with that. I'm just the maintenance man."

"Then I suggest you leave and return with someone who can."

If the man was upset by her treatment of him, he didn't show it. "Yes, ma'am. Right away."

As he left, Sylvia said, "I've had enough of this foolishness."

"From me, or the hotel?" I asked.

"In equal amounts," she said.

Sylvia grabbed her suitcase, kicked the telephone book away from the door, and walked out of her room. We had no choice but to follow.

"What are you going to do now?"

"I'm going to the front desk and demand a suite for all of the trouble they've caused me. It's the least they can do."

"Good luck with that," I said.

As she marched to the elevator, Jenny asked me, "Should we follow her?"

"No, I doubt we'll get much more out of her. Did you see her face when I told her that someone tried to kill Kelsey today?"

Jenny thought about it, and then answered, "I'd say she was hearing it for the first time, wouldn't you?"

I nodded. "I think so, too, but then again, she's mastered a game that allows her to bluff, plot, and plan, so I'm not sure how much we can trust any of her reactions."

"I never thought about it quite that way before," Jenny said. "Who's next on our list?"

"I think it's time we spoke with Brady again," I said. Sylvia was still waiting on an elevator as we walked past her.

I asked her, "Do you happen to know what room Brady's staying in at the hotel?"

She arched an eyebrow. "You don't honestly believe that sweet little Brady could be a murderer, do you?"

"I don't know what to believe," I said, "but I thought you'd welcome the chance to get me off your back."

Sylvia shrugged, and then said, "He's in the room beside mine. We checked in at the same time."

"How interesting," I said.

"Don't read anything into it, Savannah. We met to discuss Derrick's behavior before our meetings, so naturally, we checked in together."

The elevator pinged once, and the doors opened. There was a woman in a suit with a clipboard who stepped out as Sylvia stepped in.

The woman approached Sylvia's room, knocked tentatively at the door, and then knocked again, louder this time.

"She just left," I volunteered.

"What? I was told she was going to wait on me."

"I have a feeling you'll find her downstairs at your front desk," I said.

The woman bit her lip, and then turned back to the elevator. As she waited for it to open, I took Jenny's arm and we walked to Brady's room and knocked.

"I've been waiting all day for you," a beautiful young brunette in a purple satin nightgown said as she opened the door.

"You're not Lee," she added with a pout when she saw that it was us.

"Sorry, we must have the wrong room," I said.

She closed the door, and I looked at Jenny. "Too bad Zach wasn't with us. He would have enjoyed that."

"But not as much as you're going to like telling him what he missed, I'll wager," Jenny said.

I smiled at her. "You know what? You're right. This way is a lot more fun."

We walked to the door on the other side of Sylvia's room, and I knocked again.

"Yes?" a voice called out from inside.

"Brady, it's Savannah Stone. I need to speak with you."

There was a long pause, and then Brady replied, "This isn't a great time for me. Could we do it later?"

"It will just take a second," I said, wondering why Brady was stalling. Was it possible that Cary Duncan was there with him? I had to see that to believe it, but it would give Brady another reason to want Derrick dead, if it was true.

"Brady?" I asked as I knocked again.

"I'm coming," he said, and after a full minute, he finally opened the door, but just barely enough to look out through. I could see that he didn't have shoes on, his shirt had been buttoned out of order, there was a torn piece of paper stuck to one foot, and his belt was missing two loops. That was just what I could see from where I was standing.

"What can I do for you, Savannah?" He didn't even notice Jenny standing beside me.

"May we come in?" I asked as sweetly as I could manage.

"Hang on," he said as he ducked back inside.

"What's going on?" Jenny asked softly. "Is there someone in there with him?"

I shrugged. "I'm not sure, but I'm going to find out."

Thirty seconds later, Brady came out so fast that I couldn't even see into his room. He had loafers on, his hair had been hurriedly combed, but his shirt was still buttoned one buttonhole off. His door was slightly open as he stepped out, propped open with one heel, as if he thought he might need to retreat back inside without digging out his room key.

"We can talk out here," he said.

"Wouldn't we be more comfortable in your room?"

He shook his head. "No, this is fine. I should warn you, Savannah, I'm not in the mood for this." It was clear by his tone of voice that he was agitated before I got to ask a single question.

Okay, if he wanted to play it that way, I'd have to change my approach. I would have rather played 'good cop' if I could, but sometimes folks just didn't respond to that approach. It was time to stop messing around and get down to business. "Brady, where were you this afternoon?"

He looked surprised by the question. "I had a few errands to run around town. Why?"

"So you admit that you were outside the hotel?" Jenny asked.

"Yes, I just said that, didn't I?"

"Someone tried to kill Kelsey Hatcher today. Was it you?"

"What?" he asked, clearly startled by the question. "No. Of course not. That's ridiculous. Why would I want to hurt Kelsey?"

"Perhaps she planned to cancel your puzzles as well,"

I said. "That would explain why you killed Derrick, and then made a try for Kelsey."

"Savannah, have you lost your mind? I didn't kill Derrick, and I certainly wouldn't do anything to harm Kelsey."

"It's easy to claim, but your alibis aren't great, are they? You say that you were sitting in your car when Derrick was murdered, something no one can confirm, and you admit to being out on the streets when someone tried to kill Kelsey Hatcher earlier today."

He looked more worried than outraged by my accusation. "But I didn't have anything to do with either of those events."

"Why should we believe you?"

"There's no use trying to protect me," Kelsey Hatcher said as she stepped out of Brady's room.

She looked at me as she added, "Brady wouldn't hurt me, Savannah. We're in love."

"I N LOVE?" I ASKED. "HOW LONG HAVE YOU TWO BEEN TO-gether?"

"Seven months," Brady said as he took her hand in his. "I'm the one who recommended Kelsey to Derrick for the assistant's position. She needed a job, and I wanted to do anything I could to help."

That certainly put a new spin on things. If she was telling the truth.

"I'm not sure you did her any favors by recommending her," I said.

Kelsey put her arm around Brady. "Trust me; I was happy to take the job, even though Brady kept warning me to watch out for Derrick. He was a bit of a ladies' man, and my Brady is the jealous type. Derrick could be difficult to work for, but I learned so much from him. Besides, if I hadn't taken this job, I wouldn't be running the syndicate now for Cary."

"That should clear me of the attempt on Kelsey," Brady said. "I wouldn't hurt her for anything in the world."

"But you might hurt Derrick," Jenny said.

"What do you mean? Whoever killed Derrick went after Kelsey, too. You just said so."

"Not necessarily," I said, taking Jenny's point to heart. "They could be entirely different events, one a deliberate act and the other simply an accident."

"Trust me, it was no accident," Kelsey said. "I felt someone shove me hard toward the bus. If Brady hadn't grabbed me, I would be dead."

"Hang on a second," I said. "Did you tell the police that Brady was there with you?"

She shook her head. "No. We decided they didn't need to know who saved me."

A thought occurred to me, something I didn't want to voice at the moment. Had Brady shoved her, for whatever reason, and then gotten cold feet and pulled her back to safety at the last second? It would make him look like a hero, and divert suspicion away from him as Derrick's murderer. The only problem with that line of reasoning was that everyone would have to know what he'd done, and they were keeping quiet about it, at least for the moment.

"Savannah, what do you think?" Jenny asked me, and I realized that someone had just asked me a question. I'd been thinking about the ramifications about what I'd just learned, and I'd completely missed it.

"I'm sorry, I got distracted."

Jenny said, "They want to know if they should tell the police that Brady was with Kelsey today."

"No, I wouldn't say a word. At least not yet," I said, watching their reactions.

Kelsey seemed fine with it, but Brady looked a little surprised. What did that mean?

"Fine, we'll keep quiet," Kelsey said. She looked at me, and then asked, "Savannah, is there something else on your mind?"

"Maybe I've been married too long to a good cop, but something just occurred to me."

"What's that?"

"Brady, I'm sorry, but this just gives you one more motive for killing Derrick."

He looked honestly surprised by that claim. "Where do you get that, Savannah?"

"We all know how Derrick treated people, and he was no different with Kelsey. What kind of boyfriend could just stand by while he verbally abused her like he did? Added to that, you got her this job, so you were directly responsible for putting her in the line of fire."

Brady's face began to darken, and I was starting to see a side of him I hadn't witnessed before. "I didn't kill him," he said, nearly growling the words out.

"Take it easy," I said, suddenly wishing that I'd let Zach join us after all. Brady wasn't much physically, but the look in his eyes made him seem dangerous. "I'm not saying anything the police won't think when they find out you and Kelsey are dating."

"But you said we shouldn't tell them," Kelsey said.

"You know what? I just changed my mind."

"Why should we do their work for them?" Brady asked.

"Because it's going to sound better coming from you two than them hearing it from someone else, and believe me, they will. In this day and age, one of the toughest things in the world to keep is a secret."

"It's none of their business," Brady said with a surly edge in his voice.

"I'm afraid that when it comes to murder, everything is fair game," Jenny said.

"I could go get Zach," I said. "He's right downstairs." Not only was my offer a valid one, but I wanted Brady to know that my husband was just a short distance away.

"Don't do anything. I need to think about it," Brady said.

Kelsey stroked his arm lightly. "They're right. It's the best thing to do, given the circumstances."

I had another question I wanted to ask him, but it required some diplomacy if I was wrong about my assumption. I needed to get my new boss out of hearing range. "Kelsey, I'm afraid I'm feeling a bit woozy. Could you get me a glass of water?"

"Of course, Savannah."

She went back into Brady's room to get my water, and I stepped close to him and said softly, "While she's gone, I need to ask you something. Don't lie to me. Are you having an affair with Cary Duncan?"

Chapter 18

...

"**W**HAT ARE YOU TALKING ABOUT?"

"I saw you yesterday going to her room with a bouquet of flowers, and you were still there when I left the Brunswick later."

He started laughing, though I failed to see what was so amusing.

"That's not an answer," I whispered. "Hurry up, she's coming back."

Kelsey came out, handed me the glass of water, and then asked her boyfriend, "Brady? What's so funny?"

"Savannah thinks I'm having an affair with Cary Duncan," he said, still clearly amused by my question.

She smiled broadly at me. "Why on earth would you ask him that, Savannah?"

Before I could answer, Brady said, "She saw me going

into Cary's room yesterday with those flowers you picked out."

"You truly weren't hitting on her?" I asked.

"No, I was there trying to save Kelsey's job," he said. "Cary was having second thoughts about letting Kelsey run things, and I went there to convince her to give Kelsey an honest chance."

"So, there was no romance," I said.

"Not with Cary," he said. "Not in a million years."

He was still chuckling as I said, "You have to realize what it looked like to me."

"I suppose so. It's a pretty funny image, though. Are we finished here now?"

"For the moment," I said.

After the two of them disappeared back into Brady's room, Jenny said, "I didn't see that coming, did you?"

"Not if I'd had a thousand guesses. I wonder if it's true."

"What," Jenny asked, "that they're dating? They seemed comfortable enough around each other."

"I didn't see any sparks though, did you?"

"I'm not sure we would have," she said. "What should we do next?"

I looked around, and realized that there was one more guest in this hotel who was involved in our case. "Let's see if Mindi is in her room. She's in one-nine-one-eight."

"What are we going to talk to her about?"

"I'm not sure yet, but I will be by the time she comes to the door."

Jenny laughed. "That's what I like to see, confidence."

MINDI WASN'T IN HER ROOM, THOUGH. WE FOUND A housekeeping cart in front of it, and I tapped on the open door as one of the maids came out.

"Excuse me, but do you know if Mindi Mills is still staying here?"

The maid frowned as she said, "There's nothing here. I got a note to clean this room and that the previous guest had checked out."

"Any idea when she left?"

She checked her list again, and then said, "Three hours ago. Can I help you with something?"

"No, thanks," I said. "I'll catch up with her later."

We walked back to the elevator, and after I hit the down button, I asked Jenny, "Where do you suppose she went?"

"Back to Richmond?" she asked.

"I guess so, but I thought Murphy asked everyone involved with the case to stay in town."

"He couldn't order them to, though, not without more reason than he had. If he let her go, then I guess we'll have to mark her off our suspect list, too."

"Are you kidding? I just moved her up near the top. Running away is the worst thing she could have done. It just makes her look guilty."

"I suppose it could at that," Jenny said. "What should we do now?"

"Let's go back to the lobby and collect Zach. I'm dying to tell him what we've found out so far."

THE SECOND WE GOT BACK IN THE LOBBY, I SCANNED THE room for Zach, to no avail. I knew his promise to sit quietly and wait for us had been too good to be true.

"Where's that husband of yours?" Jenny asked me.

"I don't know, but I'm going to find out." I started to take my cell phone out of my bag when she put a hand on my arm.

"What are you doing?" I asked.

"Don't call him."

"Why not?"

Pointing toward the restaurant, she said, "Because there's no need to. He's right there."

I followed her gesture and saw my husband in deep conversation with Frank Lassiter.

"I thought he was going to stay on the sidelines," Jenny said.

I smiled. "I'm willing to bet Lassiter came through the lobby, so Zach decided to brace him while he had the chance."

"Should we join them, then?" Jenny asked.

I looked over at them and saw that my husband appeared to have things in hand. "No, I got tough with Lassiter the last time we questioned him. Zach probably has a better chance of getting something from him on his own. I've got another idea about what we can do next."

I glanced at the desk and saw that there was a man on duty I hadn't seen before. "I need you to do me a favor," I said.

"All you have to do is ask."

"Go to the front desk and ask for Benjamin Lowe." I didn't see him anywhere nearby, and if I started by asking for him, it would ruin the rest of my plan to get the information I wanted.

"I'll be right back."

In thirty seconds, she was as good as her word. "Benjamin's not here. He's gone for the night, and they won't call him."

"Then I'll have to do something myself. Would you mind hanging back here while I talk to the clerk at the front desk?"

"Are you going to ask him about Mindi?"

"Sure, I'll tack that onto what I had in mind, too."

"Savannah, what are you up to?"

I shrugged. "I'm trying to get some information." I

pointed to a newspaper rack beside the front desk. "If you want to eavesdrop, there's the perfect spot. Go ahead; I'll wait for you to get settled."

She was clearly confused by what I was about to do, and I didn't really want to explain it to her. It called for a bold move, and I had to work myself up to do it. It would have made life a lot easier if Benjamin were still there, but I couldn't wait until morning to ask him what I needed to.

After thirty seconds, I was ready.

I stormed to the front desk and slapped my hand down on the counter. It sounded like a gunshot as it echoed through the lobby, and I noticed a few people look up at the impact.

"I demand an explanation," I said loudly.

"How may I help you?" the man asked timidly.

"I want to know why there were duplicate food service items billed to my room yesterday."

He frowned. "I'm sure we can straighten it out. May I have your room number?"

I gave him Sylvia's room number, and then said, "The name is Sylvia Peters."

He tapped a few keys, studied the screen, and then said, "There appears to be a single charge yesterday."

"That's not what I was told," I said, again raising my voice. I saw Jenny flinch, and it took me a second to realize that she was trying to keep from laughing out loud. "Let me see that."

He complied by turning the screen around, and I saw that Sylvia had indeed ordered a salad when she said she had.

"Very well, but that doesn't explain why it was so late in arriving to my room."

He lowered his head instantly. "We had a miscommunication," he said. "All of our room service orders were delayed by over an hour because of a computer glitch."

"And that is my fault how, exactly?"

I saw the man bite his lip, and then he said, "Again, we apologize for the inconvenience. If you'll allow us, we'd like to treat you to dinner for two at our restaurant as a way to make up for it." He slid a voucher toward me, and I took it quickly.

"Thank you," I said, easing the harsh tone of my voice. "You've been very kind."

He nodded, clearly relieved to be done with me.

The only problem was, he wasn't, though he didn't know it yet.

I started to go, and then turned back to him. "My friend, Mindi Mills, seems to have checked out before she had a chance to let me know where she was going."

"Sorry, but I have no idea where she went," he said.

"Can't you find out?"

"No, ma'am. Again, I'm sorry." Funny, he didn't seem the least bit remorseful, though I really couldn't blame him.

"Very well," I said.

I walked toward the restaurant, and Jenny joined me.

"I can't believe you got him to show you that Sylvia's alibi for the attempt on Kelsey's life was valid."

"It just took a little bluster," I said. "But we still don't know where Mindi went."

"Perhaps I can help," a man's voice behind me said.

It was Benjamin Lowe, and I had some fast talking to do.

"**I** SUPPOSE YOU'RE WONDERING WHAT JUST HAPPENED," I said.

"On the contrary," he said with a smile, "I'd rather not know at all. Garrett warned me that your behavior could be eccentric at times, but that you were to be indulged whenever possible."

"Remind me to thank him the next time I see him," I said. "Did you hear everything? You weren't supposed to be here."

"Officially, I'm not, but I had some paperwork to do in back, and when I heard you claiming to be Sylvia Peters, I couldn't help eavesdropping as long as I didn't spoil the show."

"I hope the clerk isn't going to get into trouble because of me," I said. "It wasn't his fault."

"He didn't do anything wrong, given the way you presented yourself," Benjamin said. "By the way, I hope you and your husband enjoy your meal at our restaurant."

I started to hand the voucher to him when he held his palms up. "I wouldn't dream of taking that back. You earned it."

"Thanks," I said, adding a grin. "Since you're here, maybe you can help us find Mindi Mills."

"That's why I came out here. I happened to check her out myself, so I know exactly where she went."

"Go on, I'm listening."

"She wanted me to order her a limousine to take her to the Brunswick Hotel from here," he said.

"A limo? Really? I was under the impression she couldn't afford anything that nice."

Benjamin shrugged slightly. "If you'd like to speak with the car service, I used Evans Livery."

"Thanks, but I think I'll go by the Brunswick and ask her myself."

He nodded, and then retrieved a card from his breast pocket. After jotting something down on the back, Benjamin said, "To save you from further deceit, here's my personal cell phone number. I am at your disposal around the clock, so don't hesitate to call."

"You have no idea what you're opening yourself up to," Jenny said.

Benjamin replied, "I have some idea. Now, if there's nothing else, I have work to do."

"Thank you," I said.

"My pleasure."

After he was gone, I said, "I can't imagine what Garrett did for him, but it must have been huge."

"Let's not question it," Jenny said. "Are we headed to the Brunswick Hotel now?"

I glanced over at my husband in time to see him push away from the table and point one lone finger at Lassiter, who looked visibly shaken by the gesture. Zach walked out of the restaurant scowling, which lasted until he saw me. His wink told me that his fit of anger was merely a ruse to shake Lassiter, and from the expression on the man's face, it had worked.

Zach headed out the door to the parking garage, and Jenny and I followed. It appeared that we all had a lot to talk about.

"WHAT WAS THAT ABOUT?" I ASKED HIM AS SOON AS WE got out of sight.

Zach grinned. "I put a little righteous fear in him." He broke his smile for a moment. "That's okay with you, isn't it? I know I said I wouldn't interview any suspects, but he's getting ready to leave town. I caught him checking out, so I made an executive decision."

"You did great," I said. "Did you have any luck with him?"

"You won't believe it."

Noticing that Jenny and I had started walking toward my car, Zach asked, "Are we going somewhere?"

"We're heading over to the Brunswick Hotel," I said.

"What's Cary done now?"

"It's not Cary," I said. "Mindi just moved there, and we need to find out how she's suddenly able to afford it."

"Let's go, then. We can talk on the way."

Jenny said, "I've got a feeling we're going to need more than the few minutes it's going to take to drive over there. Why don't we grab some hot dogs from the Grill and then get some dessert. Does anyone feel like pie?"

Zach smiled broadly at her. "I always feel like pie." He turned to me. "Savannah, I knew there was a reason I liked her."

After we ate our fill of hot dogs at the Grill, it was time for dessert.

"Just take a left out of the parking lot," Jenny said. "I'll tell you where to turn next."

Six minutes later, we were in front of a diner that looked as though it had seen better days, say in the 1950s. The brick exterior had been painted white a decade ago if the peeling paint was any indication, and the "H" in the "Hot Food" sign was burned out. In other words, it was exactly my husband's kind of dining establishment.

We got out and went inside, and Jenny grabbed a table by the window, smiling and greeting a few folks on her way inside.

"You should run for mayor," I said. "Everywhere we go, you know somebody."

"I like it here, and they like me," she said.

A white man in his late fifties sporting a grizzled salt-and-pepper beard walked out wearing an apron that was clean, though tattered around the edges. "If it isn't Jenny Blake herself," he said as he smiled broadly at her.

"Hi, Clayton," she said.

"Sherrie, get out here."

A black woman who appeared to be around the same age came out, her cheeks dusted with flour. "Clayton, I can't keep making pies if you don't leave me to it, and then what are you going to sell?" Her expression lit up as she saw Jenny. "Jenny, it's wonderful to see you. Where have you been hiding yourself, young lady?"

"I've been working," she said. "I'd like you to meet my friends. This is Savannah Stone, and this is her husband, Zach."

Clayton offered a hand to my husband. "It's a pleasure to meet you."

Zach nodded, and then smiled broadly at Sherrie. "I hear you make the best pie in the world. That makes me an instant fan of yours."

Sherrie looked pleased by the compliment, though she tried not to show it. "Jenny, have you been spreading lies about me again?"

"Nothing but the truth," Jenny said.

"Well, it's good to see you. Can I bring you something?"

"Some coffee would be nice," she said, "and three slices of pie."

Sherrie looked at Zach. "Any kind in particular?"

"What would you say if I told you I wanted to taste one of each?"

She laughed. "I'd say your eyes were too big for your stomach."

"Then bring me a slice of your favorite," Zach said.

"And how do you know you'll like it?"

"If it's good enough for you, I'm sure it will be perfect for me," my husband replied.

Sherrie swatted at me with a rag that was flung over her shoulder. "Hold on to him, Savannah. He's one of the good ones."

"I couldn't agree more," I said.

After Sherrie was gone, a man tried to get Clayton's attention at the register. "If you all will excuse me."

"Of course," Jenny said.

After they were gone, I asked, "Are they married?"

Jenny shook her head. "No, they grew up together, but nobody from either side of the tracks liked them being such good friends, so they drifted apart. Fifteen years ago, Sherrie lost her husband in a car wreck about the same time Clayton's wife left him for another man, and the two of them decided it was high time they got to be the friends they were meant to be. They bought this place, and it's been thriving ever since they opened it." She looked around and said, "Judges eat here, right alongside trash collectors. The only rule they have is you take the next open seat if you're waiting, no matter who's around you. They pride themselves on serving the best pie in North Carolina, and offering it to anyone with the price of a slice on him."

"That still doesn't explain why they're so fond of you," I said.

"I helped them out once with a little situation, and they won't let me forget it," Jenny answered.

"You're not going to leave it at that, are you?"

"I am," Jenny said. "Look, here comes our order."

Sherrie came out with a tray loaded down with six plates. "That's too much," Jenny said.

"Only one is for you," she said as she slid a piece of peach pie in front of her. "Savannah, do you like apple?"

"I sure do," I said, and she gave me a piece of pie with a flaky golden crust barely able to contain the golden apple slices inside.

Zach looked a little worried. "Sherrie, as much as I'd love to, I can't eat that much."

She laughed again, and Clayton smiled at the register. "I'm just having some fun with you, Zach. Take your pick, though."

He studied the pie slices, and then finally settled for a slice of lemon meringue.

"That's an excellent choice," Sherrie said.

"What would you have said if I'd picked the sweet potato?"

Sherrie laughed. "The same. How do you know it's not pumpkin?"

"Pumpkin is darker, and the texture is different. It's easy enough if you know what you're looking at."

Sherrie nodded. "Not everybody can tell, though. You do like pie, don't you?"

"I told you," Zach said as he took his first bite. "Wow. This is unbelievable."

"Glad you like it," Sherrie said, and then looked at us. "Anything else for you ladies?"

"No, we're good. Thanks."

"Then I'll give you some peace."

She disappeared into the back after whispering something to Clayton, who laughed heartily. It was clear that they were indeed the best of friends.

"They'll give us some space," Jenny said as she took a bite of her pie. "The woman is magic."

I tasted mine, amazed by the texture of the crust, the crisp edge to the apples, and the blend of cinnamon, nutmeg, and some spices I didn't recognize, giving the pie a whole different level of flavor. "Wow is right."

"I told you she was good," Jenny said as she took another bite. "What did you find out from Lassiter, Zach?" Jenny asked.

He finished a bite, and had another poised for his mouth. "You two go first."

"So you can finish your pie?" I asked.

"Guilty as charged."

I didn't have a problem with that. As my husband kept eating, I began to bring him up-to-date on what Jenny and I uncovered so far.

Chapter 19

...

ITOOK A BITE OF MY PIE, AND THEN GOT STARTED. "OKAY, I'LL go. Probably the biggest thing we learned was that Kelsey and Brady have been dating for seven months. He's the one who got her the job with Derrick."

"What a lousy thing to do to a girlfriend," Zach said through a mouthful of pie.

"That's what we thought, but Kelsey appears to be grateful for it. Brady claims that when we saw him visiting Cary, he was just trying to keep Kelsey's job for her."

"So, they weren't courting flowers after all," Zach said with a smile.

"Or condolence flowers, either."

"I get it; we were both wrong," Zach said. He stabbed his fork in the air at me as he added, "But that doesn't exactly clear him in Derrick's murder. If anything, it gives him more reason to want to see him dead than we realized before."

"That's what we said. He seemed to think that because he's the one who pulled Kelsey back from the bus, he's absolved of Derrick's murder."

That caught my husband by surprise. "He was with her when it happened?"

"Yes," Jenny said, "but he claims he didn't see anything until she started falling toward the bus."

"It gives us something else to check," Zach said. "What else do you have for me?"

"We're fairly certain that it wasn't Sylvia," I said, "at least not when it comes to the attempt on Kelsey. She'd ordered a salad from room service, and it took an hour to deliver. There's no way she'd risk leaving if it would be so easy to verify that she was gone."

"Did you check with the hotel to see if it's true?"

"Yes," I said simply.

"Tell him how you did it," Jenny said with a smile.

"He doesn't need to know everything," I answered, hoping Zach would drop it.

"I just assumed you asked Benjamin."

"I tried that first," I admitted, "but he was gone; at least we thought he was."

Zach stroked his chin, and then said, "If I had to guess, I'd say that you impersonated Sylvia with the front desk clerk."

Jenny looked shocked by my husband's guess. "She did! How could you possibly know that?"

"You keep forgetting I used to do this for a living," Zach said. "That means we can mark Sylvia off the list for the attempt on Kelsey, but not Derrick's murder."

"We're having a tough time eliminating suspects for that, aren't we?" I asked.

Zach shrugged. "I'm fairly certain that we can strike Lassiter's name off all of our lists."

"How could we possibly do that? Did he say something?"

Zach smiled as he finished the last bite of his pie.

"Come on, that's not fair. We told you everything we know," I said. "Now it's your turn."

Jenny raised an eyebrow as she looked at me. "Savannah, that's not everything."

"Shhh," I said. I wasn't certain what she was talking about, but I didn't want to spoil her play.

Zach's smile disappeared. "You two aren't holding out on me, are you?"

"That depends. Are you keeping anything from us?"

He put his fork down and wiped his lips. "Fine, I'll tell you. Lassiter has a pretty good alibi for the day of the murder. He didn't want to tell me until I started putting a little pressure on him."

"How good could it be?" I asked.

"If it checks out, it's pretty solid. Lassiter claims that he was with his attorney discussing his settlement with Derrick when the man was murdered," Zach said. "That's what triggered the sale of the syndicate you all belong to, Savannah. Derrick was going to use the money he got from the proceeds to pay off Lassiter so he wouldn't sue him over their land deal that went sour. It turned out he wasn't as free and clear of it as he'd originally thought, and this was his way to make it go away for good."

"But he fired half his syndication group, including me."

"That was for show only, trust me. It was a way he could put the screws to all of you one last time, but he had no intention of firing anyone. He needed you all as part of the group to make the sale go through. Lassiter laughed in my face when I accused him of murder. His point was, why would he kill his golden goose before he got any eggs, and

I tend to agree with him. I'm going to look into it and see if it's true. Now, tell me what else you two learned today."

I looked as innocent as I could manage. "I have no idea what she's talking about."

Jenny said, "Come on, we learned something else."

"I'm just as curious as Zach is," I said.

"I just assumed you saw it, too. When Brady came out the first time, there was something sticking to his foot."

"It was just a piece of paper," I said, remembering the paper, but dismissing it as unimportant.

"Was it? From where I stood, it looked as though it had been torn out of a telephone directory. That's the same thing we found in Derrick's suitcases. It can't just be a coincidence, can it?"

"No, but I've got to admit that I missed it," I said.

"Don't feel bad. From where you were standing, you probably couldn't see it as clearly as I could."

"But what does it mean?" Zach asked.

"When we get back to Jenny's, we're going to have to take a closer look at those telephone books," I said. "But right now, it's time to go see Mindi and find out how she can suddenly afford to stay at the Brunswick Hotel."

Zach tried to signal for the bill, but Clayton was pointedly ignoring him. "Why won't he come over here?" my husband asked.

"I was afraid of that," Jenny said. "He's not going to take your money, either."

"They don't charge you? For pie like this? Are you serious?" I'd rarely seen my husband so baffled and amazed at the same time.

"Not a dime. If I try to leave so much as a tip, I get it back in the next day's mail."

"Jenny, what exactly did you do for them?"

She wouldn't answer, but simply shrugged.

"At least I can try to handle it myself," Jenny said.

She approached Clayton, who shook his head vigorously. I heard him say, "Don't make me get Sherrie out here again. I don't want to, but I will if you force me to."

"Thank you for the coffee and pie," Jenny said. "Please be sure to thank Sherrie, too."

"Don't stay away so long the next time, young lady."

"If I come back sooner, will you let me pay?"

He shook his head solemnly. "You know that's not happening. Good night, folks," he called out to us.

Zach and I both thanked him profusely, and as we were leaving, we saw another man approach Clayton. "Is the food free for everyone tonight? If it is, I want to add to my order."

"Harry, we both know you can afford whatever I charge, and if you want to keep having access to Sherrie's food, you'll pay it with a smile."

"I was just kidding," Harry said as he slipped a twenty to Clayton.

When we were outside, I said, "I feel bad depriving them of income."

"You heard me in there," Jenny said. "They won't take my money."

My husband asked, "I wonder if she makes Shoofly pie? My grandmother used to make it on special occasions, and I haven't tasted any as good as hers in a long time." He got a faraway look on his face as he added, "I bet Sherrie could do it if I asked her to."

"Come on, champ," I said as I led him to our car. "You've had enough pie for one day."

"Is there even such a thing as too much?" he asked.

As Jenny and I got in, I said, "Thank them again for us, would you?"

"The next time I'm there, I promise to," she replied.

I looked back into the diner and saw Clayton and Sherrie there, side by side, waving and smiling at my friend. I couldn't help wondering what service she'd rendered that was worth such special treatment, but then again, Jenny was like that. If she saw a friend in need, she'd move heaven and earth to help them, and I was the biggest example of that behavior in the world at the moment.

It was one of her most endearing traits, and I was thankful again for the college roommate lottery that had thrown us together in the first place. It was time to head over to the Brunswick and see what Mindi Mills was up to.

"**H**OW ARE WE GOING TO FIND MINDI'S ROOM?" JENNY asked me as we walked into the Brunswick Hotel's lobby.

"I'm going to call her on the house phone," I said.

Zach asked, "How are you going to get her to come down here?"

"I'm going to say we found Derrick's shoes, the ones she seemed to be so attached to."

"But we gave those back to Cary," Jenny said.

"Yes, but I'm guessing that Mindi doesn't know that."

I picked up one of the courtesy phones in the lobby and dialed zero.

"Yes?" a pretentious voice answered.

"Mindi Mills, please."

"One moment," he said. At least she hadn't blocked her calls. The phone rang ten times, and then went to voice mail. I decided not to leave one, and hung up.

"She's not there."

"Could she be in the restaurant or the bar?" Zach asked.

"It's worth a look."

We walked to the restaurant, which was crowded with very well-dressed diners. I didn't spot Mindi, though, or Cary, either.

"If she's not at the bar, I say we talk to Cary again,

since we're already here," Zach said. "That is, if I'm allowed to tag along this time."

"What can it hurt?" I asked.

"Wow, I can really feel the love in the room."

As we walked into the bar, it took my eyes a second to adjust to the low light level. I almost gave up when Zach touched my arm. "Well, I never imagined we'd see that."

"What?" I asked.

"Look over in the corner."

I followed his gesture, and saw that Mindi was having a drink, but that wasn't what had stunned my husband. It had to be her drinking companion.

It was Cary Duncan, and from the look of things, the two of them were as thick as thieves.

"**M**AY WE JOIN YOU?" I ASKED AS WE APPROACHED THEIR table.

Mindi looked a little intimidated by our presence, but Cary certainly took it in stride. "Actually, we were just leaving."

She stood, and Mindi followed.

"Good, I hate bars, don't you? We can talk in the lobby."

We followed them out of the bar, and Cary said, "Frankly, I'm tired of answering your questions. You've become more tedious than the police."

"We just have a few," I said. I kept obsessing over the telephone books, and I wanted to see if Cary knew why her husband might have been squirreling so many away. "When Jenny and I cleaned up Derrick's suite, we found quite a few telephone books."

Cary nodded sadly. "I wondered why you didn't give me any when you brought his suitcases. Derrick was obsessed with pilfering the things. You should see our garage.

There's one entire wall of shelves loaded down with them. It was a little quirk of his, taking souvenirs from everywhere he ever stayed."

That answered that question, even if the response was less than satisfactory.

"We just have one more, then," Zach said. "How did you two get to be such fast friends? Was it before Derrick died, or has it been since then?"

Mindi blanched a little, but Cary just smiled. "Imagine how surprised I was to find that we have so much in common. Apparently Derrick's tastes were more similar than anyone could have imagined."

"Are you saying you actually like your husband's mistress?" Jenny asked unbelievingly.

Cary waved a hand in the air. "That's all in the past, isn't it? If we can give each other a little solace in this time of need, why shouldn't we take advantage of it?"

I had a wild guess, and decided to try it before I lost my nerve. "Is that why you moved her here to your hotel?"

Cary was about to deny it when Mindi spoke up first. "She was just doing me a favor. I couldn't stand staying there after what happened."

Cary looked at Mindi as though she wanted to gag her, but I was going to take advantage of her candor. "So, nobody answered our question. How long have you two been friends?"

"We aren't friends," Cary said harshly, and then immediately backed off the bold statement when she saw Mindi flinch. "Honestly, I didn't even know she existed until she came to my room the day after Derrick was murdered. Naturally I was reluctant to speak with her, but she made some good points, and I decided to give her a chance. After all, who better to know what I'm going through than someone else who loved my husband?"

Mindi started nodding, but she kept her mouth shut.

That was too bad. I would love to get them apart so I could grill them individually, but I wasn't sure how to do it. Zach must have been reading my mind.

He said, "Cary, I'd love a moment of your time, if you wouldn't mind."

"Whatever for?"

"It's related to something Frank Lassiter told me about you. I just want to confirm it before I go to the police with what I've uncovered."

"What did that weasel say about me?" she asked, her eyes flashing with anger.

"Do you really want to discuss it here?" He gestured around the lobby, and Cary reluctantly nodded.

"There's a quiet corner over there." Before she left, she turned to Mindi and said, "I'll be right back."

After they were gone, I asked, "What's really going on, Mindi?"

"What are you talking about?"

"We're not buying your 'best buddies' act. The last time we spoke to you, you hated Cary, and now you two are nearly inseparable. Something changed. I'm just wondering what it was."

Mindi frowned. "I didn't know her before. Now that I understand where she's coming from, I'm actually starting to like her."

"It couldn't hurt that she's paying your expenses now, either."

"I earned that much at least, after the way Derrick treated me."

That answer surprised me. "Isn't it a little odd that his widow is the one covering the tab for his mistress?"

"You heard Cary. There's nothing wrong with what we're doing."

I wished I'd had more time, but Cary came storming back. "Let's go, Mindi. We're finished here."

She didn't say a word as she accompanied Cary onto the elevator.

After they were gone, I asked Zach, "What happened?"

"Sorry, I couldn't keep her any longer than I did. I had to let her know that Lassiter accused her of cheating on Derrick. She denied it of course, and when I pressed her on it, she got hostile, not that it was a long reach for her. Were you able to get anything out of Mindi?"

"Not really," I said. "She seems to be Cary's biggest fan now. When I asked her about Cary paying for her stay, she implied that it was owed to her, for some reason. I'm not exactly certain what she meant by that."

"Somebody's playing someone else," Zach said. "I just can't figure out who is doing exactly what just yet."

"Well, we'd better hurry. I'm not sure how long we can keep this up."

"Don't worry," he said, touching my shoulder lightly. "We'll figure this out. I'm sure of it."

"I'm not at all certain how we're going to do that. We've run out of people to interview," Jenny said. "Where does that leave us?"

"We go back to your place and start looking at the evidence we've collected," I said.

"Do you honestly think the answer's in Derrick's planner?"

"It could be in the telephone books, too," I replied, "but yes, there's got to be something there that can help us in our investigation. At first I thought those telephone books in Derrick's suitcase were just there as a substitute for something about the same weight, but after you mentioned that torn page stuck to Brady's foot, I'm not so sure."

Jenny said, "Listen, I've been thinking about it, and

I can't be one hundred percent positive that's what it was."

"It's another place to look," I said. "What do you say? Do we head back to Jenny's?"

"Is there any way we can stop off for more pie on our way?"

I laughed at my husband's question. "I think you've had enough for one day."

"Hey, it doesn't hurt to ask."

When we got back to Jenny's, I was surprised to see a squad car pulled up in her driveway.

Zach opened the car door as he said, "You two stay here for a second."

I wasn't even going to fight him on it this time.

He walked to the cruiser, and a young uniformed officer got out of his car. After he and Zach held a brief conversation, the officer got back in and drove off.

Zach motioned us forward, and I pulled the car up to him.

When we got out, I asked, "What was that all about?"

"Murphy had him staking the place out. He's doing what we asked him to do."

"Yes, but it's going to be hard to find someone on the videotape if he's got an armed officer stationed out front all of the time."

Zach shrugged. "We can't have it both ways. Maybe someone will show up tonight."

"At this point, I don't know what to wish for," Jenny said.

"The worst thing that can happen right now is for this guy to just disappear. We need to catch him in the act so you can resolve this once and for all."

"You're right," Jenny said as she shivered slightly. "Can we go inside now? I feel kind of exposed, just standing here."

I put my arm around her and said, "Of course we can. Don't worry, Jenny, it's going to be all right."

"I know everyone's doing their best, but I still wish it was all over, do you know what I mean?"

Thinking about the cloud of suspicion hanging over me for Derrick's murder, I could easily relate. "Yes, I kind of do."

She smiled, and then hugged me. "Of course you do. What do you say we go inside and see if we can make something happen?"

"I'm all for it."

Chapter 20

...

ZACH SAID, "I'LL GRAB THE PLANNER, AND ONE OF YOU can take the copy Jenny made. Whoever draws the short straw gets to look at the telephone books."

I volunteered, "I'll take the phone books."

"Good," Zach said. "Then let's get to work."

They took the planner and its copy out from under the pile of newspapers where I'd stashed them, and I went into Jenny's office to retrieve the telephone books. The box was heavy, but I lugged it into the living room anyway. I wanted us all to work together, and if there was a discovery made, I wanted to be in on it. I didn't have much hope for the telephone books, but I had a hard time believing that the torn page stuck to Brady's foot, if that's what it was, was simply a coincidence. Zach had taught me long ago that there was no such thing in an investigation, and I believed him.

I opened the box and reached inside for the first book. It was for all of Raleigh, and it weighed a ton. At first, I leafed through the pages, hoping something had been stuck somewhere, but there were no letters, no last-second wills, and there was certainly nothing there that even resembled a clue. Next, I started fanning the pages, looking to see if Derrick had written anything in the margins. I thought I had a hit, and I almost said something to Zach and Jenny, when I realized that someone had written a note about a business meeting three months prior.

It was going to be a long night, and I couldn't even complain, since I'd volunteered to take that task myself. I was going to need a bar of soap and a basin of hot water to scrub the germs off my hands by the time I finished.

I WAS ON TELEPHONE DIRECTORY THREE OUT OF SIX WHEN Zach said excitedly, "Jenny, turn to the entries thirteen days before Derrick was murdered."

"What did you find?" I asked as I looked up from the telephone book I was exploring.

"Hang on a second," Zach said as Jenny flipped through the copied pages.

"Okay, I'm here," she said.

"What does the entry for four p.m. look like to you?"

I put the directory down and walked over to Zach. "What does it say?"

Jenny frowned, and then said, "You might be right. Let me check." She picked her phone up and dialed a number. As I waited for her to comment further, Zach pointed to an entry with his finger.

It read, "AW&V. Settlement meeting. 4:30."

"Is that from his suit with Frank Lassiter?" I asked.

"It might be," Zach said. "That would let us wipe his name off without hesitation."

Jenny held up one hand for us to keep quiet, and after hanging up, she said, "Give me another second."

She headed back into her home office, and Zach asked, "Are you having any luck with the telephone directories?"

"No, but we figured it could be a blind alley," I said. "This might be something."

"Maybe," Zach said, but he couldn't contain the excitement in his voice. He thought he'd hit something, and I agreed. But what?

Jenny came back a minute later with a piece of paper in her hand.

Zach asked, "Was it from the settlement?"

"Yes and no," she said.

"What does that mean?" I asked her.

"It's about a settlement, but not from a lawsuit. The number belongs to a law firm in Richmond that specializes in divorce."

SO, DERRICK REALLY WAS GOING TO LEAVE HER," I SAID. "I wonder if Cary had any idea."

"If she did, it's a perfect motive for murder," Zach said. "If the divorce went through, Cary would lose her claim to Derrick's money, not to mention that life insurance policy for half a million dollars."

"Could she really be that stupid?" I asked. "She seems smarter than that to me."

Zach frowned. "Where greed's involved, sometimes intelligence goes out the window."

He reached for his phone, and I asked, "Who are you calling?"

"Shawn Murphy," he said.

I tried to stop him. "You can't tell him we have Derrick's planner."

He paused his dialing, and then said, "Savannah, he needs to know this. We'll deal with explaining how we happened to have the planner later."

"I'd like it a lot more if we could come up with something now," Jenny said. "Shawn could destroy me if he found out I've been holding onto this."

Zach thought about that, and then finally said, "I'll tell him I found it, plain and simple. If anyone takes the blame, it will be me, and you'll be free of it."

"I'm not letting you do that," Jenny said. I'd heard that steel in her voice before, and I knew she wasn't about to budge.

"We can always claim that we just found it," I said.

"How can we do that?" Zach asked.

"We cleaned out his room, didn't we? While we were there, we found this box of telephone directories, and I just now got around to looking inside it. Imagine my surprise when Derrick's planner turned up."

Zach laughed. "That's all well and good, but that doesn't explain how it was stolen from Kelsey's hotel room days later."

Jenny said, "I know. We didn't find the planner itself." She held the pages in her hand up and waved them in the air. "We found the copy."

Zach frowned for a few seconds, and then nodded. "As crazy as it sounds, that might just work." He looked at me and asked, "Savannah, do you see any problems with that?"

"Not off the top of my head," I replied.

"Then let me finish that call."

DETECTIVE MURPHY SHOWED UP SEVEN MINUTES AFTER Zach called him. Either he was an extremely fast driver, or he'd been somewhere close by. Either way, we barely had time to get our stories straight before he rang Jenny's doorbell.

"Let's see it," Murphy said as Jenny opened the door.

"Hello, Shawn, it's good to see you, too."

He stepped in, and she added, "Won't you come in?"

"I don't have time for this, Jenny. A city councilman was just robbed at gunpoint by the Capitol building, and we're all supposed to drop what we're doing and start a search party."

"The power of power is something, isn't it?" she said.

Zach stepped up. "Here's what we found." Always a stickler, my husband had turned his back and asked me to hide the copy of Derrick's planner in the pile of telephone directories I'd already looked through. When I was finished, he turned back around and "discovered" the copy in the stack. That way he was technically telling the truth to another police officer. It seemed a little ridiculous to me, but my husband had his own set of guidelines and rules that he ran his life by, and I was no one to judge.

Murphy took the pages, skimmed through them, and then said, "We've been looking for this."

"You knew there was a copy all along?" Zach asked innocently.

"Not a copy, but the original. I figure Kelsey Hatcher or Cary Duncan still has the original, but if they do, they're in no mood to share it with us." He tapped the pages. "Thanks for this. We'll jump right on it."

I wanted to tell him about the entry with the Richmond divorce attorneys, but Zach was probably reading my mind when he shook his head slightly. I kept it to myself, and Murphy headed for the door.

"Any luck tracking the teddy bear down?" Zach asked before he could get away.

"I've got a man on it, but no news yet. It might take a little time."

"Just checking," Zach said.

"When I know something, you will," he said. "I've got to run."

He left without so much as a good-bye, and I asked, "Why didn't you tell him about the divorce attorney?"

"For the same reason I didn't want you to tell him. If he finds it for himself, which he will in a few hours, trust me, it will mean more to him than if we point it out. Besides, I wanted a little deniability about reading it. Did you notice how careful he was not to ask if we'd scanned it?"

"I thought that was odd," Jenny said.

"It's so we'd be covered," Zach said. He retrieved the original from under his chair, and then said, "Now we keep digging."

"My copy is gone," Jenny said.

"You can always help me with the telephone directories I have left," I told her.

"Thanks, but I'd rather make us all a snack."

Zach perked up at that. "Snack? I could go for a snack."

I just smiled at my husband as I resumed my search of the telephone books I hadn't examined yet. My long shot was getting longer and longer, but that didn't mean I could give up. We needed more clues, and I wasn't about to turn my back on another source, no matter how remote the odds were getting.

FIVE MINUTES LATER, JENNY CAME OUT WITH A TRAY FULL of cheese and crackers and some wine. "Is everyone ready for a break?"

"Why not?" Zach asked. "This planner is giving me a migraine. Derrick wasn't the most organized man in the world, was he?"

Jenny said, "You should have seen his hotel room. That

alone would be enough to prove it. The place was a complete wreck."

"I have no problem believing that," Zach said as he took a bite of cracker. "Half his notes make no sense at all, and those are just the ones I've been able to decipher from his chicken scratch writing."

"You can do it," I said as I took a sip of wine.

"Are you making any progress with the telephone books?"

"It's slow going," I admitted, "but it's too good an opportunity to pass up." I picked up a piece of cheese, took a bite, and then added, "Why all the telephone books if he wasn't using them for something?"

"They're really heavy," Jenny said. "Maybe we were right originally and he was trying to make it seem as though the suitcases were holding something else?"

"We've already ruled out gold bars," I said. "What else could be that heavy?"

Zach said softly, "Cash might be."

"Seriously?" Jenny asked.

My husband nodded. "You'd be amazed how heavy two suitcases stuffed full of money can be."

Jenny looked at him cryptically. "When have you moved that much cash, Zach?"

He shrugged. "It came up once on the job."

Jenny looked at me, but I shook my head slightly, silently pleading for her to drop it. Zach didn't like to talk about the time in Charlotte ten years before when he'd been forced to act as a courier for kidnappers. It had turned out badly, with the money taken and the victim never found, so I'd been surprised when he'd brought it up.

"Anyway," I said, "I doubt Derrick ever had that much cash on him in his life. Besides, he'd have to take the telephone books out as soon as he was ready to leave."

Jenny asked, "Why would he have to do that?"

"He had to get his clothes home, didn't he? Those suitcases were just a temporary storage place."

"I don't know. I just don't get it."

"Me, either," I said. I slapped my hands together, and added, "I've got two more telephone books, and then we'll know for sure if they're important or not."

"I'll help," Jenny said.

"Thanks, but it's become a matter of personal pride for me now."

"Or stubbornness," Zach said.

"Aren't they the same thing?" I asked with a grin.

"Sometimes they are," Zach said. "Jenny, maybe you can help me with the planner. How good are you at reading hieroglyphics?"

"I'll do my best," she said.

I took another sip, and reached for the fifth telephone book in the pile. As I fanned the pages, expecting nothing to happen, I was startled when an envelope slipped out and fluttered into my lap.

"I think I just found something," I said as I finished fanning the pages of the directory. Nothing else dropped out, so I set the phone book aside and picked up the envelope.

"What is it?" Zach asked as he came over to join me on the couch.

"I'm not sure. Let's see," I said as I turned the envelope over and broke the seal on it.

The letter inside was brief and to the point, and I read it out loud to Zach and Jenny.

To: Kelsey Hatcher
From: Derrick Duncan

As of the end of business today, your services will no longer be required. Your final check will be sent to you via registered mail within ten days.

It was signed by Derrick, and dated the day of his murder.

"Am I wrong, or is that a strong motive?" I asked.

Zach took the letter from me, careful to handle it around the edges. "We need to call Murphy back."

"He's going to love this. How are we going to tell him that we found something else in the telephone books we had? It's a little too coincidental, don't you think?"

"That can't be helped," Zach said. "He has a right to know. Jenny, do you want to go catch a movie or something while we do this? It might help keep you out of it."

She smiled gently. "It's a little too late for that, wouldn't you say? Call him, Zach. I can take it."

"First, I'm going through the last book," I said.

I did a quick examination, but it turned up empty. "Okay, now you can call him."

Zach made the phone call, and two minutes later, I was surprised to see a car outside Jenny's tear up the driveway with its police lights flashing.

"What's going on?" I asked. "Surely he's not doing that just to get this letter."

"There's more to it than that. I'll be right back."

Zach walked out the front door, and Jenny and I followed him. He noticed, but didn't comment.

As we stepped out together, a piece of paper was fluttering on the wooden porch floor. It looked like a note, and there was something holding it to the board.

It didn't take a second glance to see that a knife had been stabbed through its center.

"I didn't do anything," a voice kept protesting from the yard, now lit by Murphy's headlights.

"That's not how it looked to me," the detective said as he cuffed the man.

"I was going to see if I could do anything to help her,"

Charlie protested again. "When I saw that knife sticking up, I couldn't even warn them. Why did you put it there?"

"Me?" Murphy looked surprised by the implication. "I didn't do it. You did."

Charlie acted equally shocked. "You did! I watched you from my kitchen window. Just because you're a cop doesn't mean you can railroad me into this. I'll testify in court that you're the one who did it."

"What's going on?" Zach asked.

Murphy said, "When I drove up, I saw him creeping around the porch. My lights hit the knife, and he started running back to his house the second he saw me."

"I had to get away from you!" Charlie shouted. "You did it! I saw you!"

"Screaming louder isn't going to get anyone to believe your lies," Murphy said.

"It's your word against mine," Charlie said, finally calming down a little.

I could tell he was nervous by the quiver in his voice, but he was standing his ground. Was he telling the truth? Murphy had a history with Jenny, one that might suggest something like this was possible. I leaned toward believing the policeman, though. But could Charlie be right? Was it going to boil down to one man's word against another's?

Zach said calmly, "I can help here."

"How?" Murphy asked. "You weren't looking out the window when it happened, were you?"

"Better than that," Zach said. "I've got video cameras set up on the porch. We'll be able to see who did it in just a few seconds."

Charlie said, "I don't believe you."

Zach reached under the railing and removed one from its perch. "How about now?"

That was all it took to break the man. Through his tears,

he told Jenny, "When you moved in next door, you were so nice to me. No one else even bothered to wave ever since I rented this place. I knew that the two of us had a special bond." His expression grew angry as he added, "But then you changed. You started treating me like everyone else."

"I don't know what you're talking about. I wave to you all the time," Jenny protested.

"But not with the same vigor you used to. Something changed in you, Jennifer."

"I've heard enough of this garbage," Murphy said as he led Charlie to the back of his car.

"I loved you," Charlie shouted, and I felt a shiver run through me.

Murphy forced him into the back of his car, and then rejoined us. "Nice work, chief," he said to Zach.

"You, too," my husband said.

"I owe you one. If you hadn't been taping, that could have gotten messy for me."

Jenny said softly, "I didn't honestly think that you were the one stalking me, Shawn."

"Thanks for that, but a good defense attorney could have put enough reasonable doubt without the tape to get him off." He nodded toward us, and then asked, "Where's that letter you told me about?"

"I'll go get it," Jenny said.

Zach added, "I'll get you the tape for evidence, too."

After they were gone, I said, "It's a good thing you came by when you did. Thank you."

He raised one eyebrow as he said, "Sometimes timing is everything. There's something that's bothering me, though."

"What's that?"

"How come you just found the letter, if you'd already searched through the telephone books you found in Derrick's room?"

"We didn't search all of them when you were here before," I said, something that was the absolute truth.

"Okay," he said. "Have you finished searching now?"

I nodded. "We went ahead and looked through the last one before you came."

He seemed to think about that for a minute, and then said, "I'll have an officer here in ten minutes to pick them up. You don't mind, do you?"

"Why should I mind?"

He shrugged, and then said with a grin, "I just want to make sure you didn't miss anything else."

Or have an excuse to find anything else, I added silently to myself.

Zach arrived with the tape and the letter we'd found. The envelope was now in a large clear plastic bag. "Here you go. If you need me to testify, I'll be happy to do whatever I can."

"Thanks," he said. "I appreciate that."

Before he could get to his car, another squad car pulled up. Murphy directed him to collect the telephone books while he took photographs and then collected the knife and the note on the front porch.

In ten minutes, they were both gone.

"Are you all right?" I asked.

Jenny was staring at Charlie's house, noticeably shaking. "It's just so creepy. He was living right there, watching me the whole time, and I didn't even know it."

"It puts a bad twist to the concept of a Neighborhood Watch program, doesn't it?" Zach asked.

"You're not helping," I said to my husband.

"Sorry. Why don't we go inside?"

"In a minute," Jenny said.

I motioned for Zach to go on, and he nodded in understanding. Jenny and I stood out there for a minute, both our gazes on the house next door. "Did you have any idea he was just renting the place?"

"Not a clue," she said. "I can't believe I didn't suspect a thing."

"The man is nuts," I said. "He fooled all of us."

"I suppose," she said. "But on some level, I don't think he fooled you or your husband."

I hugged her, and then I said, "Let's go make some hot chocolate and do our best to forget about this."

She smiled slightly at the suggestion. "Now that I think about it, I don't believe I've had any since college."

"Then it's high time we brought back an old tradition, isn't it? We'll send Zach out to the store for some, and we'll make it a party."

"I'm not sure I'm up for that."

I laughed. "Jenny, by party, I mean we make a long grocery list of food we've sworn off for ten years and make pigs out of ourselves. We can even tell stories from our dorm days and torture Zach with them. What do you say?"

"It sounds wonderful. I'm so glad you're here. I just can't believe it's finally over." A frown crossed her lips. "Not that it's really over. There will be sworn statements, and I'll have to testify. You will, too. I'm so sorry about dragging you into this."

"Come on, I pulled you into a murder investigation. Testifying on your behalf is the least I can do. You can consider it a down payment on the legal fees I'm sure to amass."

"Don't worry. I'm worth every penny you'll have to pay me."

"I hope you're worth more than that," I said, and Jenny laughed again, this one full and genuine. It wasn't much, but it did prove that she was going to get through this, and that was enough for me.

Chapter 21

...

AFTER WE'D ALL HAD OUR SHARE OF HOT CHOCOLATE, Doritos, and fudge ripple ice cream, Zach said, "I can't believe you two used to eat like this."

"Come on, this was lightweight compared to what we used to do," Jenny said.

"It's true. I don't have the stamina for it that I used to," I admitted.

"I'm glad about that," Zach said. "If we're finished gorging, can we discuss where we are now in the case?"

I sighed. "Zach, can't we take one night off from our investigation?"

Jenny shook her head. "He's right. We can't afford to let up just because we found out who was stalking me. Derrick Duncan's murder case is more important than that."

"Fine," I said, pushing the empty bowl away from me.

"Let's talk about it. That termination letter certainly changes things, doesn't it?"

"Does it?" Zach asked. "We know Derrick wrote it, but we can be fairly certain that he didn't deliver it. There's a good chance Kelsey didn't even know she was about to be fired."

"If he was even going to pull the trigger and do it," I said. "Derrick loved to threaten people, we know that."

"So, you're saying we're right back where we started from?" Jenny asked.

"No, it definitely adds another layer to our investigation," Zach said.

Jenny bit her lower lip, and then said, "Maybe it would help if we made a list of our suspects. If we have motives, that might help clarify things as well."

Zach nodded his approval. "That's a great idea."

"Let me get something from my office. I'll be right back."

When she left, Zach asked softly, "Is she going to be all right?"

"She's shaken," I replied, "but she's tough. That was brilliant, taping the porch. You saved the day."

Zach shrugged. "I'm just glad it worked."

Jenny came back in carrying an easel and an enormous pad of paper. "I use this when I'm prepping for a trial," she said. As she handed Zach a thick black marker, she asked, "Would you care to do the honors?"

"Sure," he said. He drew a vertical line down a third of the way over on the paper, and then divided it horizontally into six sections.

"Why six?" Jenny asked.

"Six lines for six suspects," he said as he started filling in the names. After he'd written Cary Duncan, Kelsey Hatcher, Mindi Mills, Brady Sims, Sylvia Peters, and Frank Lassiter down the list, he moved to the open sections.

"Now we put down the motives," he said as he added another line to the grid, making an elongated tic-tac-toe board with three equal vertical divisions.

"For Cary, we've got love and greed," I said.

Zach nodded as he wrote that down. "Brady and Sylvia can be revenge for the firing," he said.

"Mindi could be panic over being dumped," Jenny added.

"And Lassiter has to be revenge," I said.

Zach wrote it, and then drew a line through Frank Lassiter's name.

"Hey, why did you do that?"

"I confirmed his alibi today. He was in Richmond when Derrick was murdered. Sorry, I forgot to tell you. I got the call while I was out shopping for your little binge."

"You can mark Sylvia's name off, too," Jenny said. "We know she was in her room when someone tried to push Kelsey Hatcher in front of that bus."

"Don't be so hasty," I said. "That might clear her for Kelsey's attempted murder, but not for Derrick."

"Are we going to assume the two things are unrelated?" Jenny asked.

"We aren't even positive anything happened with Kelsey," Zach said.

"But we have witnesses," I said.

He shrugged. "Who saw anything except Kelsey and Brady? And what proof do we have that Kelsey was actually pushed?"

"You don't trust anybody, do you?" Jenny asked.

"Not when it comes to a murder investigation," Zach replied. "I can't afford to."

"Then Lassiter's name is off our list, but the others are all still viable."

I frowned. "We have alibis for some of them, but I don't know how we can verify them. Brady said he was sitting in his car when Derrick was murdered, and Sylvia claimed to be in her room. I'm not sure how to confirm either one of those alibis."

"What about Cary, Mindi, and Kelsey?" Zach asked.

I thought back to our conversation. "Cary told me that she got to town after Derrick was murdered, but how can we believe her? If she can kill, she can certainly lie."

Zach wrote it down on the list. "Maybe we can prove she was here before she said she was."

"How can we do that?"

"I don't know. Maybe she got a speeding ticket on the way down, or there could be receipts for gasoline purchases. There might be something."

"But you'd need the resources of the police department to determine that, wouldn't you?"

He smiled. "I might just have them. You heard him; Murphy owes me one. It just might be time to collect."

"Just because you helped him tonight doesn't mean he's going to bend a single rule in an active police investigation," Jenny said.

"I'm not asking for much."

"Why don't we see what else we can come up with before you start calling in favors?" I asked. As I stared at the sheet of paper, I asked, "Have we even heard Kelsey's alibi yet? Don't forget that Mindi acted honestly surprised when we told her about Derrick's murder, but I suppose she could have been acting."

Jenny shook her head. "I don't think she's that good."

"And Kelsey was getting her own tray of food when I found Derrick." I remembered that scream, and how genuine it had sounded.

Zach wrote it down, and then he said, "There's still a great deal we don't know, isn't there?"

"How do we go about finding anything else out?" I asked.

"We keep digging," he said.

"Tonight?" I asked, beginning to regret the amount of junk food I'd just consumed.

"No, I think it will wait until morning. I believe we've all had enough excitement for one day."

"I agree," Jenny said. As she started to clean up, I said, "You go on to bed. I'll take care of that."

"I'd love to fight you over it," she said as she tried to stifle a yawn, "but I don't have it in me."

"I'll give you a hand," Zach said.

After Jenny went to bed, we finished cleaning up, and as I wiped down the counter, I asked, "Do you think we're ever going to solve this?"

He nodded solemnly. "I do, and what's more, I think it's going to be soon."

"How can you say that?"

Zach just shrugged. "Call it a cop's intuition, but I think something's about to break."

THE NEXT MORNING, I AWOKE TO FIND THAT MY HUSBAND has slipped out of the bed at some point in the night. I threw on a robe and found Jenny already up and dressed in a handsome suit, sipping a cup of coffee and scanning the newspaper.

"Hey, sleepyhead," she said with a smile.

I glanced at the clock. "It's only seven thirty. Have you seen Zach?"

"He left an hour ago."

Jenny handed me a cup of coffee. "Here, this will wake you up."

I took it gratefully, inhaled the aroma for a second, and then drank deeply from the cup.

"Better," I said. "Did he happen to say where he was going?"

"He went for a run with Shawn," she said. "Those two are forming some kind of odd friendship, aren't they?"

"They're both cops, no matter what Zach's current status is. With so much in common, I'd be amazed if they weren't getting along."

Jenny watched me for a few seconds before she spoke. "Have you two come to any conclusions about that job offer he got?"

"No, we're both pointedly ignoring it for now," I said, and then took another sip. "Why, do you want to discuss it?"

"Hey, I was just asking," she said.

"Sorry, I don't mean to be so crabby about it. I'm sure we'll talk about it at some point, but I'm guessing not before we've untangled this mess." I glanced again at her suit. "Are you going into work today?"

She nodded. "I thought I might be able to work the phones and see if there's anything going on with the investigation. Sometimes the courthouse is the best place to pick up on what's happening."

"I don't want you going out on any limbs for me," I said.

"What kind of friend would I be if I didn't?" she asked as she rinsed her cup and put it in the sink. "I'm late. See you later?"

"Count on it," I said.

After she was gone, I took a shower and changed. Where was Zach? If he was just going running, he should have been back at least an hour ago. I knew his heart was healthy enough for most things, but if he got into some kind of macho contest with Shawn Murphy, he might not fare so well.

I was about to call his cell phone when he walked in the door. He was sweaty from his run, but there was a broad smile on his face.

"Hello, sunshine," he said as he leaned forward to kiss me.

"You are a mess," I said as I limited it to a quick peck.

"Give me five minutes and I'll be good as new." He took a glass from the cupboard and filled it with water from the purifier on Jenny's tap. After taking a long swallow, he said, "I guess you heard where I was."

"Out with Shawn Murphy, unless your plans changed. Did you have a good run?"

"He tried to kill me," Zach said with a smile, "but I managed to keep up most of the way."

"I'm glad you didn't fall over dead," I said with a straight face.

"That makes two of us. I got some good information out of him as we jogged."

"He actually told you something?"

Zach nodded. "I'll tell you right after I get out of the shower."

"You'll tell me now," I said, blocking his way.

"I can pick you up and move you, and we both know it," Zach said, "but that's going to get you sweaty, too."

"Go," I said as I moved out of his way. "And don't take too long."

"You could always join me," he said with a wry grin.

"I could, but who knows if your heart can take it. If you can wait, then I can, too."

Five minutes later he came back, well groomed and smelling a world better than he had before. "Wow, you clean up nicely."

He bowed at the waist. "Thank you, ma'am."

As Zach took a seat beside me, he asked, "Is there a chance I can get something to eat? I hate to ask, but I'm starving."

"I'm sure I can whip up something for you," I said. "What would you like, eggs or an omelet?"

"Scrambled eggs will be fine, with some toast and some orange juice."

"Let me see what I can do," I said as I started rooting around in Jenny's kitchen. She had everything Zach had requested.

"You're in luck. Now talk."

"But I'm still hungry," he protested.

"If you don't tell me everything you know, and I mean right now, I'm not even going to boil water for you."

"Fine, I'll cooperate."

As I put his toast in the toaster and started scrambling his eggs, Zach said, "Murphy was pretty happy we taped Charlie on the porch. By the time they got to the station, Jenny's neighbor was claiming that his confession had been coerced. Shawn watched the tape, and then showed it to Charlie. We caught him doing it, so there's no denying it now."

"I can't believe Jenny has to live with that man right beside her."

Zach grinned. "That's one of the good parts. This morning, he was evicted from his rental, but not his jail cell. The owner's going to move him out while he's still in police custody, so Jenny won't ever have to see him again."

"I hope you're right," I said as I plated his eggs and added the toast. After I poured him a tall glass of orange juice, I asked, "Will there be anything else, sir?"

He surveyed it all with a smile. "No, this looks great."

As he started to eat, I said, "We can wait with the questions and answers until after you've eaten."

"No, I don't mind talking while I eat," he said, and then promptly took another bite.

"Did Murphy tell you anything about the case?"

Zach nodded, finished chewing a bite, and then took a sip of juice. "It turns out we can cross Sylvia off our list."

"For the attempt on Kelsey," I said.

"For both of them. Sylvia was in her room, on the house phone, talking to her interior decorator in Charlotte the entire time. The police confirmed it through phone records and a personal interview with the decorator."

"Okay, then that's good. Sylvia's name gets crossed off. Did you find anything else out from him?"

Zach took one last bite, and then pushed his empty plate away. "That was great, Savannah. I was starving."

"Running can do that to you," I said. "What else did Murphy tell you about the case, Zach?"

My husband smiled softly. "It's more of a hunch than a fact, but he's got good instincts, so I'm willing to bet he's on the money with it."

"Don't sit there grinning like a fool," I said. "What did he tell you?"

"The police believe that the reason Mindi Mills moved to the Brunswick was so Cary Duncan could keep a closer eye on her. It's odd that the widow's paying the mistress's way, isn't it? Shawn is under the impression that Mindi thinks the relocation was her idea. He believes that Mindi is blackmailing Cary into paying her bill, and that's just for starters. She knows something, he's pretty sure of that. Nobody knows exactly what it is yet, but they're digging into it, and Shawn has faith they'll find out what it is, and fairly soon."

"Could she have witnessed Cary killing her husband?" I asked.

"I suppose that's one possibility." He got up and rinsed his plate and glass, and then put them in the sink beside the mugs Jenny and I used. "It could be a secret Derrick told Mindi before he died, something that Cary doesn't want to get out. Who knows?"

"Cary and Mindi do, at this point."

"And we'll know ourselves soon enough."

"Then we can't exactly strike their names off our list, can we?"

He shook his head. "No; besides Cary and Mindi, we've still got Kelsey and Brady." Zach smiled at me and tapped me lightly on the cheek. "We've narrowed it down from six to four, though. I'd say that's something, wouldn't you?"

"If the police are focusing on Cary and Mindi, should we spend some time on Brady and Kelsey?"

He laughed, and I asked, "What's so funny?"

"Sometimes it's like you can read my mind," Zach said as he wrapped me into his arms and kissed me.

Chapter 22

...

LUCKILY, WE FOUND KELSEY AND BRADY IN THE HOTEL restaurant and didn't have to go upstairs to one of their rooms, or worse yet, chase them all over Raleigh.

"Mind if we join you?" I asked as I pulled out a chair at their table.

Zach took the last free seat. "That breakfast buffet looks great."

I'd just fed him, but I knew my sweet husband was willing to take one for the team, especially if it meant he got to squeeze in an extra meal or two.

"Actually—" Kelsey started to say, when I interrupted her.

"It's so sweet of you to make room for us. There's a great deal we need to talk about, and this is the perfect time."

Kelsey deferred to Brady, who nodded slightly. As soon

as she had his approval, she smiled at me. "Of course you're welcome to join us. What exactly do we need to discuss, though?"

"Our future working relationship," I said. I really had nothing else I could use to get her to open up, so I was going to have to discuss things I'd rather not. "I don't want us to end up like I did with Derrick." Okay, that didn't sound right.

"What Savannah is trying to say is that she doesn't want there to be any acrimony between you," Zach said.

I smiled tightly at him. Was he seriously going to start going around explaining me to people? "What Zach is trying to say is that he's going to the buffet."

Zach looked startled for a split second, and then turned to Brady. "Why don't you join me so they can talk a little business?"

Brady didn't look all that certain he wanted to be away from Kelsey, but I had to give my husband credit for trying to turn a negative into a positive. Though Brady didn't seem pleased with Zach's suggestion, he really had no choice as my husband put a hand under his arm and practically levitated him off his chair.

After they were gone, I said, "I need to talk to you for a second."

"What is it? Do you have another problem with the way I'm running things?" Her emphasis on the word "another" gave me a moment's pause. I had to let that go, though. This really wasn't a business meeting; it was a fact-finding mission.

"No, as of now, we're good. It's about Derrick."

She looked even more annoyed by the change in topic. "What about him? Can't we just drop that subject and move on?"

"Soon," I promised. "Once I get the answers to a few

questions, I'll be finished," I said, which wasn't exactly the truth, but how could she possibly know that?

"Go ahead," Kelsey said, the exasperation clear in her voice. "I'm not sure what else I can tell you, but I'll try."

"How long was Derrick alone when you left to get your food the day he died?"

"How did you know I got his food for him first?" Kelsey asked.

I smiled at her and tried to soften my words. "Don't forget, I worked for Derrick, too. I can't imagine he'd let you eat before he was served."

She nodded. "I was gone maybe twenty minutes," Kelsey finally admitted.

"Hang on a second. You both ate from the hotel restaurant's menu, right?"

"Yes, it was right there, and Derrick was in no mood to wait. He was so mad at you, Savannah. He told me that he thought you were being disloyal to him, and I honestly think it hurt his feelings."

"He fired me, remember? And that's after he tried to sell me to the highest bidder. Was he really that concerned about loyalty?"

"Maybe not," Kelsey admitted after a moment.

"So, the question remains. Why did it take you twenty minutes to get your own food?"

Kelsey glanced at the buffet, and I saw her looking at Brady with an odd expression.

"You were waiting for him, weren't you?" I asked.

"What?" she asked as she looked back at me. "What are you talking about?"

"You didn't get your food sooner because you were waiting for Brady."

"He was supposed to come back after his meeting with Derrick," she protested, "but I waited twenty minutes, and he never showed up. We were so careful that no one knew about our relationship. You saw him walk right past me when Derrick fired him; he didn't even glance in my direction."

"In his defense, he'd just been blindsided. Did you know that was coming? It didn't look like he'd been warned beforehand."

"I had no idea what Derrick was up to, and that's the truth," Kelsey said. "You've got to believe me."

I patted her hand. "I do," I said, and I meant every word of it. If she'd known what was coming, she would have prepared Brady for it, and from our conversation before the meeting—and his reaction to it afterward—there was no way he knew anything for sure, though he did seem to suspect that something was awry when we'd first spoken.

The men came back to our table, and from the sparse amount of food on his plate, Zach had barely touched the buffet. Was it possible he was actually slowing down? My husband put his plate down, and then said, "I'm not feeling one hundred percent. Do you two mind if we do this another time?"

The enthusiasm of their agreement was almost obscene.

I wasn't ready to go, but apparently my husband was.

After we were out in the lobby, I asked him, "Are you really sick?"

"Sick of them," he said.

"I wasn't finished with Kelsey."

"Wait until you hear what I just learned. You'll be thanking me in a second."

"I doubt it, but go ahead and try."

"Brady was supposed to meet Kelsey after she served Derrick his meal, but she never showed up."

"Don't look so smug," I said. "Kelsey just told me the exact same thing about him."

Zach frowned. "So, instead of giving each other an alibi, they've found a way to divide the suspicion between them."

"It's not a stupid tactic," I said. "Who would a jury believe? If they could build up enough doubt about the other's innocence, it could sway a pair of verdicts."

Zach shook his head. "Why wouldn't they just say they were together, if that's the case? It's a lot easier than casting suspicion on someone else."

I shrugged. "I know; you're absolutely right. It doesn't make sense, at least not if they're trying to cover for each other."

"So you're saying that either one of them could have done it," Zach said.

"It makes sense that way," I said as we moved to a corner of the lobby. "One of them is telling the truth, and the other is clearly lying."

"Not necessarily. What if they both showed up for their little tryst, but got the location wrong?"

"So, we're no further along than we were before," I said.

"I wouldn't say that. We know for sure now that either one of them could have done it."

"But we don't know which," I said.

"There's always that," Zach agreed. "Where does that leave us?"

"Two steps forward, and one back." I started thinking about what we'd learned, and how we could use it to our advantage. If the police were focusing on Mindi and Cary, we couldn't do anything about that. It wouldn't bother me one bit if they solved the case before we did. We weren't in a race, unless I considered it a competition to free me from suspicion.

But what if they were wrong?

Zach and I could have the best chance of learning what had really happened to Derrick Duncan.

I took my husband's hand. "It's time we stirred the pot a little, don't you think?"

"What did you have in mind?"

"We need to let them know we found the planner, and that we've got a copy of it."

Zach looked at me oddly. "What good is that going to do?"

"Stay with me," I said. "What if we claim there was something tucked away in it, an entry that pertains to the day he was murdered?"

"So, we use ourselves as bait," Zach said.

"Exactly." I frowned, and then added, "I'm not comfortable using Jenny's place, though. She's been through enough lately."

Zach grinned at me. "We can always get a room here ourselves. As a matter of fact, why keep all of the fun to Brady and Kelsey? I think we should tell Cary and Mindi the same thing. That way we're covering all of our remaining suspects."

"Somehow I don't think Shawn Murphy is going to approve," I said.

"He'll get over it pretty quickly if we hand him the killer. How should we do this?"

I headed back toward the dining room. "I think a breathless announcement is the best, don't you?"

He grabbed my arm before I could make it two steps to the door. "Aren't you forgetting something?"

"What's that?"

He grinned. "We need a pair of rooms to lure the killer to first."

"Why two?"

"If we get them with a connecting door, we can leave it unlocked and see who takes the bait."

"That's brilliant," I said.

"I'm just trying to figure out how to keep us safe."

"You don't have to apologize for that. I appreciate it," I said with a smile. "Sorry. Sometimes I get carried away when I'm excited."

"Don't apologize. That's one of the things I love best about you. Let's get the rooms, and then I'll go upstairs and set things up. After that, I'll call Cary Duncan."

"How are you going to let Mindi know?"

"If I'm right, I won't have to. I'm guessing they're still together, so we should find something out soon."

A FTER WE GOT THE CONNECTING ROOMS, 1421 AND 1423, it was time to set our trap.

I rushed into the restaurant alone, and was relieved to see that Kelsey and Brady were still there.

"I'm glad I caught you," I said as I joined them, not even having to pretend that I was out of breath.

"What is it? Is something wrong?" Kelsey asked.

"No, exactly the opposite. Zach and I found a copy of Derrick's planner among the telephone books that were in his suitcases."

"It couldn't be the one I had. Do you think there was a duplicate somewhere all along?" Kelsey asked me.

"It wouldn't surprise me. We're going to start going through it now in our room."

"You're staying here as well?" Brady asked.

I nodded, glad for the opportunity. "We're in one-four-two-one. Zach thinks there's something written in the planner that's going to blow the lid off things. Sorry I can't stay, but I've got to go."

I took off before they could ask any more questions and took the elevator upstairs.

I knocked lightly on 1423, and then said, "Zach, it's me."

He opened the door and let me in. After I was safely inside, I asked, "What do we do now?"

"The other door's unlocked, and I got some papers from downstairs and shoved them into a folder. It won't fool anyone if they actually look at it, but from across the room, they'll be fine. I moved the desk so we could see it from this door without being seen."

"You've thought of everything, haven't you?"

Zach frowned. "I'm still not positive this is going to work. We may have a long morning ahead of us."

"It's the best idea we've had so far," I said.

We pulled the desk chairs to the door, and took up our positions. I started to talk in a whisper a few times, but Zach kept shaking his head and shushing me, so I quit trying to talk to him. I thought about tackling another puzzle as we waited, but I knew I'd be too distracted to do it.

I knew cops staked places out all of the time, but I didn't know how they managed it without going completely insane with boredom.

SOMEHOW, I MANAGED TO NOD OFF, BUT I WAS JERKED sharply awake when I heard the fire alarm sound.

"I thought that could happen," Zach said. "Somebody's trying to get us out of here."

"They're doing more than that," I said as I smelled the air. "That's smoke. Zach," I added, my voice rising, "they're trying to burn us out!"

Zach looked in the other room instead of exiting like I wanted him to. The smoke was stronger in there, and I wondered if the hallway was on fire. "What are you doing? We need to leave."

"Don't worry. We're going to be fine," he said. He moved past me to the door where we'd been watching, and took my hand. "Come on, Savannah."

"I'm hurrying," I said, not sure how happy I was about running toward a fire, instead of away from it.

Zach pulled the door open, and as he did, the smoke got stronger and the smell of something burning intensified.

I was expecting to see a hallway engulfed in flames, and was preparing myself to stop, drop, and roll, just like I'd been taught as a child.

Instead, I saw a small guest trash can leaning against the door to the other room, with paper or something smoldering inside of it.

Zach grabbed a fire extinguisher and had the fire out by the time Hotel Security got up there.

"What happened here?" the lead man asked as he surveyed the damage. The name tag on his gold jacket said, "Greg."

"It looks like somebody's idea of a prank went too far," Zach said.

I stared at my husband with open disbelief. I was about to say something when he shook his head sharply, so against my better judgment, I kept my mouth shut.

"We've been vandalized a few times this week already," the lead man said. "I guess I shouldn't be surprised." He examined the scorched door, and then said, "It's just on the surface. Jason, go get the fans and the maintenance crew. I'm going to reset the alarm."

After his partner left, Greg turned to Zach and said, "That was quick thinking on your part."

"Just trying to lend a hand," Zach said. "Are we done here?"

Greg shrugged. "Did you see anything or anyone up here?"

"Not a soul," Zach said. "We were in our room."

"And which one was that?" Greg asked. Maybe he wasn't as slow as he appeared.

"That one," Zach said as he pointed to the one beside the room we'd been staking out.

"And that one," I added.

Zach looked angry, but there was nothing he could do about it. If Murphy got involved, he'd find out we rented both rooms, and I didn't want to have to explain that.

"Two people, two rooms?" Greg asked. "Are you two married?"

"We are, but he snores," I said. Greg looked at Zach for confirmation, who sheepishly admitted, "Can't help myself."

"They have those strips I use," Greg said. "So, whose room is this one?"

Before I could claim it, Zach said, "It's mine. I can't imagine who might have done it. We just checked in an hour ago, and nobody knows we're staying here."

Well, at least half of that was true. We had just checked in, but I knew four people who were well aware of our presence.

"Fine. We'll be glad to find you two more rooms on another floor," Greg said.

"If it's all the same to you, I don't think we'll be staying here tonight."

Greg nodded. "I understand completely. Don't worry about a bill. I'll talk to the manager as soon as we get this taken care of."

I was about to head for the elevator when Greg asked, "Aren't you going to need help with your luggage?"

Zach smiled. "We're traveling light. We can get it ourselves, but thanks for asking."

We went back into the room, and Zach said, "I need to get that folder."

"But there's nothing but junk in it," I said.

"We know that, but whoever tried to smoke us out

doesn't. I want them to see us leaving the hotel with it tucked under my arm."

"How'd you get so sneaky?"

"Fighting bad guys all day will do that to you," he said.

He collected the folder, and I asked, "What about luggage?"

"We're going to have to explain that on the fly."

Fortunately, Greg and Jason were setting up the fans, while a crew was starting on the door. They had power sanders out, and I suspected it would be as good as new in no time. We were able to slip onto the elevator, and I let a lungful of air out as the doors closed.

"That was close," I said.

"Come on, we could have handled it."

As the elevator descended, I asked, "Why would someone try such a cheesy trick to get us out of our room?"

Zach frowned. "I have a feeling we weren't meant to get out that easily. I should have gone straight to the hallway when we first heard the alarm. Going out through the other room might have cost us the chance to find out who set that fire."

"Do you think they were trying to hurt us?"

He shook his head. "Actually, I'm pretty sure they wanted us dead. If we'd opened that room door when we first smelled smoke, something very bad could have happened to us, and I don't mean getting a burn."

"Then I'm glad you thought to get two rooms. It appears that we've managed to push someone beyond their limits."

Zach nodded as the elevator opened on the ground floor. "Let's just hope we can push them again. Do you have any ideas?"

"Maybe one," I said.

"That's more than I've got. I'm listening."

Chapter 23

. . .

"IT'S TOO RISKY," ZACH SAID AFTER I TOLD HIM MY PLAN. WE were sitting in the parking garage discussing it away from anyone who might want to listen in.

"We've just lost our best chance to find out who killed Derrick," I said. "Do we really have that much choice?"

"We could always sit back and let Murphy solve it," Zach said. "After all, that's what he's getting paid to do."

"I can't just wait for someone to burn Jenny's house down. Isn't that next? Somebody's willing to commit murder to shut us up."

Zach shook his head. "That fire was meant to be a distraction, nothing more. Once we got to the door, the real fun was going to start."

"Who knows what would have happened if you hadn't been smart enough to get a connecting room?"

Zach frowned, and I could tell that I was starting to

wear him down. It was time to step it up. "You'll be right there in case anything happens. I'll be perfectly safe."

"Savannah, as much as I'd like to, I can't protect you from everything," he said.

"I know that," I said softly. "I have to do this. You see that, don't you?"

He tapped the dashboard, and after a huge sigh, he said, "Go on. I'll make the telephone calls as you drive."

AS I DROVE BACK TO PULLEN PARK, ZACH PHONED KELSEY Hatcher. I listened in on his side of the conversation as I drove, and hoped my plan to smoke out a killer worked. He'd really have to sell it, but I had faith in him.

"Savannah asked me to call you to tell you that we've just about got this solved. There's something in the planner that's going to blow the lid off the case and help the police arrest the killer."

There was a pause, and he replied, "Detective Murphy is meeting Savannah in Pullen Park in an hour to get the planner. As a matter of fact, she's already over there waiting for him." Another pause, and he replied, "I can't. I'll be downtown with an old friend. We'll be leaving soon, and I need to say good-bye before we go back to Asheville." Another pause, and then Zach said, "That's right, by the monument to *The Andy Griffith Show*, as a matter of fact. Gotta go," he said quickly, and then hung up.

"How'd I do?" he asked me.

"You were wonderful."

"Brady was with her, I could hear him in the background asking questions, so that just leaves Cary and Mindi."

Zach called Cary and had much the same message, conveying the information we wanted them to believe was true. I pulled into the parking lot as he hung up.

"Well," he said, "we've set the trap."

"Let's just hope someone gets caught in it this time."

A S WE LEFT OUR CAR, I WAS SURPRISED TO SEE THAT THE park was nearly empty. I'd been counting on having enough people around to add another layer of defense, but apparently that wasn't going to happen.

Zach and I would manage, though.

We stepped over the embedded railroad tracks and back onto the herringbone laid pavers. As we neared the ticket office where they sold entries to the carousel, the kiddie boats, and the train, I saw that the booth was closed for the day. That explained the absence of cars in the parking lot. We came around the corner and onto the open expanse of grass encircled by the same brown pavers, with the statue we wanted on the other end of the green. There was a grouping of heavy shrubs just behind the statue, and I could see that my plan just might work. Zach would be close enough to hear anything that was said, yet still be protected from sight.

Now it was just a matter of waiting to see if anyone turned up.

"Do you have the folder?" Zach asked.

"It's in my bag," I answered.

"You might want to get it out so everyone can see it," he said.

I did as he asked, and then tried to look everywhere at once. Zach caught me looking. "Relax. Nobody's had time to get here yet. We can still call it off, you know."

"I'm fine. I promise."

Once I was settled in, Zach moved behind the cluster of bushes and vanished from my view. A moment later, he stepped back out. "This isn't going to work."

"Why not?"

"I can't see you." He looked around, and then pointed to another cluster of bushes nearby that partially shielded some kind of large green electrical box. "That might work."

He walked quickly to the spot, and a moment later, Zach asked, "Can you see me?"

"No. If I hadn't seen you go in there, I never would have known you were there."

"Good, that's the way we need it."

"What do we do now?"

"It's the easy part; we wait."

THIRTY MINUTES LATER, I WAS BEGINNING TO DOUBT IF anyone was going to show up. I almost said something to my husband when I heard a telephone ringing in the bushes.

"Sorry, I forgot to turn it off," he said. I heard a few whispers, and he surprised me by coming out from his hiding place.

"What's going on?"

"That was Murphy," Zach said. "He's ready to make an arrest."

I felt the air go out of my lungs. "Who did it?"

"Cary killed him for the life insurance, and Mindi found out. She was blackmailing Cary, which explains her change in attitude. Evidently Cary refused to give her half the money, so Mindi came to Shawn with her story. He's going to arrest Cary for murder, and he asked me if I wanted to come along for the arrest."

"Of course you do," I said, seeing the gleam in my husband's glance. "Go."

"I hate leaving you here by yourself, but there's no way I can bring you along," Zach said.

"Don't worry about me. If the killer's there, I *have* to be safe here. Why don't you go, and I'll phone Jenny to come by and get me. She can be here in a few minutes. Would that make you happy?"

"Probably, but I still want to wait with you here until she shows up."

I hated being coddled. "Zach, go on. I'm a grown woman. I can take care of myself."

He looked like a puppy, he was so eager to go. "Go on."

"If you're sure," he said.

I threw him my car keys. "I'm positive."

He caught them midair, and then said, "I'm not going anywhere until you call her. If she can't come, I'm staying with you."

I called Jenny. "Hey, I need a ride."

"Sure, where are you?"

"I'm at Pullen Park."

"The carousel's not open now," she said. "I don't think the boat dock is, either."

"I'm not asking you to go on a picnic with me," I said. "Can you come get me?"

"I'm on my way," she said.

After I hung up, I said, "See, she'll be here in no time."

"If you're sure," Zach said as he kissed my cheek.

Before I could answer, he was sprinting down the path toward the parking lot. My husband could be such a child sometimes.

I was marveling at how Cary could have killed her husband when I suddenly realized that the police had to be wrong. Mindi may have been blackmailing Cary— that didn't surprise me one bit—but her sense of self-preservation was too strong to risk her own freedom just to get back at Cary. And then I remembered how Cary had reacted to the mere mention of a knife being used on her husband. Cary hadn't been acting then, I was certain of it. She might have bludgeoned her philandering husband with something, but I doubted seriously that she would stab him.

And if I was right, then neither Cary nor Mindi had done it.

That left Brady and Kelsey, my last two suspects. Kelsey certainly had the most to gain from Derrick's death, but only if she'd known she would soon be getting his job, instead of being about to be fired herself. How could she have possibly known that she'd end up taking over for him, though? Could there have been anything romantic between them? I doubted it, no matter what a hound dog Derrick was. He liked his women flashy, and he proved it with both his wife and his mistress. I doubted that he'd ever take a second look at Kelsey. I honestly couldn't see her doing it.

But what about Brady? He had nothing to gain by Derrick's death on the face of it, but he did stand to lose everything he cared about. Kelsey had told me herself that he was the jealous type, and I didn't doubt he might have suspected Derrick had made a play for his girlfriend. That alone might not trigger an act of violence, but couple losing his livelihood with an active imagination, and he could have easily killed our syndicator.

It all made sense when I looked at it that way, but how could I ever prove it?

I was about to telephone Zach to tell him my suspicions when Brady stepped out from behind the bush where Zach had originally stood. He had a gun in his hand, which he showed me just before sticking it back into his pocket, though it was clear it was still pointing at me.

"I thought he'd never leave," Brady said, and there was something in his voice that told me that every last one of my suspicions had been right. "If your husband had stayed around much longer, I'm afraid you both would have died tonight."

* * *

"**I**'LL TAKE THAT PLANNER," HE SAID. "AND YOUR TELE-phone, too."

I looked around, but there was no one within shouting distance of us. What a time for the park to be deserted.

"Take it easy, Brady. I'd be glad to give this to you. There's no reason anyone has to get hurt."

He laughed at that. "I'm afraid it's a little too late for that, Savannah. Derrick wouldn't change his mind, so I had no choice. He had to be dealt with, and so do you." He looked around us, and then motioned me with his head. "Let's move over by the lake. I want it to look like we're a couple out enjoying the evening."

"Sorry, I'm not that good an actor."

"Just do it, Savannah."

I couldn't argue with that. As we moved toward the white railing that guarded the lake from the pathway, I had to buy myself some time. If I could draw him out, I might be able to save myself until Jenny could get there. "You stood Kelsey up at the hotel so you could kill Derrick. You never had any intention of talking him out of anything."

"How did you know about that?"

I shrugged. "My husband and I have been asking questions, you know that. You told me you couldn't find Kelsey, and she told us the same thing. That was pretty clever of you to put suspicion on her, too. Was that her idea, or yours?"

"Don't talk about her that way," Brady said, his voice becoming agitated. We were a few feet apart now, with the railing in front of us, and the water just beyond it. Brady kept glancing back over his shoulder, as if he were expecting someone. So was I. He said, "Kelsey wasn't involved in it at all. She still has no idea that I did it for her, and if I have my way, she'll never find out."

"It worked out pretty well for you, didn't it?" Where was Jenny? I was hoping she'd see Brady with me and call Shawn Murphy, or Zach, or anyone who could help, for that matter.

"Do you think that was just a coincidence? I gave Cary the idea to hire Kelsey and suggested she give her a chance to take over for Derrick. The woman was so pliable, it was almost too easy."

I kept scanning all around me, but the closest people I could see were on the other side of the lake. They were so far away, Brady could have probably shot me and they'd just think that they'd heard a car backfire.

"Come on, Savannah. Hand me your telephone, or I'm going to take a chance and shoot you to get it. Neither one of us wants that, now do we?"

I thought about using it as a weapon, maybe try to hurl it at his head enough to distract him so I could run away, but I doubted I could throw it hard enough to have any real impact.

I reached into my pocket for my phone, hitting the 2 button as I did, which would call Zach.

"Now," he commanded.

I hoped the call had time to go through, as I had run out of time to stall. I tossed it toward him, missing his outstretched hand on purpose, and it landed at his feet. Before I could say anything, Brady took the heel of his boot and smashed it into a dozen pieces. When he was satisfied that it was dead, he swept the remnants of it into the lake water.

"I need some of those numbers," I protested.

"If you don't hand me that planner, you're not going to need anything ever again."

I looked at the folder in my hands. What would he do when he discovered the truth, that Zach and I had been using it as a ruse? I had a feeling that when he looked at those papers, I wasn't going to live long enough for them to leave his hand and hit the ground.

"Why do you need this?"

"If you'd had any brains, you would have found it yourself."

I thought about the entries I'd read. "Sorry, I still don't get it." And then I remembered the note I'd found written in someone else's handwriting, a note that didn't match Derrick's scrawl, or the usual yellow paper he liked. The words on the lime green paper virtually glowed in front of my eyes.

"You were the one who threatened him," I said. "I bet you were surprised when you saw that he kept your note."

"He was hitting on Kelsey," Brady said. "I couldn't let him take her from me. Derrick had two women already. Why did he have to go after my girlfriend, too? She's all I've got, and I wasn't going to let him have her without a fight."

"And then on top of that, he fired you," I said.

"I couldn't believe it. I had no idea it was coming. I went to my car afterward, just like I said I did. The longer I thought about it, the more I realized that I couldn't let him get away with it. He hadn't signed the papers yet, he told each of us that, so if I couldn't get him to change his mind, there was another option. Cary doesn't care about the business end of things, and from what I'd seen, she never had. I knew I'd have a fair shot at getting her to keep Kelsey on, if I had the chance. Savannah, can you honestly say the world's not a better place without that louse in it?"

"That's not up to me to say," I said. "That was a cute trick with the trash can by the door."

I was surprised when he smiled. "I had to get that note back. It's the only thing that links me directly to Derrick's murder."

"Not quite the only thing," I said.

He shrugged. "Without the note, it's going to be a case of he said/she said. All of us hated him."

"Not enough to kill him, though," I said. "Did you really try to kill Kelsey, or was it just staged?"

He smiled. "I had to muddy the waters a little. Besides, she was never in any real danger. I'm getting tired of this. Give me the planner," Brady said. "I'm not asking you again."

It was now or never. I started to offer the folder to him when I pretended to trip on a stone. The papers came out, and Brady instinctively used both hands to reach for them, leaving the gun in his pocket.

That was my one chance. As he tried to react to the fallen papers, I threw myself at him, doing my best to drive him over the rail and into the water.

I almost made it, too, but he managed to fend me off and right himself before he went over the edge.

And that's when Jenny jumped out and hit him, too, sending him over the railing and into the water.

"Run," I screamed, and I glanced over to see that Jenny was right behind me.

"It was Brady?" she asked breathlessly.

I glanced back to where Brady had gone into the water.

With one hand, he'd managed to grab the top rail, and he was quickly pulling himself back out of the water.

We were in serious trouble now, with nowhere to go that he couldn't catch us. Jenny's car was in the opposite direction, so we didn't have a chance running for it. We were going to have to come up with something else if we were going to live to see the next sunrise.

"He's coming after us, Jenny," I said as I led her to the shuttered carousel.

"How are we going to get away?" she asked.

"Run to the other side."

We did, and as we rounded the corner of the building,

I saw that Brady was much closer than I would have expected. There was a look of fury on his face that was clearly driving him on.

As I looked back, Brady fired a shot at us, and it buried itself into a wooden pillar of the building less than two feet away from me.

"Run," I screamed at Jenny again.

When we got to the other side, I saw that she'd done something to her ankle.

"I think it's sprained," she said quietly. "Go on. Save yourself."

"Not a chance," I said as I looked around for anything I could use as a weapon. The only thing I saw was a long worn wooden stick with a nail poking out one side. It was clearly used to pick up trash on the ground, but I was going to use it for something else, or die trying to save my friend.

The only hope I had was to catch him by surprise. Running around the other side of the rounded building, I held the weapon in front of me as though it were an ancient lance, and I was on horseback.

I caught up to him just as he turned toward Jenny.

Brady barked out, "Where is she? Don't try to save her, or you'll die, too."

"You're going to kill me anyway," she said.

I heard Brady laugh, a sound that was completely devoid of humor, or even humanity. "You know what? You're right."

As he lifted the gun, I knew I was going to be too late. I was fifteen feet from where he stood, and I didn't have a chance of getting there in time.

But my lance did.

I threw it with everything I had, praying that it would find its mark. I'd been aiming for his head, but I struck his leg instead. It found some purchase in the muscle and flesh there, and Brady went down in a heap, clutching his leg. The gun had clattered out of his hands on impact, and we both dove for it.

As our hands touched, I heard the most beautiful sound I'd ever heard in my life.

Zach said, "One more inch, and you're dead. Just give me a reason. I'm begging you."

Brady knew he was beaten. He stopped reaching for the gun and pulled the impromptu spear out of his leg.

I'M SO HAPPY TO SEE YOU," I SAID ONCE HE HAD BRADY tied up with his own belt.

"You were doing fine on your own," he said.

"Did you get my call?"

He looked puzzled by that. "No, I realized halfway to Murphy that I must have lost my mind leaving you alone. By the time I got here, I figured it had to be Brady, but I'm guessing you beat me to it, didn't you?"

"I knew two minutes before he showed up," I admitted. "I just ran out of time."

He hugged me. "I think you did just fine. I called Murphy, and he's on his way. He realized Mindi was lying to him the second he heard Cary's story. Mindi was blackmailing her, but it had nothing to do with murder."

"What else was it?"

Zach grinned. "I'm glad you don't know everything. I was starting to get an inferiority complex. Cary was having an affair with a married man."

"But Derrick was dead," I said. "How could she blackmail her?"

"Well, I guess I should admit that my initial instincts were wrong. The man she was sleeping with was Frank Lassiter. Mindi told Cary if she didn't pay up, she was going to the police with some fabricated evidence that Cary and Frank had conspired to kill Derrick."

"So, his murder prompted yet another crime," Jenny said as Zach helped her up.

"Throw a rock in a still pond and the ripples go all the way to shore," he said. "Should we get you to the hospital so someone can look at that ankle?"

She laughed. "No, all I need is an ice pack." Jenny glanced over at Brady, who'd been silent since I'd stabbed him. "What about him?"

Detective Murphy came up to us, with four uniformed officers. He took the scene in, and then said to Zach, "You were right."

He shook his head. "She got it before I did."

Shawn saluted me with two fingers. "Then you're the one I owe an apology."

"Seeing him locked up is all I need."

"That we can make happen. Take him downtown."

As two of the officers lifted him to his feet, he screamed, "My leg is killing me. That witch stabbed me. I need to go to a hospital."

"Come on, Brady," I said with a grin I didn't feel. "I barely nicked you."

After he was gone, I asked, "Does anybody mind if we go back to Jenny's now? I need a long, hot soak in that tub of hers."

"You've earned at least that," Jenny said.

"Tell you what, ladies," Zach added, "I'll even cook for us tonight."

I looked at Jenny and smiled, and as my husband helped her walk back to my car, I said, "If you really want to reward us, get takeout."

"Hey, I'm an excellent cook," he said, with a hint of faux hurt in his voice.

"Sure you are," I said as I patted his chest, "but it might be nice if we're all pampered a little tonight."

Chapter 24

• • •

"**I CAN'T BELIEVE YOU'RE LEAVING**," JENNY SAID TWO DAYS later as she walked us out to the car. Her ankle was fine now, and from our latest report from Shawn Murphy, Brady was confessing to everything he'd ever done.

"It's time. I'm behind on my puzzles, and Kelsey is turning out to be a real taskmaster."

"How is she doing?" Jenny asked, as Zach finished putting our things in my car.

"She still can't believe Brady killed Derrick, but she's not going to stop running things for Cary, at least for now." I looked over at the now-empty house where Charlie had been. "Are you going to be all right?"

"He's in jail, and even if he gets out, I doubt he'll come after me again."

"How can you know that?" I asked.

Jenny lowered her voice. "I'm not supposed to know this, but Zach had a talk with Charlie in jail, and then Shawn spent a little time with him, too. I'd be amazed if he didn't leave North Carolina when he gets out."

Zach came back to us. "We're ready." He hugged Jenny, and then said, "Take care of yourself. Don't forget, it's your turn to visit us the next time."

She smiled at him. "I might just take you up on that. Now that I'm a partner, I've got a feeling I might actually take a vacation or two every now and then."

I hugged her. "You're welcome anytime."

Zach looked surprised when I tossed my car keys to him. "You drive."

"Seriously? You hate it when I drive your car."

"I'm learning to adjust," I said.

We got in, and Jenny waved to us until we couldn't see her anymore. "Don't worry about her. She'll be fine," Zach said.

"I know she will. I'll miss her, though."

"We could always retire in Raleigh instead," he said. "We've got some good friends who live here."

"Don't get me wrong; it's nice," I said as he pulled out of her development and onto the main highway that would soon lead us to I-40 West, going home, "but the mountains always call me home."

"I'm glad, because I'd hate to leave our little place in the woods."

I reached behind the seat and pulled out a legal pad and the special type of pencil I loved.

As I started creating a new puzzle, Zach said, "Hey, nobody said you could work all of the way home."

"Would you rather talk about that job offer you got in Asheville instead?" I asked as I put my pencil down.

"No, do your puzzle, and I'll drive."

As I worked on a new puzzle, I kept wondering what he would do. A full-time job would dramatically change our lives, and not for the better, as far as I was concerned. But in the end, it was Zach's decision, and I knew that unless I was dead-set against it, he'd make the best decision he could, for both of us.

WE WERE NEARLY TO STATESVILLE WHEN ZACH SAID, "I've made my decision about the job."

That was it? There wasn't even going to be a discussion? "What did you decide?"

"Unless you are completely against it," he said, his voice low and resigned, "I'm going to turn them down."

"I understand," I said, and then it caught up with me. "What did you just say?"

Zach laughed. "Sorry, I couldn't help myself. Savannah, I like the way our lives are right now. Why would I want to get behind a desk again? Things are good, so let's not mess them up."

I put my puzzle down and kissed his cheek. "That sounds wonderful to me."

"I thought it might," he said.

By the time we got near the Hickory exit, I thought about my uncles, and their great Alaskan adventure. I wondered where they were at that moment, and Zach surprised me by slowing down and getting off the exit. I glanced at the fuel gauge and said, "We don't need gas."

"No, but there are a couple of men who'd love to see you. Tom and Barton called this morning. They're at Tom's, and they asked me if we'd stop in and see them."

"And you didn't tell me?" I said, slapping playfully at his arm.

"They wanted it to be a surprise." He just grinned at me as he added, "Surprise."

I had to laugh. It would be good having my family together again. I'd come close to dying at that park, and there wasn't anything in the world that made me more thankful for what I had than coming close to losing it all.

Puzzles

...

NUMBERS HIDE AND SEEK

Find the pattern, and then discover the missing number!

PUZZLE 1

7, 11, 33, 37, ____, 115, 345, 349

PUZZLE 2

24, 96, 48, 192, ____, 384

SOLUTION 1

7, 11, 33, 37, 111, 115, 345, 349

Pattern: add 4, multiply by 3

Formula: $7 + 4 = 11$; $11 \times 3 = 33$; $33 + 4 = 37$; $37 \times 3 = 111$; $111 + 4 = 115$; $115 \times 3 = 345$; $345 + 4 = 349$

SOLUTION 2

24, 96, 48, 192, 96, 384

Pattern: multiply by 4, divide by 2

Formula: $24 \times 4 = 96$; $96 / 2 = 48$; $48 \times 4 = 192$; $192 / 2 = 96$; $96 \times 4 = 384$

BLOCKHEADS

Discover the missing numbers! Two touching blocks on one level add up to the block above it.

PUZZLE 1

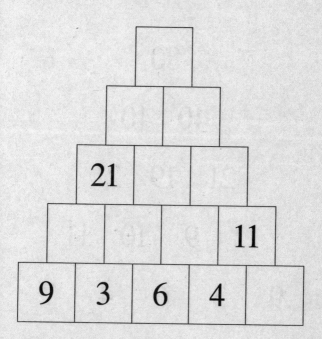

SOLUTION 1

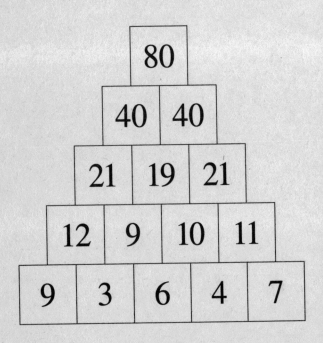

PUZZLE 2

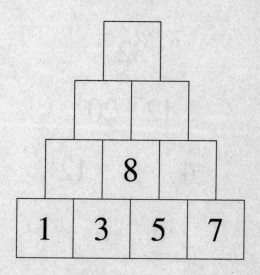

SOLUTION 2

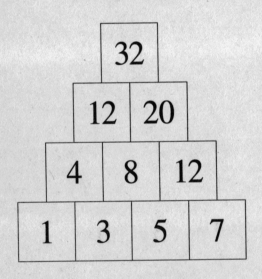

CHAPTER & HEARSE

Mystery bookstore owner Tricia Miles has been spending more time solving whodunits than reading them. Now a nearby gas explosion has injured Tricia's sister's boyfriend, Bob Kelly, the head of the Chamber of Commerce, and killed the owner of the town's history bookstore. Tricia's never been a fan of Bob, but when she reads that he's being tight-lipped about the "accident," it's time to take action.

DON'T MISS THE FIRST NOVEL IN
THE BOOKS BY THE BAY MYSTERIES FROM

ELLERY ADAMS

A Killer Plot

In the small coastal town of Oyster Bay, North Carolina, you'll find plenty of characters, ne'er-do-wells,
and even a few celebs trying to duck the paparazzi.
But when murder joins this curious community,
writer Olivia Limoges and the Bayside Book Writers are determined to get the story before they meet
their own surprise ending.

M769T0910

M2G0610